WICKLOW GOLD

RAY CRANLEY

KB
KESTREL BOOKS

Book Publishers & Distributors

Cover: Painting by Val Byrne

'for Jacinta'

First published 1999
by

KESTREL BOOKS

48A Main St., Bray, Co. Wicklow, Ireland.
Tel: +353 1 2863402; Fax: +353 1 2860984
Email: sales@kestrelbooks.com

Printed in Ireland by
Falcon Print & Finish Ltd.

ISBN:
Pbk: 1-900505-41-X
Hbk: 1-900505-46-0

WICKLOW GOLD

CHAPTER 1

837 AD

Bresal shaded his eyes from the noonday sun and gazed aloft to where several men worked some fifty feet above him. He hoped he would be forgiven for allowing a certain degree of pride to swell his breast; his brain-child, his great round tower was progressing beautifully, already rising almost halfway to its ultimate intended height. If the Viking hordes should decide to attack the community of Kevin again after the tower's completion they would not find such easy axe-fodder as heretofore. The doorway was Bresal's chief source of satisfaction and had on several occasions necessitated the suppression of a chuckle on the part of its architect as he contemplated the savage frustration on the faces of the raiders when confronted with this impenetrable edifice. He was sure he had sensed the same stifled mirth in the good Abbot himself when shown the plans.

More precisely the reason for this happy enthusiasm was not the doorway itself which was of fairly simple design, but rather its location; Bresal had set it upwards of eleven feet above ground level. The tower would serve many purposes: a bell-tower for the newly-built Cathedral; a watch-tower to provide early warning of an attack, and most importantly a tower of refuge for the monks and sacred vessels from the many small churches in the monastic settlement. Once inside with their ladder pulled up behind them it would be impossible for the pagans to get at them. There would be no more scrambling up mountainsides laden with bags of precious objects.

As the builders chipped away, hammer-dressing the stones to the curvature of the tower, Bresal prayed they would be finished before another attack shattered the tranquillity of their beloved valley, for if there was a place on earth that could be said to embody the very essence of peace it was this sequestered vale of Glendalough — the glen of the two lakes, cradled by lofty oak-wooded mountains of great beauty. Two and a half centuries before Bresal's time good Kevin had come here to live the solitary life of the hermit and had founded the monastery which had blossomed into one of the most influential centres of learning in the known world. The princes of countries now groping their way through terrible ages of darkness sent their sons here to be educated alongside the sons of Irish kings and chieftains, for the monks of Glendalough had traversed the seas and its name was spoken with reverence in the most remote places. The Greek and Latin tongues were as commonly heard among the students who strolled in chattering groups by the engrossed Bresal as Gaelic Irish was, the common bond of all being a love of learning and literature.

They were aware of the importance of the community; aware that Ireland bore the torch of knowledge in a world struggling under an overwhelming onslaught of barbarism and ignorance. They would keep that torch burning until the dark times passed away. Bresal was barefoot, sandals being worn only when travelling outside the stone cashel or boundary wall. His habit of undyed wool was uncomfortably hot in the present heatwave but hopelessly inadequate when the winter winds howled up the valley. The small eminence on which the central group of buildings stood inside the cashel was at the delta formed by two rivers — the Glendasan on the north side flowing close by the gateway, and the smaller Glenealo skirting the cashel to the south beyond Kevin's Church. Outside, the valley floor was dotted with the wattle-and-daub huts of students.

Deep in the glen, close to the upper lake, was the burial place of the Mocholmog clan, local chieftains and generous donors of the monastery lands, and deeper still the now abandoned Templenaskellig — the Church of the Rock — the first church built by Kevin, perched on a rocky ledge under the cliff by the lakeshore and only accessible by water. Close by, set thirty feet above the lake in the beetling rock of Lugduff Mountain was the little cave carved out by unknown hands ages before Kevin's time and utilised by him as a retreat on coming to the glen. Lulled by the lapping waters of the lake below, a spot more conducive to solitary contemplation would be difficult to imagine.

Bresal turned his gaze to his most recently completed architectural achievement — the gateway to the settlement. He had designed and built it last summer to replace the vulnerable old wooden structure. An archway of stone was topped by a gatekeeper's chamber under a corbelled roof, and immediately inside the gateway stood a small bell-tower, the whole when viewed from outside giving the impression of a smaller version of Kevin's Church, from which he had borrowed the roofing technique.

The great cross-inscribed Sanctuary Stone set beside the paved way inside the gate marked the point at which the law of the church replaced the law of the land, and this was observed by chieftain and peasant alike. The Viking barbarians, of course, had no such scruples.

Bresal scanned the skyline along the mountain ridges; no cloud had marred the blue perfection of the heavens for more than two weeks. His eyes took in the richly wooded slopes of Derrybawn, the steep craggy side of Lugduff and rising majestically behind the workmen on the tower the great hump-backed bulk of Camaderry where sparse stunted trees stood out against the undisturbed blue. Undisturbed, that is, except for the puffs of white smoke ascending from between the trees.

Such was Bresal's mood of contentment that the significance of what he was seeing took a second or two to register, then his heart staggered in mid-beat. The beacon fire!

He scrambled up a ladder that stood against the side of the partly-built tower and looked back towards Brockagh Mountain to the east. Yes. There could be no doubt about it. No possible mistake; plumes of smoke rose from the summit of Brockagh also. Oh, sweet Jesus protect us.

'Vikings!' he yelled, falling down the last four steps of the ladder in his haste and sprawling on the ground. 'It's a raid! A raid!'

He picked himself up and dashed to the gateway, startling the drowsy keeper with frantic shouts to sound the bell. Its tolling at this hour would be automatically interpreted as an alarm by workers outside the cashel, there being no ecclesiastical reason for it. All would repair to the cashel where they would be advised to escape to the mountains with all possible haste. At the first peals of the bell workers began pouring from the corn mill on the Glendasan River just yards from the gateway.

Donal and Cormac, two monks chosen for their youth and fitness, swiftly made their way to the large stone cross close by the Cathedral and waited. Each held a capacious leather bag. At the same time monks in various parts of the valley were hastily removing the more precious objects from the churches in a pre-arranged plan that had evolved painfully over decades of raids. They had at most one hour before the terrible hordes swarmed over the cashel lusting after blood and gold.

Donal and Cormac held their bags open as monks bearing the community's treasures arrived from all directions, sweating in the baking heat of the day. Bresal helped with the treasures from the Cathedral, foremost among these being the golden shrine containing relics of Kevin himself. The Abbot and several older monks stood by with squares of linen in which each object was wrapped separately to prevent damage. Smaller chalices and goblets along with brooches, pins and various small altar implements were placed inside the fabulously decorated large chalices which numbered six. The sacred books, painstakingly handwritten by the scribes of the community, were distributed evenly between the two bags, each book encased in its own shrine of gold or silver. All were packed on top of the sacred vestments which were folded in the bottoms of the bags.

When full the bags stood as tall as an average man, but their handlers were not average men. Donal, the son of an important member of the Mocholmog clan, was a powerfully built six feet seven inches and twenty five years of age; the twenty two year old Cormac only slightly shorter and just as broad. They laced and knotted the leather thongs used to close the bags and willing hands helped hoist them onto their backs placing the carrying straps over their heads and across their shoulders. 'Go, my dear sons, and may God and Holy Kevin guide your feet,' the Abbot said, blessing them with the sign of the cross as they moved off.

Although unwieldy, the bags were not very heavy. The two men crossed the wooden footbridge over the Glenealo, breaking into a loping trot as they started along the way known as the Green Road. High among the trees rising on their left they could hear the shouts and scramblings of fleeing monks and students as they made their way to the crest of Derrybawn. Donal and Cormac continued for more than a mile on the Green Road before turning upwards beside Poulanass waterfall which tumbled in the cleft that divided Derrybawn and Lugduff mountains.

Donal knew exactly where he was making for; these mountains were his home territory and he remembered an ideal hiding place discovered when a boy at play with his friends.

Higher and still higher they went, their strong limbs never flagging, their pace steady until, cresting the hill, they followed the ancient track called Borenacrow that led across the mountain to the rugged fastnesses of Glenmalure. All was utterly quiet now except for the faint drumming of the warm breeze in their ears. They were mercifully out of earshot of the horror that in all probability was at that moment being enacted back at the monastery.

When they had gone more than halfway across the mountain and could now look down into Glenmalure, Donal left the track and made off through the scrubby heather and broken rocks. Sure-footed as they were, extra care had to be taken here; a careless slip could mean damage to the sacred vessels. Great boulders dotted the mountaintop as if abandoned there by giants who had become bored with some game. Donal stopped and surveyed the scene.

'There!' he exclaimed suddenly. 'See yonder windswept holly?' He pointed to a misshapen tree that looked as if some monstrous suction from the east was attempting to tear it from its roots. 'The great rock behind it is our destination.'

Coming up to the massive boulder they laid their burdens carefully on a cushion of purple and white heather. Donal began pulling away the scrub in the narrow space between the tree and the rock. In seconds he had revealed an opening large enough to admit a crawling man.

'I will climb down and you can pass the bags to me,' he said as feet first he edged himself into the hole until he had vanished completely from sight. The cool air in the small cavern beneath was welcome after his exertion. He stood up, mildly surprised the cave still allowed him to do so, his height having increased very considerably since his last visit. Up to ten men could squeeze in here in the unlikely event of such a measure becoming necessary. The Vikings had never followed their prey as far as the high summits on any of their raids, venturing only into the woods on the lower slopes to seek out and butcher any unfortunates who did not have the strength to climb high enough. Many older monks had been lost in this way during previous raids, and some young ones too who tried to save large amounts of their belongings then found themselves too heavily laden to reach safe heights.

Sloping downwards from the cave entrance was a groove in the rock which in wet weather carried rainwater down one side and into the bowels of the mountain through a hole in the floor of the cave, leaving the main part of the little chamber dry at all times; a circumstance of vital importance where the precious manuscripts were concerned.

'I am ready, Cormac. You may lower the bags to me now,' Donal called.

'You are indeed full of surprises, Donal,' Cormac remarked, bringing the first bag to the entrance. 'No man would find this place easily.'

'No man will need to except ourselves when this day of evil has passed.'

Cormac pushed the bottom of the bag at the entrance.

5

'It will not go in.'

'Do not force it. Open the bags and pass the items to me one at a time. That way no damage will be done.'

Half an hour later Donal climbed out from beneath the rock, having carefully placed the precious objects around the floor and folded the bags beside them. He pulled the scraggy growth back into position concealing the entrance.

They lay back on the heather and rested, the sun still high in the sky sending waves of shimmering heat down on the mountain in warm radiating heartbeats from heaven.

'Pray none of our brethren fall into the hands of the evil ones,' Donal said gravely, 'for they are a merciless horde.'

'One wonders,' Cormac observed gazing appreciatively around him at the hills rolling away in all directions into the sun-hazed distance, 'when such beauty exists in the world how the hearts of some men can be filled with a lust to destroy.'

'Ignorance,' Donal replied. 'Wherever knowledge blossoms in the world ignorance rises up against it, tries to extinguish the flame. The barbarians feel they must destroy what they do not understand. Have you noticed how an ignorant person will mock and deride a wise one who, though eminently qualified to mock, will never do so? Ignorance is the most wicked abomination on the face of the earth; all evil springs from it.'

'Surely greed plays a part? They never go away devoid of plunder,' Cormac pointed out.

'And is greed not a direct consequence of ignorance?' Donal replied sadly.

As the sun sank towards the mountains beyond the upper lake Bresal watched from the heights of Derrybawn and saw the first smoke and flames issue from torched buildings as the Vikings overran the settlement far below, the din of destruction reduced to tinklings by distance. The bakery, the scriptorium, the carpenter's workshop and the hospice were all now ablaze, along with many smaller huts of timber construction. Outside the cashel smoke belched from the roof of the corn mill. Helmets and weapons glinted in the fading sunlight and the black raven of Odin's banner flapped proudly over the savagery and devastation.

The thin, barely audible squeals that rose now and then on the air amidst the sounds of vandalism froze Bresal's blood for he knew they were the death-screams of men he knew. Friends. Being slaughtered for nothing more than the lustful entertainment of savages, He prayed so intensely his head hurt, while the prayers of the monks around him lulled the mountain air. His gaze rested upon his half-completed tower which from this height looked like an ink-pot. It was the only hope for the future of the community and a grim determination filled him. He would live. Every ounce of his energy would be channelled into finishing it. He would bring the slaughter to an end; this would be the last time.

Donal and Cormac darted cautiously from tree to tree as they descended towards the cashel. Silence reigned over the ruins except for the odd crackle of still smouldering timber and the eerie creak and splash of the mill-wheel. The raiders seldom delayed any longer than it took to loot, burn or kill whatever was convenient, having no desire to give the local chieftain time to muster forces for a counter-attack.

'They have surely departed by now,' Donal said as they drew ever closer to the cashel. A sudden overpowering revulsion brought him to his knees gagging as he came upon the hacked pieces of what had recently been a man scattered around like a butchered beast on the ground before him.

A human being did this!

Recognition of the dead monk was as impossible as understanding the minds of those who had perpetrated the atrocity. Donal had witnessed similar horrors after earlier attacks; he should have been prepared. But could all the preparation in God's universe render a body insensible to such ferocious inhumanity?

Recovering as best he could he continued downwards between the trees, Cormac, pale as a ghost, following close at his heels. They were now down to the level of the Green Road and Donal stopped behind a tree to watch and listen again for any sign that the raiders might still be around.

There was a swishing sound followed by a slight thud on the ground just behind him. Something rolled past him and out of the trees onto the Green Road. As his numbed brain identified the object as Cormac's head he felt something at his back. Terror did not have time to register. He glanced with a vaguely puzzled look at the ugly blade that protruded from his chest impaling him to the tree. He tried to collapse but could not, his impaler holding the sword firmly and shrieking with hideous laughter.

Blackness released Donal.

CHAPTER 2

1798

The ghostly moonlight that had bathed the glen for the earlier part of the night was slowly, almost imperceptibly, driven across the narrow valley floor and up the rock-strewn side of Lugduff by a creeping black shadow as the moon sank behind the massive ridge of Carrawaystick Mountain. Glenmalure slept. No light flickered from a window in any of the cottages in the glen. The Avonbeg gurgled and sang its way down the valley, fed by the rain-swollen waterfalls that tumbled from the mountains on either side. Except for the never-ending lullaby of the waters, all was still.

A couple of hundred yards from the road a rickety old wooden footbridge spanned the river and led to the tiny two-roomed cottage where Darby Byrne, a man in his seventies gnarled and misshapen by rheumatism, lived with his twenty-year-old son, Matt. When the old man had become too crippled to work five years ago it had fallen to young Matt to keep hunger from the door which he did by milking their four cows and keeping a large potato and vegetable patch. They were luckier than many of their neighbours in that they had about five acres of good grassland spread in a long strip beside the river. At harvest time Matt found work on larger farms outside the glen but never travelled further than would allow him to return home each evening to tend the cows. He had grown to a handsome six feet four and had he been of a fierce disposition would have made a formidable enemy.

Old Darby still managed to do their cooking and on occasion would venture out with the help of a stick and bring the cows in for milking. He had no inclination to sit back and take advantage of his son's willingness, only a sometimes overwhelming frustration at his own disability. He had been over fifty when he married old Jackson's daughter, thirty years his junior, and she had died giving birth to Matt less than a year into the marriage. He knew nothing of babies but neighbours wives had rallied round and Matt found himself being reared by half a dozen eager mothers. 'A good neighbour,' Darby would say, 'is worth a hundred head o' cattle.'

He was proud of his son, whose muscular frame now dwarfed him. They got on well and sat before the fire together in the evenings talking and smoking their pipes.

Only since the recent rebellion had uneasiness impinged upon their contented existence. On random nights a couple of soldiers would be quartered at their house in an attempt to prevent the harbouring of rebels still outstanding on the fastnesses of the surrounding hills. Matt had taken no part in the rebellion. He had resisted all entreaties to join the rebels knowing his father could not run the farm without him.

The rebels, however, considered the Byrne house a safe one and on an inclement night up to four of them might arrive after dark seeking shelter which was never refused. On more than one occasion the rebel Captain Michael Dwyer himself had spent the night there.

Tonight father and son were alone in the house. Darby snored in a small bunk near the fireplace, a pot of porridge nearby on the hearth ready to heat when he rose and revived the fire in the morning. On the double bed in the room behind the fireplace Matt slept the sleep that is the reward of honest toil.

'Get up, Darby Byrne, you old villain. Come out here!' The sudden barking shout rent the stillness and echoed back and forth between the rocky slopes.

Matt opened his eyes. Somebody shouting. Had he been dreaming? His answer came in a violent banging on the door.

'Open up, you old bastard!'

'Matt...' his father's voice came hoarsely from the other room.

'All right, father. I'm awake, I hear,' he said, rolling from the bed and peering out into the darkness through the small window in the bedroom. He could make out the shapes of several horses, one with a soldier in the saddle.

'It's yeos, father,' he said, running to the door and calling: 'What do you want?'

'If you don't open this bloody door in the name of the King we'll burn you alive in there.'

Without waiting for a reply the terrific crashing against the door of rifle butts and boots recommenced. The masonry around the heavy iron bolt began to crack and crumble.

'Dear God, protect us,' Darby prayed as the splintered door flew inwards on its hinges.

Two soldiers burst into the room, a third stayed in the doorway. 'Corporal Edward Baker at your service,' the leader introduced himself with an undisguised sneer. 'Get a light burning. Quickly now.'

'Yes sir, yes,' Darby shuffled to the fireplace and uncovered a glowing turf. He picked it up with the tongs and lit the small crusie lamp that hung in the chimney beside the fire. Baker took a stub of candle from the window-sill, lit it and checked the bedroom. The bright red of their coats-seemed to fill the place and they reeked of drink. Matt was filled with a terrible dread; these men were strangers. Most of the local yeomen were known to him, many of them neighbours who regularly harboured Dwyer and his men and had made possible his escape from capture on many occasions. But Matt had heard stories from the rebels of horrific atrocities committed by yeos of a very different disposition, some so shocking he refused to believe, taking them as understandable rebel exaggerations.

'So, Mister Darby Byrne, no rebel scum at home tonight, sir, eh?' Baker put the candle back on the window ledge. 'A great pity,' he shook his head, 'a great pity indeed, for now we are disappointed, and wouldn't you agree, sir, that it's a shameful thing that soldiers in his Glorious Majesty's service should be disappointed?

'Leave him alone,' Matt intervened, 'what has he ever done to harm you?'

'Keep your croppy mouth shut or it will not go well for you,' Baker almost screamed at him, his eyes wild, 'as you very well know, this old dog harbours filthy murdering rebels, and you know too what we do with his kind.' Matt saw the mad blood-lust in the man's eyes and his heart sank. He made a lunge at the sneering face and was brought down by a vicious blow to the side of the face from the gun-butt of the second yeoman. All three soldiers laughed as he rolled on the floor clutching his head in agony.

'In the name of God, why do you disgrace your uniform like this. We

11

want no part of your war,' Darby pleaded, tears welling in his eyes at his son's ill-treatment. 'What choice do we have when soldiers or rebels come to our door with guns in their hands demanding shelter? We treat you all in the same manner, God help us.'

'Aha! Did you hear that, boys? Did you hear that?' Baker exclaimed, the expression on his face like that of a prospector who has just extracted a gold nugget from the earth. 'A clear confession to harbouring, and in front of most reliable witnesses.' He placed his hand mock-friendly fashion on Darby's shoulder. 'Well, my proud old ruffian, I'm afraid it's time to go.'

'Where are you taking me?' Darby enquired.

What in different circumstances would have been described as a childish giggle escaped Baker's lips as he reached for his musket where he had left it leaning against the wall.

'Williams!' he addressed the man in the doorway. 'You and Murphy hold the young buck, and hold him well, mark you.'

They lifted Matt to his feet and twisted his arms behind his back. Baker turned back to Darby.

'Now, my good fellow, if you will oblige me removing your rags, sir,' he ended the sentence in a semi-hysterical chortle. Matt, despite the searing agony of his smashed face, sensed his father was as good as dead and struggled violently to free himself from his captors.

'No!', he cried, his bloodied mouth distorting his voice. 'For the love of Jesus, I beg you leave my father be. Take me instead.' Baker left Darby be long enough to drive a well-aimed boot into Matt's groin. Matt screamed and tried to double over but the two yeos held him upright. His head buzzed and he came close to passing out, the laughter of his tormentors fading in and out of his consciousness.

'Why do you protest so, lad? We are here only to amuse you. Watch! Watch closely. I am sure you will find the entertainment memorable.' Through his raging pain and delirium Matt heard his father's voice crying piteously: 'Matt... Matt, I'm so sorry, son...'

The old man stood naked, pathetically thin, tears streaming down his face. His weeping seemed to infuriate Baker who flew at him, bayonet at the ready, and screamed into his face: 'Die! You filthy old reptile. You foul scum of a whore's bastard. Die!'

Spittle flew and foam bubbled at the corners of his mouth.

'Ma...' His son's name died in a choking squawk on Darby's lips as Baker plunged his bayonet into his stomach, ripping it upwards under his ribcage. The yeoman's maniacal laughter was now completely out of control as with the strength of madness he drove Darby's writhing form back against the chimney breast, lifting him off the floor and holding him there on the bayonet. 'Die! Die! Die!' he shrieked, blood sputtering into his face and running down the rifle onto his hands and arms, until Darby's body hung limp and lifeless. He withdrew the bayonet and the body collapsed across the fireplace. There was silence for several seconds except for the heavy rasping breaths of Baker. Even his own comrades were shocked speechless by the bloodthirsty ferocity of the murder. 'He... confessed,' Baker finally gasped, 'you heard him, he didn't deserve... to live.'

'Maybe it would have been better for us to have brought him in,' ventured Williams.

'Oh yes,' sneered Baker, 'and have him appeal to our gracious Viceroy. He'd be back here with a protection within a week. That Cornwallis is too easily swayed by the whining of these villains, No. We have done what is best. Now, outside and fire the place.'

'What about this one,' Murphy asked.

Matt now hung unconscious between the two soldiers, having passed out, his mind incapable of coping with the horror as his father was bayoneted.

'Bring him along. We'll leave him hanging at the Rock where he can bid good morning to his croppy friends.'

Cullen's rock, a huge granite boulder at the roadside nearby was regularly utilised as a gallows for the dispatch of rebels.

They dragged Matt outside and threw him to the ground some yards from the house. A fourth soldier, the one seen by Matt from the bedroom window, was still mounted on guard. Murphy and Williams lit some papers and pieces of Darby's torn clothing and stuffed them under the thatch above the doorway. In seconds the dry straw was an inferno, the yeomen performing a whooping war-dance around it. Matt regained consciousness in time to see the roof fall in sending a shower of sparks and flames skywards. The soldiers cheered. Matt could see them clearly against the glare and could feel the heat on his battered face.

Above the roar and crackle of the fire he thought he heard the sound of a whistle being blown and seconds later the mounted soldier fell with a heavy thud to the ground within two feet of him.

'Matt... I'm dying, Matt,' the soldier croaked his name. 'For God's sake, forgive me.'

Matt's confused brain struggled to formulate a reply to something he would have found difficult to comprehend even in his proper senses; one of the men who had come here to murder his father was now imploring his forgiveness!

'It's Jack Woods, Matt... I had no choice. They said it was just a routine search for rebels. I knew there were none at the house... thought that would be the end of it.'

Jack Woods. The name registered. Jack Woods...! His first cousin from Imaal, the next glen. Aunt Jane... father's sister. Oh, God in heaven, was there to be no end to the miseries of this night? 'Jack... they've killed father. How could you just stand by. You could have tried...' Matt realized he was speaking to a corpse; Jack had given a long sigh and stopped breathing.

Williams turned from the blazing house and called: 'Woods, come join... By Christ, he has Woods down. I'll finish the villain now.' He made a run towards Matt and tumbled to the ground before he had covered three paces. He lay absolutely still. This time Matt had heard the musket shot, had seen Williams's head whip sideways as the ball smashed into his right temple.

Baker and Murphy stood and looked at each other in shock for a second, the mad look in Baker's eyes turning to one of terror as he realized they made perfect targets for their unseen attackers against the background of flames.

'Run!'

As the word left his mouth a volley of musket-fire rang out and he screamed as a ball shattered his thigh throwing him to the ground. Murphy managed to mount his horse but was brought down almost immediately by another volley.

Four men carrying muskets emerged from the darkness. One ran to where Baker lay moaning, kicked his gun out of reach and stood over him. As Matt attempted to get to his feet another brought his weapon to bear on him. Matt recognized him.

'Don't shoot, Vesty, It's me, Matt Byrne.'

His face was now so swollen and stiff it took a desperate effort to get the words out.

'Praise be to God,' exclaimed Vesty Byrne, relaxing and dropping on one knee beside him. 'Oh, but they've done a fine job on your face, Matt, I wouldn't have known you. Lie there now and don't stir yourself until we've done here.'

'Father... they bayoneted him. That one there...' he pointed to the whimpering Baker.

'And right dearly he'll pay for it, never fear.'

All four rebels were known to Matt. When they had checked and found the other three yeomen to be dead they gathered around Baker and deliberated whether to shoot him where he lay or hang him at Cullen's Rock. Listening to them, the scene of his father's horrific murder flashed upon Matt's mind and he was seized by a violent blinding rage. Before the rebels could do anything he had scrambled to his feet, pushed his way between them and was kicking frenziedly at the face that had so recently sneered and taken delight in the murder of a fellow human being. By the time they managed to haul him away Baker's head was just a bloody mass, but he was still breathing.

'Well, that settles it anyway,' Martin Burke said raising his musket, 'we can't hang him in that state,' and he sent a ball through the mutilated head. Baker's body shuddered and was still. 'Do you think you can sit a horse, Matt?' Vesty asked, 'We have a fine selection of mounts now.'

'I think so. Just give me a hand up.'

Vesty lifted him single-handedly onto the horse.

'These fellows will have no more need of horses in this world, the Devil can supply his own. We'll take you to Pierce Harney's place at Baravore. You'll be safe enough there, and we'll get somebody to have a look at that jaw. I'll wager by the look of it the bone is in smithereens.'

'Did you blow a whistle?' Matt mumbled. 'Thought I heard...'

'Not I, avick,' Vesty replied. 'That was the Captain's signal for us to attack. He has an old sea-whistle he uses for that purpose so there can be no mistaking that particular order.'

Matt looked around, his eyes questioning.

'He'll be on the road ahead of us. We were making for Harney's when we saw the fire. Those yeos had little sense to go and signal their whereabouts like that.'

Martin Burke and Sam McAllister gathered the weapons of the dead yeomen while the fourth man, whom Matt recognized as the formidable John

Mernagh, was stripping harness and saddles from their horses. His pock-marked face shadowed by great beetling black eyebrows tended to confirm the expediency of having him on your side. He had been born and reared in Glenmalure.

'Now, let us be away from here,' he said when the loads were shared out. They rode slowly in the darkness along the narrow road, passing the ghostly white granite of Cullen's rock. Near the head of the glen they crossed Baravore Ford and after a few hundred yards turned left up a steep stone-flagged path to Pierce Harney's cottage. Mrs. Harney settled Matt on a palliasse by the fire and set about making him comfortable. She ladled out bowls of hot soup for the men but Matt found himself quite unable to open his mouth wide enough to take any.

'God love you,' she murmured, stroking his hair, 'God love you.' Footsteps approached the door and Michael Dwyer entered the cottage. 'Pierce is watching the ford,' he said, leaving his musket on the table. A little under six feet in height, broad-shouldered and straight-standing, his almost black eyes took in the room and came to rest on Matt.

'A cruel night for you, Matt Byrne,' he said, approaching the bed, 'but ne'er a one of them will gloat over it.'

Matt could only summon a grunt in reply.

'When you are recovered you can decide what you want to do. We would not force you out on your keeping with us, but I think it likely that you now have a better understanding of why we are out in the first place.'

Matt grunted again.

'I would caution you, however,' Dwyer continued, 'against branding all yeos as devils, for this is far from being the case. I have it on good authority that in the event of a successful rising they would desert in their hundreds and join us. Besides, it's true to say that we are as safe in many a yeoman's house in this area as we are here at Harney's. Our friend McAllister here has already deserted from the Antrim Militia and can vouch for what I say.' Sam McAllister nodded in affirmation, pulling his bright green cravat, which he was seldom seen without, from around his neck in the heat of the room.

'Ay,' he said in his sharp northern accent, 'there are some who would burn their own mothers, but many more just biding their time until the moment is right.'

'It should not be forgotten either,' Dwyer went on, 'that among our men we have those who would plunder and murder and who care not one whit for justice, which is all we seek. When they become known to us these people are dealt with right severely.' Mrs. Harney produced a jar of whiskey from a small cupboard. 'If we can get some of this into you it should help ease the pain, Matt, asthore.'

'Begod,' Martin Burke exclaimed, 'I believe I feel the very divil of a pain coming on meself!'

The others laughed and Dwyer remarked that he too had just now felt a definite twinge.

'Well, you can all wait awhilst I see to this poor lad. I doubt he finds your oul' prate very funny.'

She took a bulrush from a bundle that had been collected for lights and broke off a few inches of stem which she cleaned out and placed between Matt's swollen lips.

'Now, which of you boys has the steadiest hand? This jar is heavy and I don't want to waste good whiskey on the floor.' Dwyer took the jar.

'I'll hold the reed steady. You just let the whiskey trickle in, nice and easy now,' Mrs. Harney instructed. 'The rest of you hold your tongues a minute.'

Dwyer lifted the jar, his face set in concentration as the first dribble entered the reed. Matt felt the warmth in his throat but when he swallowed the whiskey went against his breath and he coughed and spluttered, then whined through his nose with the pain.

'Slowly. Slowly, Michael.'

They started again, and whiskey dripped and trickled down Matt's gullet for the next quarter of an hour. Its glow spread through him, soothing and calming, and he felt himself drifting away from the pain, the room, the voices of his rescuers. He vaguely wondered if he was falling asleep or dying; he didn't really care which.

CHAPTER 3

For long hours after the house had become quiet except for the snoring of his men, a troubled Michael Dwyer sat perusing a piece of paper in the flickering firelight, occasionally taking a draught of whiskey from a mug on the hob.

'This is to certify that the bearer hereof, Michael Dwyer, of the parish of Donoughmore, County Wicklow, by occupation farmer, has surrendered himself, confessed his being engaged in the present Rebellion and Michael Dwyer has given up all his arms and discovered of those which he knew to be concealed; has taken the Oath of Allegiance to his Majesty, his heirs and successors, and has abjured all former Oaths and Engagements in any wise whatsoever contrary thereto, and has bound himself for the future as a peaceable and loyal Subject; in consequence whereof this certificate is given to the said Michael Dwyer in order that his person and his property may not in any wise be molested.

All His Majesty's loving subjects are hereby enjoined to pay due Attention thereto, in Pursuance of the Proclamation issued by Major-General John Moore, dated the 9th day of August 1798; and this Certificate is to be in full force so long as the said Michael Dwyer continues to demean himself as a peaceable and loyal Subject.'

Dated at Imaal the 9th day of August 1798.

At last, looking across at the sleeping disfigured face of young Matt Byrne, Dwyer let the Protection slip from his fingers into the flames. Three short weeks ago he had ridden into the English camp at the head of the Glen of Imaal where Lord Huntley and Major-General Moore were camped with the 100th Regiment of Highlanders. The camp had been set up there to facilitate the distribution of Protections to rebels outstanding in the Wicklow Mountains since the failed rebellion.

Dwyer had been well received by Huntley and Moore and they made him an offer of a foreign commission if he so desired. Lord Huntley had gone so far as to warn him of the inadvisability of sleeping at home, even with the Protection under his pillow. The warning was unnecessary; Dwyer well knew that while the Highlanders on the whole conducted themselves in an honourable manner, a large number of yeomen appeared to have divested themselves of any vestige of humanity and were out of control, terrorizing the countryside, perpetrating the most horrific atrocities on those who had handed in their arms and were now without means of defending themselves.

The truth was most of those who had taken up arms would never have done so had they not been driven to it by the barbaric actions of the yeos in recent times.

Lord Cornwallis, the new Viceroy and Commander-in-chief of His Majesty's forces in Ireland, had remarked that 'the ferocity of our troops who delight in murder most powerfully counteracts all plans of reconciliation.' He also condemned the folly of endeavouring to make it a religious war. General Moore, speaking of the Militia said: 'The tendency to pillage is great... the moment the men were allowed to pile their arms they began plundering all round until the exasperated inhabitants took arms and killed three of them. The conduct of the Militia in this respect is dreadful. The composition of the officers is so bad that I see it will be impossible to make soldiers of them.'

Dwyer drained his whiskey-mug and watched the Protection erupt with a whump, the flames muttered their seven-second life away and the black remains lifted from the glowing turf and wafted up the chimney. It was no good; he would have to remain out on his keeping. No man, however peaceable, could lie down under such brutality.

Some men, having received their Protections at the camp had had the misfortune to meet with groups of yeomen on their way home. The yeos had forced them to eat their Protections, then shot them and left them to die by the roadside. This had happened only a short time before to Andy Doran, a neighbour of Dwyers from the Glen of Imaal, but the murder of old Darby Byrne and near-murder of young Matt, neither of whom had ever been out, was the last straw. Even some of the clergy were now out; men who had passionately pleaded against insurrection until the murders became so blatant they felt they had no choice but to help defend their flock.

Dwyer felt better having made his decision. He would call a meeting of his most trusted men at the cave on Keadeen Mountain; after tonight most of them would surely be of the same mind as himself. His decision to stay out left him with a personal problem to sort out; his wedding was due to take place in a month. What would Mary say to this reversal of events? He did not relish the thought of facing her, remembering how overcome with joy and relief she had been when he had finally agreed to take out a Protection.

'Mary Doyle,' he said to himself as he rose from his chair, 'you are a lovely creature, but it was a misfortunate wind that blew you to John Cullen's house that night. You little knew the trouble you were storing for yourself.'

John Cullen's cottage stood on Knockgorragh Hill, a remote spot in Imaal which made it a much-favoured place of refuge for Dwyer. Mary had been there visiting when he had found it necessary to avail of Cullen's hospitality one stormy night and he had fallen for her dark looks straight away. Both storm and night had passed before they left the fireside. The exciting promises her dark eyes made during that first meeting had been fulfilled and Cullen's had become their regular rendezvous. Thoughts of her had steeled his determination to get out of some extremely perilous situations which might otherwise have proved fatal.

He gently shook the shoulder of big Vesty Byrne. Vesty woke with a great snort from a sound sleep. He groaned as he stood up from his awkward squatting position in the corner of the room. 'By Christ, Mick, my very bones hurt like the devil.'

'Ay, Vesty, a common complaint among cave-dwellers. It's almost dawn. Time we moved on and let Pierce Harney into his bed for an hour or two.'

They roused the other three men and Sam McAllister ran down to the ford and informed Harney they were leaving.

'And right relieved I am to hear it, Sam avick. The weather is turning a mite chilly for a body to be out strollin' by the river all night.'

The four rebels rode off in the opposite direction to that from which they had come, making their way over the mountains into the Glen of Imaal by the high trail known as the Black Banks. There were four great glens in the vicinity: Imaal, Glenmalure, Glendalough and Glenmacnass, radiating like spokes in a cartwheel and separated by steep rock-strewn mountains which concealed many a cave known only to rebels on their keeping.

The sun was rising over Imaal when Dwyer parted from his companions having arranged a meeting in the cave on Keadeen to discuss their plans for the future. He turned his mount in the direction of John Cullen's place.

Vesty Byrne looked after his friend and leader as he rode away. 'There's no doubt of it,' he remarked, shaking his head, 'that Doyle one has him bewitched, but then it must be admitted she could bewitch any man of us if she took it into her pretty head.'

CHAPTER 4

John Cullen hacked some generous chunks of bacon from the smoke-browned flitch that hung in the chimney and threw them onto the big iron frying pan. The delicious smell of cooking wafted out over the half door to greet Dwyer as he approached. His stomach growled and he allowed the hunger to register. Long months on the run when a meal could never be guaranteed had trained his mind to ignore hunger for extended periods and although he had taken food at Harney's last night the aroma of frying bacon made his legs feel weak.

'Good morning in there, John Cullen,' he shouted as he came up to the door. Cullen leaned over the half door, the fork he had been turning the bacon with steaming in the morning air.

'Michael,' he smiled broadly, 'it's good to see it's yourself. When anyone else rides up I'm pepperin' for fear they're comin' to tell me you're dead.'

Dwyer laughed. 'It's a great comfort to know you have such unshakeable confidence in me, John, old friend.'

'Think nothin' of it. Get that horse out of sight around the back and we'll breakfast together.'

'You'll not have to twist my arm, John, I'll be with you right sharply.'

Cullen forked the hunks of dripping bacon into a dish and cracked half a dozen eggs into the pan. Since his wife had passed on two years ago, looking after Dwyer, who was a relative, had given him heart to go on. He was proud of the trust the rebel leader placed in him. The Cullens had no children of their own but the young Doyles from Knockandarragh had come to play around the little cottage on the hillock from the time they could walk. They were all married now except for Mary who still called to see him and more often than ever now since Dwyer had come into the picture. A second pan of bacon popped and sizzled over the fire as Dwyer and Cullen made short work of the first lot.

'Has Mary been by of late?'

Cullen gave a knowing chuckle. 'Divil a day passes but she's here askin' me the same question about yourself. If you can manage to stay aisy until about midday I'll hould a shiny guinea you'll see her traipsin' up the hill.'

Dwyer looked solemn. 'I'm afraid she may not be very pleased with what I have to say to her this day, John, and God knows it pains me greatly to cause her grief, but I'm staying out. I burned the Protection.'

'Ah, no, Michael,' Cullen's cutlery clattered on his plate and he sat back from the table, his face slack with disbelief, 'I thought you were safe at last and you for the altar in a few weeks time. Faith, and this'll break the poor colleen's heart all right, and she's been as happy as a kitten in a dairy since you took out that protection. But why? For God's sake, Michael, tell me what came over you at all that you did such a thing?'

'Yeos murdered old Darby Byrne last night and burned his house...'

'God rest the poor man,' Cullen interjected, 'he that never spoke a bad word about a soul.'

'They would have done for young Matt as well', Dwyer continued, 'had we not seen the fire and intervened. It was God's doing that Vesty and the other boys had not taken out Protections yet, for if they'd been unarmed as I was Matt would be dead now. Vesty gave me a spare musket he had but by the look of it I fear it may be a greater danger to myself than to the enemy. Matt is in a bad enough state over at Harney's, but that's not all. A different band of yeos murdered Andy Doran on his way home after collecting his Protection, made him eat it first, and he is one of many, I regret to say. Somebody called to my father's house and warned him that if I showed myself there they would get me. Now tell me, John, what earthly good is a Protection to a man if he can't sleep in his own bed?'

'God protect us then,' Cullen sighed resignedly. ''It seems there's to be no peace for this poor country no matter which way we turn.'

They finished the meal in silence, then Dwyer rose and yawned. 'I could do well with a few hours sleep.'

'The bed is ready, and you can sleep aisy. I'll keep my eye to the hill.'

'I sleep no easier anywhere than I do under this roof of yours, John,' Dwyer replied as he entered the smaller of the two bedrooms which stood at either side of the kitchen. Here Cullen had recently built in an opening window at the back in case Dwyer should ever need to make a hasty escape; he could be on his horse, which was tethered outside the window, in seconds. It was late afternoon when he was awakened by the sound of clattering pots and crockery and the voice of Mary Doyle chatting to John Cullen. He threw Cullen a questioning look as he came into the kitchen and Cullen shook his head.

'I'm right glad to see you here, Mary.'

Mary turned from the fire where a big iron pot of potatoes was on the boil. 'Oh, indeed, Mister Dwyer,' she said playfully, 'and I suppose that's why you've spent the five hours I've been here snoring like Pat's pig being driven to market.' She ran and embraced him, then, sensing that all was not as it should be, held him at arms length.

'Something's wrong, Michael. Out with it.'

'In truth, Mary, I hate to tell you, but I won't beat about the bush. I have decided it is impossible for me to keep the terms of the Protection. It could mean being murdered in my bed.' She slumped away from him onto a chair and with her face in her hands said quietly:

'Are you going to tell me now that we shouldn't get married, Michael? Does this change all our plans?'

'I'm going to tell you nothing of the sort. We'll be married on the day as planned if you'll still have me, but I'm afraid it cannot be in church, Mary, it would be foolhardy to expose our people to danger. If Father Dick Murphy and John here will agree I think the best place for the wedding would be in this house.' She rose and embraced him again.

'Michael Dwyer, of course I'll still have you, but it's the divil of a hard thing to have to be all the time worrying about you just when we thought things were looking a bit brighter.'

He told her about the recent murders.

'I knew you wouldn't go back on your promise lightly,' she said. He kissed her forehead. 'I must be off soon to the cave on Keadeen.'

'Faith, and do you know what I'm goin' to tell you, young Dwyer,' Cullen said, 'if you and your friends are not finished off by a ball from a yeo's musket, then the damp of them caves you spend so much time in will do the job. John Mernagh was here last week and he was barkin' like an oul' dog, the man. A graveyard cough if ever I heard one.'

Dwyer laughed.

'Ay, Mernagh laughed too. I might as well be whistlin' a jig to a milestone as showin' concern for such an ungrateful pack. You'll fill your belly before you go, anyway,' he said as he turned a huge pile of potatoes into a bowl on the table. 'There's plenty of buttermilk to wash the praties down.'

CHAPTER 5

Riding towards Keadeen Dwyer came up with Sam McAllister who was also making his way to the meeting. Together they gave the lie to the propaganda emanating from some high quarters determined to label the troubles in Ireland a religious war, for McAllister was a Presbyterian and Dwyer a Roman Catholic. The Society of United Irishmen, the organization to which they both belonged, had been founded by the Protestant Theobald Wolfe Tone in the north of the country.

They left their mounts in a little grove of stunted oaks as darkness fell and started up the mountain on foot, a warm September breeze stirring the heather as they climbed. On the open hillside which appeared devoid of any sign that humankind had ever set foot in the place, Dwyer stopped, turned his back to a big rock and kicked it with his heel. Almost immediately a large clump of heather appeared to uproot itself and the head of Vesty Byrne was suddenly there in its place.

'All here?' Dwyer enquired.

'Ay, you're the last.'

They climbed one by one through the small opening and down a short ladder, Sam McAllister pulling the clump of heather into place behind him. The cave opened from a short narrow passageway into a small chamber capable of holding a dozen or more people comfortably with space enough for a small table around which some of the men present now sat on various types of roughly-made stools playing cards by the light of a candle stuck in an old bottle and a couple of rushlights stuck into the moss that lined the walls in an attempt to keep the damp at bay. A series of large nails had been driven into one wall and these served as hangers for the variety of 'uniforms' and accoutrements of the men. In the flickering light the cave evinced an atmosphere of cosiness, but this impression would soon be dispelled by the approach of winter. The cards were gathered and put away as Dwyer took his place at the table.

Along with Dwyer, McAllister, Vesty Byrne, John Mernagh and Martin Burke were John Healy from Annamoe, Paddy Grant who owned a large farm in Glenmalure, Big Arthur Devlin of Cronybyrne, Little Paddy Bryan, the black-bearded tailor from Imaal and Wat McDonnell from Baltinglass.

McDonnell produced a bottle of whiskey and it was passed around. When the appreciative coughing and spluttering had died down Dwyer addressed the little gathering.

'Well, boys, there is little need to make any fancy speeches about why we are back in this cave tonight. You are all well aware of what has been happening around here, and I have it from a man who travelled out recently from the town of Bray that there have been many murders there, and that between here and that town the countryside is almost deserted. He saw cabins burning in all directions, the inhabitants shot as they tried to run away. Now while Cornwallis himself appears by all accounts to be a fair and decent man, it's clear that he finds it impossible to control the bloodlust of the lower orders of the yeomen who don't share his humanity. In such circumstances I can see no alternative to staying out and fighting, as we are all marked for murder whatever we do. We'll fight on in the hope that the French will eventually succeed in coming to our assistance.'

As Dwyer spoke a slow silent procession of seven local women bore what was left of old Darby Byrne through the darkness far below in Glenmalure. They carried the charred corpse, wrapped in sacking, to the head of the glen and over the Black Banks pass to the ancient graveyard of Kilranelagh where a makeshift coffin and an opened grave awaited them. Here and there along the way more women appeared out of the night with a murmured prayer and joined them.

They lowered the coffin and took turns with a shovel to fill the grave, then stood and prayed in hushed tones. From the surrounding trees and bushes the voices of jeering yeos, disappointed that their hours of waiting had yielded no rebels, cursed the women.

'Croppy sluts! Rebel whores!' they hissed, unseen in the blackness. The women ignored the taunts, finished their praying and retreated in silence from the graveyard.

Close to Baravore Ford Pierce Harney's wife left the group and climbed the steep path to her cottage.

'Your father's at rest now, Matt' she addressed the prone figure on the palliasse, his face now grotesquely swollen and any attempt at speech impossible. He blinked his acknowledgement through a haze of pain. His stomach growled hungrily having known nothing but whiskey and warm milk for more than twenty four hours. Mrs. Harney poked the fire and poured some more milk into a small iron pot.

'I got a message for you while I was out, Matt. Paddy Grant has arranged with a young lad to take care of your cows. He has taken them over to Grant's farm at Kirikee and you're not to be worrying your head about them. A few extra to milk will be no trouble to them over there.'

That itself. The fate of the cows had been on his mind but he had been unable to communicate his concern to anybody. The fact of his homelessness and loneliness in the world now bore down on him, mental agony vying with the physical for supremacy in his tortured brain. He knew little or nothing about politics, his life up to now having been completely taken up with farming. From the conversations of sheltering rebels he had learned of the failure of the rebellion earlier in the year, and of at least two abortive attempts by French fleets to come to the aid of the insurgents. He now owed his life to the rebels, and it seemed only right that he should strive to be of whatever service he could to them. Besides, a great rage burned inside him at the senseless murder of his father, and riding with Dwyer and his men could provide opportunities for revenge.

'Now, asthore,' Mrs. Harney said soothingly as she eased the reed between his swollen lips.

CHAPTER 6

FEBRUARY 15TH 1799

Sam McAllister pushed the furze stopper from the cave-mouth high on Keadeen and let a sudden squawk out of him. The men back in the chamber who had been slapping limbs to keep their circulation going or holding frozen fingers over the pathetic heat of candle flames suddenly leapt for their weapons. McAllister came stumbling and spluttering along the passageway shaking lumps of snow from his face and hair.

'A blizzard!' he gasped. 'It's thick on the ground already out there. The oul' lady's plucking her geese in earnest tonight.' They laughed at his misfortune and relaxed.

'If you create such a din when a bit of snow falls on your head,' Dwyer chuckled, 'I hope not to be in the same county if you ever find yourself on the wrong end of a pike. I suggest we lose no time in getting out of here and finding proper shelter. We'd freeze to death here overnight.'

'Where will we go?' asked Wat McDonnell. 'We can't go trekking across the Black Banks in that weather, and anyway there's a dozen of us, Harney wouldn't have room.'

'We'll not attempt to get to Glenmalure. Hoxey's farm at Derrynamuck is our safest bet. It can't be much past nine o'clock so they'll not be abed yet. Hoxey can take several of us and the rest can divide between Toole's and Connel's further up the lane. They're friendly enough, and that way we'll all be within hailing distance of each other.'

'They'll not be over-pleased at having us barge in on them,' said Sam McAllister.

'True enough, Sam,' Dwyer replied, 'but I'm afraid neither we nor they have a choice. However, we can assure them that no yeo will be anxious to forsake his fireside this night."

They wrapped themselves in cloaks, some supplied by friendly yeos, others reluctantly by their less amiable comrades, and climbed out into the white swirling night. The wind was not as strong as they had feared but the snow fell in huge flakes clogging their eyes in seconds making them sharply aware of the urgency of getting to lower ground. They picked their steps cautiously through the deepening blanket of white that covered treacherous holes and loose stones that could crack an ankle like a piece of rotted wood in such low temperatures. By the time they reached the floor of Imaal their feet and legs were soaked and frozen.

Here the wind was all but non-existent and, apart from the sound of the mens' footsteps in the snow and the infinitely gentle settling of countless millions of snowflakes, the glen had been transformed into a world of white silence. Dwyer was apprehensive as they approached Derrynamuck; the householders had had no notice of their coming and there could be no guarantee that some soldiers would not be free-quartered in one or more of the cottages. The more corrupt element of the military welcomed free-quartering as a perk, as many houses would boast some good-looking females who would be looked upon as fair game, and rape was widespread. Complaint could result in the torching of one's home.

Leaving the group at the entrance to the farmyard Dwyer advanced alone to Hoxey's door. The glow of candlelight from within on the falling flakes had an almost hypnotic effect and Dwyer stood for some moments contemplating the peaceful beauty of it, then shaking himself he knocked on the door.

'Who is it?' a male voice enquired.

'Michael Dwyer. Let me in, Pat Hoxey, before I perish.'

Bolts were pulled back and the door opened.

'Have you lost your reason altogether, Mick, to be abroad on a night like this? Get in there with you.'

'Rest assured it's not for divarsion we're out there. Listen, Pat, there's a dozen of us needing shelter. I dislike tempting trouble to your door but we'll be off early in the morning, and by the look of things outside it could be days before a patrol comes this way again.'

'A dozen!' Hoxey was aghast. 'You know I'll help if I can, Mick, but we've already got some extra people here. All the beds are taken up.'

'Don't bother your head about beds, we'll be only too glad to get in out of that weather. If you can manage two or three the rest can stay at Toole's and Connel's.'

Hoxey agreed to take two men and Dwyer went to fetch the group who were huddling in the shelter of the roadside hedge. A short distance beyond them, also keeping close in to the hedge and unseen in the swirling snow by the shivering rebels, a rider watched and waited. With muffled goodnights Ned Lennon and Tom Clerk gratefully entered Hoxey's and the others trudged through the farmyard and on up the lane to Toole's, a distance of about thirty yards. Here Wat McDonnell, John Ashe, Pat Toole, Darby Dunn, John Mickle and Hughie the Brander Byrne were put up. Miley Connel's cottage was at the top of the lane, a further thirty yards from Toole's. Dwyer, McAllister, Pat Costello and John Savage arrived at his door.

'I'll not turn you away, Dwyer, for I wouldn't turn a stray dog from my door on the class of night that's in it, but remember I have a wife and children here and if word of this gets out we'll be evicted. It'll be on your head.'

Dwyer knew the man spoke the truth; eviction was one of the less harsh penalties for harbouring. They entered the blessed warmth of the kitchen and Connel's wife hung a huge cauldron of rabbit stew on the crane over the fire. Boots and trousers were pulled off and left near the hearth to dry and the men sat around in their long underdrawers and bare Feet. 'Miley,' Dwyer sighed, luxuriating in the heat from the blazing turf, 'you may not appreciate it, but your address is Paradise.'

Back down on the main road the lone horseman moved away, disappearing into the snowy night in the direction of Rathdrum. Despite the weather, Pat Hoxey decided he would take no chances and around midnight he and Matt Byrne who had been helping out at the farm and was lodging there came out of the house to mount a watch. All prints of man and beast had long been completely obliterated.

'I'll get into the ditch a little way on the Stratford side,' he said to Byrne, turning left at the entrance. 'You do the same on the Rathdrum road.'

They each wore two long, high-collared coats one over the other against the weather, and old slouch farm hats pulled down over their heads so that by hunching their shoulders they were completely protected from the falling snow. It was already deep enough to make walking difficult and Matt lifted his feet high at each step as he searched for and found a suitable spot where he burrowed his way into the hedge as far as he could. Although his face had healed well and showed no outward sign of his injuries, the cold made his jaw ache and he resented this extra torture being inflicted on him. Hoxey was being over cautious. Mother of Jesus, who in their senses would be out chasing rebels on a night like this? He hunkered down, hugging his knees, his face bent over to catch the warm air from his body coming up between the coats. Four months now since he had told Dwyer he would ride with him, and all he had been allowed to do so far had been picket duty, spending his nights on watch outside while the rebels snored in warm beds. He had approached Dwyer about the possibility of going on raids and had impressed upon him his desire to avenge his father. It had only earned him a lecture.

'Until you empty your head of that revenge nonsense there will be no raids for you, my friend. You would only prove a hot-headed liability to us, so just calm yourself and bide your time.' An hour passed and nothing moved in the hushed glen. Occasionally he raised his head and peered along the unbroken white of the road. Not that he could see very far; the snow was falling so heavily it brought visibility down to a few yards. He rocked back and forth to keep himself from freezing; the cold seemed to have penetrated his bones. He felt as if he wouldn't be able to stand up if every soldier in the county of Wicklow came marching into Imaal. He stretched one leg out in front of him, balancing on the other, then reversed his position to exercise the other leg. Finally managing to get into a standing position he moaned with the pain in his frozen hands and feet which now rivalled that in his jaw.

'This is sheer madness,' he hissed between his chattering teeth. He hauled himself out of the hedge. Thorny briars, reluctant to release him, showered him with small avalanches of snow as he tore himself free. He shook himself, stuffed his hands deep into the large coat-pockets and stumbled back down the road to the farm entrance. In the yard a little way up from the house stood a small pigsty and over the sty was a tiny wooden-floored compartment where passing tramps were sometimes given permission to spend the night. Matt climbed in and collapsed onto the thick layer of straw that covered the floor. He could see the entrance from here through a hole in the wall where a stone had been dislodged, probably for air more than light. He quickly realized why the place was so popular with tramps; the compartment was warmer than his room in the house, the body heat of the pigs rising between the loose boards into the straw. He whimpered with relief as the pain in his hands and feet gradually faded with the return of circulation. His jaw still throbbed but he settled himself as comfortably as he could, keeping the road in sight through the hole. As the night wore on and his comfort increased, he dozed off.

CHAPTER 7

He woke up with a start and for a moment didn't know where he was in the darkness. Something had wakened him. There it was again. Scuffling, shuffling sounds. He looked out through the hole in the wall and his heart faltered; it was no longer snowing and the yard was full of Highlanders, two of them holding a struggling Pat Hoxey, one holding his hand over Pat's mouth.

Matt's brain whirled. Jesus Christ, he had let them all down; Dwyer and the whole lot of them would be taken without a chance to fight. He cursed himself for a fool to go and fall asleep on duty. Hoxey must have heard the approach of the soldiers and tried to get to the house but thanks to Matt's incompetence they had advanced close to the entrance by the time he got there and had captured him. It would be piling stupidity upon stupidity to reveal himself now; there was nothing he could do. And this was no chance raid by undisciplined yeos; those were the Glengarry Fencibles out there, the First British Highland Regiment, garrisoned at Hacketstown. Only the most reliable intelligence would have brought them all this way in such inclement conditions.

They had evidently already surrounded all three houses as the number of horses in the yard far outnumbered the thirty or so Highlanders he could see around Hoxey's. A man he heard addressed as Captain Beaton rapped on Hoxey's door and called out: 'You are surrounded. Surrender in the name of the King or the house will be burned down around you!'

The crying of the younger Hoxey children and the screams of their mother and older sisters came faintly across the yard to Matt's tortured ears. Then the voice of Ned Lennon: 'We will surrender and come out if you will give your word not to shoot.'

'You have my word,' Captain Beaton replied and turned to Pat Hoxey, 'Mister Hoxey, you will be so kind as to enter your house and hand out the weapons of your friends.'

The men who had been holding Hoxey released him and he went in. 'You will open the door a few inches,' Beaton's voice was firm but not too loud for fear of alerting the rebels in the other cottages, 'and hand the weapons out butt end foremost.'

The stock of a carbine appeared at the door and a soldier very cautiously approached and took it. They waited for the next weapon and when none was forthcoming Beaton went up to the door and called: 'Pass out the rest of your guns or suffer the consequences.'

'That was our only weapon,' came the voice of Ned Lennon.

'Do you take me for a fool, sir?'

'I do not, but I would ask you to believe that we have no wish to be the cause of suffering to this innocent family and so would not attempt to deceive you.'

'Very well. Open the door wide and stand back.'

Beaton waved several soldiers forward and with muskets raised they advanced to the door and entered. Finding there were indeed no more arms inside they proceeded to tie Lennon and Tom Clerk together back to back with hay ropes, and, after thoroughly searching the house, roughly pushed them outside.

Leaving three men on guard at the farm entrance the Highlanders, pulling the prisoners along with them, moved on up the lane to Toole's. On hearing the challenge Wat McDonnell and the other five rebels at Toole's were in favour of fighting it out, but again the pleadings of the women and children won the day and they surrendered. Tied back to back and shivering in the wet clothing they had been compelled to put back on, they were hustled through the deep snow to the top of the lane where Captain Roderick McDonald and his men had Connel's surrounded. The full force of soldiers, numbering close to one hundred, now ringed the cottage and, the need for silence now gone, McDonald roared at the top of his voice: 'Michael Dwyer, surrender in the name of His Majesty the King.' Dwyer was on his feet before McDonald had completed the sentence, the others close behind him. Miley Connel's wife, who had been too nervous to sleep, sat by the fire and cried quietly. Several times she had ventured out into the snowy night and listened for any sign of danger, but her vigilance had been in vain.

Dwyer peered through the small window and saw against the white background of snow the dark shapes of soldiers everywhere, three and four deep in places. They were hopelessly surrounded. Never before had he felt it was the end. His mind flashed to Mary, now carrying his child; a child it seemed he was destined never to see. He turned to the others. 'Highlanders,' he said. 'Scores of them by the look of it. Some dark work has been carried out this night.'

'We await your reply, Dwyer. Come out now and your life will be spared, but be quick about it. This is not the kind of night that lends itself to patience. All your friends have surrendered. Here they are. Look if you will.'

Dwyer strained his eyes and saw the forms of men tied together being pushed to the front of the soldiers.

'What have you brought upon us, Dwyer,' Miley Connel asked accusingly. 'Those fellows out there will burn us all alive. The poor children...'

'I am truly sorry, Miley, and if I had the low villain who betrayed us he would die before your eyes. I will do my best for your family. The Highlanders are honourable men. If they make a bargain they will stick to it.'

He unlatched the door, opened it slightly and standing back behind the wall called: 'May I know your name, sir?'

'Are you Michael Dwyer?' McDonald asked.

'I am.'

'My name is Captain Roderick McDonald of the Glengarry fencibles.'

'Captain McDonald, I wish you to know we were driven here by the inclemency of the weather and imposed our presence upon this household. I would earnestly request, therefore, that you allow these peaceful people to leave here unharmed. When this is done I will inform you of our intentions.'

There was some hushed conversation between McDonald and Beaton, then McDonald addressed Dwyer again. 'Very well, send them out one by one. Are there children?'

'There are. Three.'

'Let them come first, then.'

As coats were hurriedly thrown around the Connel children, Dwyer turned to his three companions who stood with muskets at the ready. 'I'm going to fight,' he said. 'We're dead men anyway, so we may as well sell our lives dearly.'

Costello was agitated, his face full of dread. 'But you said yourself the Highlanders were not like the yeos, and won't shoot us if we surrender.'

'True, Pat, but we would only be saving ourselves for the hangman. Our heads would be spiked on the walls of the Flannel Hall in Rathdrum before the end of the month. What about you, Sam?' McAllister spoke with a strange sad resignation in his voice:

'Very well. Very well.' He turned to Costello and John Savage. 'He's right. At least let us go with some dignity.'

Agreement was reached to fight on, albeit reluctantly on the part of Costello.

The Connel family had now all left except Miley who approached Dwyer and shook his hand.

'We will lose our home, Michael, but yours will be a greater sacrifice. I salute your courage but despair for the safety of the mountain people left unprotected when you have gone.'

'Goodbye, Miley, I can only repeat that I heartily regret bringing this trouble on you and your family.'

Connel shook hands with the other three and left. McAllister bolted the door. An eerie silence settled on the cottage for a few moments, the men inside standing looking at each other, the soldiers outside listening for the rebels' decision, then Dwyer said quietly: 'This is it, boys, let us give a good account of ourselves.' Raising his voice he called: 'Captain McDonald.'

'I am listening.'

'We have heard your call to surrender and your terms, but we know full well that surrender would only delay our deaths for a short while and would serve no good purpose. Therefore, we have decided to fight to the end.'

'I am sorry you have come to such a decision, Captain Dwyer, for where there is life there is hope. Will you not reconsider?'

'I will not, but I thank you for the offer,' replied Dwyer, noting the tone of genuine respect in McDonald's voice. Seldom if ever had an enemy addressed Dwyer by his rank.

Almost immediately the windows were shattered by musket-fire, the balls striking the opposite walls with dull thuds. Volley followed volley in rapid succession making it extremely difficult for the rebels to get a shot away. Dwyer and McAllister crouched one at each side of the kitchen window, Costello and Savage were in the bedroom. Dwyer knelt on the earthen floor and poked his musket over the corner of the window-sill. He raised himself slowly until he could see outside with his right eye. Some of the soldiers were crouched behind the low stone wall that surrounded the yard, others behind the cowhouse in the right-hand corner of the yard. He fired, aiming as best he could at the corner of the cowhouse and before he ducked saw a figure fall outwards from the wall. A shout of rage went up and the musket-fire suddenly increased in its ferocity. Lead hailed through the windows and battered the heavy door, the flashes of exploding gunpowder creating a fireworks display around the cottage.

Every so often the rebels managed to get a hurried shot away but the battle had raged for more than an hour when a second soldier fell. McDonald was furious at the idea of his large force being held off by a mere four rebels who as yet had suffered no apparent injury. He barked an order and some men ran to the rear of the cottage. There were no windows at the back so the rebels could not see the flickering of torches held under the eaves where the thatch was dry beneath its layer of snow.

Costello was first to notice.

'Smoke!' he cried. 'They've fired the roof. We'll burn alive!'

'Easy, Pat, easy, 'Dwyer shouted from the kitchen, 'It won't burn too quickly with the best part of a foot of snow on top of it.' He was right, but as it smouldered smoke soon became the deadly enemy. McAllister dipped his green cravat into the water-bucket and covered his nose and mouth with it, the others followed his example with various pieces of rag. A cheer went up outside as the Highlanders saw the smoke rise from the roof.

In the ceilingless cottage the men could now see the fire running across the underside of the thatch over the chimney corner. With a sudden whoosh and scattering of sparks a clump of thatch fell onto a clamp of turf that had been stacked beside the fireplace. The thatch flared up and within minutes the turf, being bone dry, was ablaze. Dwyer knew the time was fast approaching when they would have to make their final choice between burning or being shot to death.

McAllister grabbed the water-bucket with the intention of dousing the fire, but as he crossed the room he felt a sledge-hammer blow to his right arm. The bucket flew from his grasp sending the water in a useless runnels across the floor. McAllister instinctively tried to raise his arm but it dangled loosely by his side, shattered by the ball that had found its target by sheer bad luck. The pain exploded in his brain and an involuntary yelp escaped his lips: 'I'm hit, Mick, my arm is done.' He staggered back and slid to a sitting position against the wall beside Dwyer.

Another great clump of smouldering thatch dislodged itself and fell to the floor. Dwyer dragged the table into position under the gaping hole in the roof and pulled himself up between the smoking rafters to see if there were any weaknesses in the ranks outside which might allow a fighting chance of escape through the rear side of the roof. He was disappointed; there were as many soldiers behind the house as in front. Captain McDonald was taking no chances; Dwyer had escaped from too many seemingly hopeless situations to allow for complacency now.

Costello came screaming from the bedroom, Savage endeavouring to hold him back. 'We're finished! Oh Christ Jesus, we're finished. I don't want to die. Do something. Do something!'

He grabbed a short-handled spade that stood against the chimney-breast and crouched under the table where he began frantically hacking and digging at the earthen floor as if there were some remote possibility of tunnelling to safety that way. He wept hysterically as he dug.

'He has lost his reason. Leave him to it,' John Savage said. Dwyer jumped down from the table, took hold of Costello and shook him violently. 'Listen to me, Pat Costello, this is no good. However desperate our situation panic will not help at all. Now, please, man, get your gun and defend yourself.'

'We're finished,' Costello wailed.

'We're finished when we're dead, Pat, and we're not dead yet.'

'Mick!' The weak voice of McAllister who now sat in a spreading pool of his own blood came from across the room. Dwyer let Costello slump to the floor and crawled to McAllister. Burning thatch was now falling all around them and the clamp of turf blazed furiously. Dwyer choked and spluttered as the smoke burned his lungs and stung copious tears from his eyes.

'What is it, Sam,' he gasped, 'I'm afraid our time has come, my good friend.'

'That's just it, Mick, I'm nearly passing out... loss of blood. I have no hope of making any sort of run for it, but maybe I can give the rest of you a fighting chance.'

'How in God's name...'

'Listen. Quickly now. Get my musket and put it in my good hand.' Dwyer did as he was asked. The restored possibility of escape had calmed Costello who had retrieved his gun and was listening eagerly to McAllister. The room was now becoming an inferno, the heat unbearable.

'Now, stand me up at the door.'

Savage helped Dwyer lift McAllister into a standing position.

'This is my plan,' he coughed. 'First, unbolt the door, then all of you get down on the floor. One of you can pull the door open from the bottom. I'll turn myself around into the centre of the doorway and with the help of God most of them will empty their guns at me. If you can jump up and away smartly enough you might make it through them and get away before they can reload.' Dwyer could see it as a slim but worthwhile chance.

'Sam...' he began.

'Do it now or we're all dead. God bless you, Mick.'

The three crouched down and Dwyer used a crooked stick to open the door. McAllister, leaning against the jamb, swung himself around until he was standing fully in the doorway, silhouetted against the flames in the room behind him. He discharged his musket. There was a prolonged, deafening volley and McAllister was thrown backwards into the kitchen as if struck by a cannon-ball.

As the echoes of the gunfire reverberated from the surrounding hills the three remaining rebels leapt from the doorway and ran wildly in different directions. The sudden shock of freezing air after the suffocating heat seemed to sharpen Dwyer's senses and he spotted a break in the line of soldiers at the side of the house where a narrow laneway led to the open fields. He turned for the gap and in doing so his bare feet slipped on ice which had formed on a drain hidden beneath the snow and he went sprawling. It was a lucky slip; a volley rang out at that instant and he heard the lead whistling above him.

Springing to his feet he headed for the laneway only to find that a ladder had been placed across the entrance from wall to wall. He put one hand on the ladder with the intention of vaulting over it. His hand slipped on the frozen wood and again he fell. This time a ball from Beaton's weapon grazed him, ripping a long gash in his waistcoat. Scrambling madly he came up beyond the obstacle. He made it through the laneway into an open field and heard a cry of 'I'll get him' as a large Highlander threw down his gun and lunged after him.

A cold grey dawn was breaking over the white mountains to the east. Dwyer could not afford to let himself think of the numbing cold as he ploughed through the deep snow downhill towards the road. He wore nothing apart from what he had been sleeping in when they had been surprised by the call to surrender — a flannel waistcoat and a pair of long drawers of the same material. The Highlander was about fifty yards behind Dwyer and gaining all the time, the main body of soldiers creating a commotion some way behind him. Dwyer could not believe his luck as he realized they dared not fire on him while their own man was between them and their quarry. His heart leapt; there was a chance. There really was a chance.

He launched himself through a hedge, heedless of the thorns ripping into his flesh. He crossed the road, running through Lynch's farmyard and into the fields beyond, still travelling downhill towards the Little Slaney river. The Highlander was closing on him fast. He felt a hand grasp for his shoulder and leapt sideways sticking one leg out behind him. The Highlander tripped and went down heavily and Dwyer was away to the end of the field and into the freezing cold waters of the Little Slaney. Sharp stones lacerated his feet as he stumbled across the stream. He ran along the side of a hedge where he was invisible to his pursuers. Knowing every inch of the fields he had played in as a child he managed to increase the distance between himself and the Highlanders until finally they gave up and returned to Derrynamuck disappointed. But Dwyer was not yet out of danger. A detachment of soldiers who were stationed at the far end of the valley was making its way along the road towards Derrynamuck to investigate the gunfire. They spotted Dwyer as he struggled across the snowy landscape and decided to give chase.

Dwyer, unaware of their presence, gritted his teeth against the agonizing pain from his torn feet and headed in the direction of Seskin where Thaddeus Dwyer, a first cousin of his father, lived. He came in sight of the house and as he hobbled the last few yards great convulsive sobs shook his body. He fell against the door which was opened almost immediately by an amazed Mrs. Dwyer who was alone in the house at the time.

He was a sorry spectacle; his smoke-blackened face bleeding from numerous thorn-slashes, tears streaming down his cheeks through the grime, blood spots seeping through his pitiful clothing from countless other thorn-wounds all over his body, and the soles of his feet like raw bloody meat.

'Holy Mother of God, Michael alanna, what has happened to you at all?'

She helped him to a chair by the fire and went to pour some milk into a pot to heat. Looking across the fields from the window she saw the soldiers on the road less than a quarter of a mile away. 'Michael, they're coming up the road,' she cried. 'Oh, God help you. What can you do, alanna, there's no place here for you to hide.'

For a long moment he felt that all he could do was to sit there by the fire until they walked in the door and took him. His body did not want to resist anymore; enough was enough. With a superhuman effort he suppressed his agony, grabbed an old shirt that hung on a string above the fireplace, tore it in two and wrapped one piece around each foot.

'I'll not stay and cause you grief, Hannah, tell Thaddeus I called and may yet see him again.'

'Oh, poor Michael. I'll torment Heaven with me prayers for you.' She threw an old jacket over his shoulders. He put his feet to the floor and fiercely sucked in his breath to prevent himself from crying out. He made his way like a man walking on hot coals out through the byre at the back of the house and once again took to the open fields, staying as close as he could to the hedges in order to make his trail less obvious.

Hannah Dwyer busied herself tramping around her yard to obliterate his footprints and the telltale drips of blood. When the soldiers knocked on her door and walked in she was sitting calmly by the fire drinking hot milk.

'Pardon the intrusion, ma'am,' the officer addressed her, 'but we are in pursuit of a dangerous felon. His tracks lead to your gate. I must ask you if he is in this house, and warn you that harbouring rebels is a serious offence.'

'There's only meself in it, sir. Me husband is out on the mountain tryin' to get some hay to the sheep, but I'll not hinder you if you have a mind to search the oul' place. '

'We'll just take a look in the other rooms, ma'am, if you've no objection.'

'Plase yourselves.'

The officer waved some men on to search the rest of the house but stayed in the kitchen himself.

'Tell me, ma'am,' he enquired, 'what would your husband's name be?'

'Thaddeus, sir, Thaddeus Dwyer.'

'Is it, by God! Then you'll no doubt know of Michael Dwyer, the man we are chasing.'

'Ay, sir, I do. His father and Thaddeus are first cousins.'

The officers tone became noticeably cooler.

'Well then, Ma'am, I'm afraid we shall have to conduct a more thorough search of your residence than we had intended.'

'Sir!' Hannah sounded offended. 'I am gettin' a bit close to meetin' the Almighty to be riskin' me immortal soul with lies. I have tould you he is not in this house and you will find it is so. Mind you,' she added, taking a sip from her cup, 'I couldn't swear that the rascal hasn't concealed himself in the barn or one of the outhouses, if you know what I mane, sir.'

The soldiers spent a fruitless two hours forking and prodding hay in the barn, crawling into the inner sanctum of the pigsty, scattering squawking fowl in their coops and chasing cows out of the byre. Some had begun dismantling the large clamp of turf that was built against the gable end of the house, but shamefacedly replaced the sods when the officer pointed out that it would have been impossible for the outlaw to have hidden himself in the clamp and have it rebuilt around him in the time since they had seen him crossing the fields, and besides, even if he had managed to somehow carry out this feat there most certainly would not be an undisturbed eight-inch layer of snow covering the clamp.

Dwyer was by now struggling painfully up the steeply rising ground on the other side of the glen almost opposite Derrynamuck. He could see the heavy black smoke still rising from Miley Connel's cottage. The snow, becoming deeper the higher he climbed, hid treacherous rocks which threw him down time and again until in his weariness he wanted to stay down; to just let it all drift away. He came to the Hairy Man's Brook a little way above where it flows into the Knickeen River. His head sang and buzzed from the searing pain and cold of his feet and he feared he might pass out and freeze to death on the open hillside, a cruel irony considering he had just escaped being burned to death. He did not dare stop for rest in case he should fall asleep which would have the same outcome. He got into the brook and started to climb against the rushing water, crying out as the uneven stones tortured his lacerated soles. He stayed in the water as long as he could, only leaving it to get around some impassable obstruction; it would help confuse anyone who might follow this far.

Leaving Hairy Man's Brook at its source he continued over Cavanagh's Gap, the highest point of his journey. Here on the mountaintop the snow lay so thickly his progress was agonizingly slow and he pulled the old jacket around him against the freezing wind. Eventually the ground began falling again and the rocks gradually gave way to fields, making his going somewhat less difficult.

The last reserves of his strength were fading fast, and even as he came in sight of his destination, the tiny mountain hamlet of Corragh, his legs repeatedly went from under him. In a semi-conscious haze he dragged himself the last few yards to Red Jem Kelly's cottage and for the second time that day collapsed weeping against the door of a friend.

CHAPTER 8

Biddy Dolan gasped and whined out her orgasm as the soldier pounded her backside against the cold stone wall of the Flannel Hall in the town of Rathdrum. Biddy was as fond of men as she was of breathing and her voracious appetite was amply catered for as long as the rebels remained outstanding in the mountains ensuring an inexhaustible military presence in the area. She was nineteen years of age and had been hopelessly addicted to sex ever since at the age of sixteen she had enquired of a Highlander what he wore underneath his kilt and he had invited her to investigate for herself. Having satisfied her curiosity with the Highlander she found herself impelled by irresistible urges to repeat the experience with the men of as many regiments as possible. Within a year of her Highland fling there was nothing anybody could teach Croppy Biddy. The soldiers in their neat uniforms looked so handsome compared to the local lads in their ill-fitting rags, and she delighted in her power to make a stiff-lipped high-ranking officer lose control.

But the honey on the bun as far as Biddy was concerned was the astonishing fact that they paid for it! She knew in her heart that had things been otherwise she would willingly have robbed her own mother to pay for it herself, and so her amazement knew no bounds that men would part with good money for her to perform an act that made her almost lose her mind with pleasure.

At first she had had no need of their money, but since that miserable old priest had read her out from the altar one Sunday she had been glad of it. She didn't care a farthing what people thought of her lifestyle, which she considered a more natural one than most of them led, but it had hurt her deeply when her parents had stood up in the church that morning and moved away from her. The door of their home in the village of Carnew where her father carried on his trade as a thatcher had been locked to her, and no words, nor even a nod of recognition when they met in the road, had passed between them since.

She had moved away from the village and now lived quite comfortably in a rented room on the steeply sloping main street of Rathdrum where she entertained to her heart's content. Once she had brought a sergeant and five privates back from the public house. The sergeant, pulling rank on the privates, insisted on going first claiming he was doing them a service by 'buttering the bun' for them. Then there was that soldier who had lost both legs, carried up to her room by two of his fellows who had hired her as a going home present for him. She had been morbidly excited at the prospect and had not been disappointed, finding his lack of limbs facilitated some unusual and highly erotic manoeuvres.

She furthered her basic education by reading books borrowed from friendly officers, and developed a healthy pride in her independence. Anyway, she reflected, what would an old dried stick of a priest know, that never joined giblets with a woman in his life? What could he know of a woman's cunt-itch, as the soldiers called it, that persistent itch that Biddy unashamedly kept well scratched?

An hour's pully-hauly with a good woman would either kill or cure him. It was the same with those self-righteous old hags who spat at her in the street as she danced past with her eyes full of mischief and her great wild mane of flaming hair crowning her tall graceful figure. They called her a whore and a hobby-horse, a dirty lick-spigot, but she laughed at them and skipped on, rejoicing in the knowledge that she had visited worlds they would never know. Their men, of course, looked upon her in a different light, leering at her with hungry eyes, nudging one another and saying what fine bit of muslin she was.

She spent most evenings at the public house singing and dancing and seldom had to open her purse, so she could afford to dress well and at the same time keep adding to her nest egg which she kept in an old leather bag under her bed. Some of her most rewarding enterprises financially had involved large sums paid to her for swearing against rebels, her most recent appearance being at the trial of Billy Byrne of Ballymanus who had danced a fine jig on nothing at the Gallows Rock last September. That one had paid handsomely.

Perjuring herself did not trouble her conscience, having been assured by the authorities that these people were inhuman murderers who would escape paying for their horrible crimes unless somebody like her good self was willing to help convict them.

'You fuck well, Antrim man,' she gasped as the soldier withdrew from her with a grunt. She had acquired a wide vocabulary of sexual slang-words from the soldiery and used it with relish.

Feeling a cold trickle on her thighs in the night air she pulled her skirts down around herself. She had long dispensed with underwear as a nuisance in urgent situations and now only resorted to wearing drawers when the Cardinal was at home.

'Biddy Dolan,' the Antrim Militia sergeant pressed a coin into her hand. 'That wee scut of yours will be the death of me. You have me worn out.'

'Oh, poor you!' she exclaimed with mock sympathy, playfully taking him in her hand. 'Left with a dead thing that's no use to a girl at all, at all. What's poor Biddy going to do for the rest of the night now?' She suddenly gave his testicles a firm squeeze.

'Ow! You wee witch. That hurts.'

She laughed, squeezed a little harder and let go.

'A fine pair you have there, soldier. Do anyone proud."

'Well, my beautiful bobtail, you would be the one to know.'

'Ay, I've weighed enough men in these hands to know when I'm holding an exceptional baste.'

'Tell me this, Biddy, what is it like with a rebel?'

'I don't fuck rebels.'

'Oh?'

'Maybe I prefer a man in uniform,' she licked her lips suggestively, 'besides, Rathdrum being red with soldiers, they're afraid to come into town much. They stick to their shebeens in the hills. Hold hard, though, I lie! I once did it in a field over Greenane way with a fellow who was someways connected with Dwyer. Rolled off me and ran away telling me to put it on the Commanding Officer's account. Wasn't up to much, anyway.'

'Well, listen to this now. There's a young fellow called Matt Byrne who was recently rescued by Dwyer and his gang during a raid in Glenmalure. They murdered four yeomen. It would be reasonable to believe that, being in

Dwyer's debt, he may at the very least be in contact with him and so may possess valuable information. Now for some unknown reason I have lately seen him drinking heavily at the inn up the street and looking very sorry for himself, and it occurred to me that a pretty wee girl like yourself would have no trouble befriending this young man and affording him some comfort in his misfortune, whatever it might be. If you managed to extract some useful information on Dwyer the reward would be much greater than anything you have received so far.'

'Is that so now, sir,' she grinned at him, 'well then you'd better point out this Matt Byrne to me so I can be about my duty. Now, let's get indoors before my arse freezes entirely.'

CHAPTER 9

Except for the drips of whiskey Mrs. Harney had administered through the reed, alcoholic drink had never passed Matt Byrne's lips until the weeks following the disaster at Derrynamuck. Now he found that whiskey was the only means of getting away from his conscience for a while, and as he was not a wanted man he was reasonably safe in Rathdrum.

He had lain in his apartment over the pigsty at Hoxey's all through the following day and then sneaked away under cover of darkness. Since then he had been sleeping in the old barn at the back of the burnt-out shell of his father's house. Whiskey was slowly but surely burning its way through the little tin box of sovereigns that had been his father's savings. It had escaped the fire because old Darby had taken the precaution of nailing it to a beam in the roof of the barn.

Matt sat at Harney's table eating the mountainous pile of dinner Mrs. Harney had set before him. The Harney's had invited him to stay with them until he got his house re-roofed and made habitable again, but he had declined the offer owing to the awkwardness he felt in the presence of the rebels who were regular visitors there. It was now two months since that shameful night and he still did not know for certain whether Dwyer was dead or alive. He could elicit no information from Vesty Byrne, John Mernagh or Martin Burke, who were frequently around but treated him with indifference and he wondered if they had spoken to Pat Hoxey and if so, what he had told them. Not that Hoxey could be sure of what exactly had happened to Matt that night, but he must surely be suspicious at Matt's failure to contact him with an explanation.

He had made several attempts to talk to Vesty and the others but they just waved him off as if they had no interest in anything he might have to say.

Rumours had spread through the county: Dwyer was in Clare recuperating; Dwyer had somehow escaped to America; Dwyer was dead. The latter rumour derived some credence from the reports of blood seen on the snow by his pursuers. As time passed Matt noticed that one or another of the three rebels would go missing for a few days at a time, and he suspected they were visiting Dwyer somewhere not too far off, maybe in one of the neighbouring counties. Now, as he washed down his meal of potatoes and bacon with a large mug of milk, Vesty Byrne appeared at Harney's door.

'Matt,' he said, 'the Captain wants to see you.'

It was a full three weeks from the day of his arrival at Red Jem Kelly's before Michael Dwyer could put a foot under him. Red Jem had taken care of him like a baby, and made an overnight trip to Dublin in his trap to obtain ointment and dressings for Dwyer's feet which had turned septic. He also brought a large jar of whiskey which they made good use of by the fire in the evenings while Jem, who was over seventy, succeeded in lifting Dwyer's spirits with his quaint anecdotes. He changed the dressings every day and made a pair of crutches when it became possible for Dwyer to try moving about the place. He was proud of the hiding place he had constructed for the rebel Captain some years ago. In the Ingle nook he had built what looked like a rather large log-box and had broken through the wall and made a similar box on the bedroom side. He dug the floor down about two feet, making a little room six feet square and five feet high. The cover for the log-box was a sort of inverted lid six inches deep which was piled with logs giving the illusion of a full box, and on the bedroom side a wooden cover was nailed onto the box with a circle cut out of it in which was placed the receptacle utilised to eliminate the necessity of visiting the field during the night. It was usually left half full when the Captain was below to discourage further probing by suspicious soldiery. A large hinged wooden lid came down over the receptacle.

Dwyer slept on a palliasse in the little compartment, its proximity to the fireplace ensuring a constant comfortable warmth. On the nights when Vesty or one of the others stayed over it hid two in reasonable comfort. They had relayed to him Pat Hoxey's story of the events at Derrynamuck and he had resolved to hear what young Byrne had to say for himself. Dwyer had been surprised to hear there was a watch that night, he himself deeming it unnecessary in the circumstances.

By the end of March he had dispensed with the crutches and a week later took his leave of Red Jem Kelly and started back across the mountains in conditions that could scarcely have been any further removed from those that had prevailed when he had crossed Cavanagh's Gap in February; a clear blue sky hung over the hills and gentle spring sunshine bathed the countryside. Hardy little mountain flowers of every hue nodded in the soothing breeze as he passed along. His feet still troubled him a bit with the unaccustomed climbing, but he knew that in a week or two they would be as good as ever.

Resting awhile on a rock beside the Hairy Man's rook he was lulled by its tumbling waters as it cascaded down the mountainside, its spray transformed into a million dancing diamonds in the April sunlight. He savoured the healing peace of the mountains and looked forward to seeing Mary, now six months pregnant, at John Cullen's house. While at Red Jem's he had asked Vesty to bring her across the mountains to visit but Vesty had declared that it would be foolish to the point of madness to attempt such a thing as the authorities were certain to have a watch on Mary in the hope that she might lead them to him if he indeed lived. Vesty had warned Dwyer before about the dangers of having Mary visit him in their various hiding places since the marriage, and the two men had had some angry exchanges on the subject.

Word was conveyed to Mary, who had been staying with her parents, to visit John Cullen as often as she could in the weeks before Dwyer was due to arrive there. This she did, and was followed by the military every time for over a week until, growing tired of wasted journeys, they left her alone.

Dwyer scooped a handful of water from the brook and drank it. He splashed his face with another handful and continued his way down to Cullen's.

It was a strange and wonderful thing for him to feel his baby kick against his hand, but his joy was tinged with guilt as he pondered the kind of life this new human being would have with its father a proclaimed outlaw on the run.

'Vesty and the lad are comin' up the hill,' John Cullen shouted from the yard.

Dwyer went into his usual room, asking Mary to send Matt Byrne in to him.

'Well, Matt, come in and sit down,' he said as the obviously nervous lad opened the door.

Matt did not know what to expect and offered a gauche 'I did not betray you, Captain Dwyer.'

Dwyer couldn't help smiling.

'I never thought of that as a possibility, nor did the boys or you would have known of it before now. I just wanted to hear from your own lips what happened that night.'

Matt decided it would be best to relate truthfully all that had transpired and Dwyer listened without interruption.

'A costly mistake, Matt,' he commented gravely, 'do you know that all of my party of that night are dead bar one? I lost some good friends.'

Matt hung his head. 'I heard at Harney's. I haven't been able to live with myself since.'

'They shot the lads who had deserted from the militia and hanged the rest,' Dwyer continued. 'You complained to me of not being included in raiding parties. If you cannot be trusted to stand picket how could we depend upon you to follow orders which might well involve risk to your life?'

Matt could find no reply to that.

'Nevertheless, a mistake it was and I made a mistake myself that night in not ordering a picket out in the first place, so I do not intend to impose any punishment upon you. Be right careful, however, that the like never happens again or it will not go well for you. You may not attach much importance to the job of picketing but I hope you have learned from this bitter lesson that at times you hold our lives in your hands, and you may be assured that is of the utmost importance to us! Now, we will join the others and say no more of it.'

Matt was elated at this unexpected leniency. He had expected at the very least to be dropped from any further involvement with the rebels, and resolved to die at his post rather than abandon it in future, and so it was with great shock and trepidation that he found himself brought before the Captain again the very next night.

CHAPTER TEN

After his lecture From Dwyer, Matt went straight into Rathdrum, and evening found him singing along with the ballads and bawdy songs a group of off-duty soldiers were performing in the opposite corner of the room; tonight the whiskey was for celebration, not consolation. A great weight had been lifted from his mind and he sang out with gusto, grinning his broad boyish grin which was now slightly lop-sided due to his beating.

Before, the tavern had been to him no more than a vague, noisy backdrop to his misery, but now it was alive and vibrant, and he noticed the other patrons for the first time: Their faces; their laughter, their banter with the landlord as he poured their drinks. And that beautiful girl sitting at the bar. He knew she had been there most of the other nights, but tonight, the veil of guilt removed from his eyes, he saw her. His eyes took in the rich mass of red hair that fell about her pretty face, and the way she tossed her head every now and then to get it out of her eyes. Once or twice during the performance of this attractive mannerism he could have sworn she looked directly at him and his heart thudded in his breast. He had never had anything to do with girls, and the closest he had come to a female was when he had kissed a cousin of his goodbye as she left to live in America with her new husband.

The girl looked at him again and this time left him in no doubt that it was deliberate. She held his gaze and smiled. God, her eyes were incredible. That look! Telling him things he could only try to guess at. His heart lurched and he gulped and choked on his whiskey. The girl laughed and turned back to the bar.

Biddy Dolan wasn't certain she had the right man. The description she had been given by the militiaman seemed to fit except for the fellow's obvious good spirits; he certainly didn't appear to be in need of comforting. Still, that crooked grin of his was uncommonly attractive and she wasn't about to look a gift horse in the mouth. She would have him before the night was out, rebel or no. She stepped down from her stool.

My God, she's coming over here.

Matt stood up as good manners demanded and awkwardly proffered his hand as she approached. Biddy was tall but his powerful frame towered over her. She took his hand and felt waves of lust wash over her. By Christ, he was a mountain of a man, most of the soldiers puny in comparison.

'And who have we here, may I ask, sitting by himself while everybody else enjoys the merry company of friends?'

'Matt Byrne, ma'am,' he swallowed hard.

'And if I were to sit beside you now, Matt Byrne,' she smiled coquettishly, 'would you have any objection? I'm without a companion myself this night and it's no place for a lady to be alone.'

'Yes... I mean no, no objection. Sit down, ma'am, yes, sit down. What will you be drinkin'?'

'Whiskey, if you please, and listen to me now, I have no intention of drinkin' with a fellow who is going to call me 'ma'am' all night. My name is Bridget, though most call me Biddy.'

'Biddy. Yes. All right. Biddy.'

'And then I won't have to be calling you 'sir' all night,' she laughed.

'Oh no. Oh begod, no!'

She watched him hungrily as he walked to the bar, her breathing heavy. Right then she could not have cared less about information, rewards or all the soldiers in His Majesty's army; she would worry about these things after she had tended to more urgent matters. Matt's nervousness made him drink faster than usual and he visited the bar three times before a half hour had passed.

The girl sat very close to him and the heat of her body came through his clothes. The smell of her excited him and he shook like a leaf, splashing his whiskey over the edge of his glass when she let her hand brush against his thigh as if by accident. He had no idea how to respond. He wanted to do something, say something, hold her hand maybe, but he was afraid of being too forward and frightening her away so he just sat there and swallowed and shook.

'Matt,' she said in a whisper husky with restrained desire, 'would you like to go somewhere we can be alone?'

He nodded, not trusting his voice to work. They went out into the night and walked down the steep, narrow street between candle-lit windows. His legs felt like water and he feared he would lose the power of them entirely before they got to wherever she was taking him. Biddy's legs felt weak too, but whereas his weakness stemmed from a mixture of fear and excitement, the cause of hers was unadulterated. She stopped at an unpainted heavy oak door, reached into the front of her dress, looking into his eyes, tongue at the corner of her mouth as she did so, and pulled out a key. Laughing, she pressed its warmth to his lips and then opened the door.

A candle-sconce stood on a little wall shelf inside and the draught from the door as they closed it behind them almost blew the candle out. She lit their way up the stairs and he followed in a daze. She opened a door and stood aside, gesturing him in.

'Pray enter, kind sir.'

The room was tastefully furnished and carpeted; no sleazy dossing-room this. Biddy Dolan spent her money well. A small oak dressing-table stood under the window that overlooked the street. On it were arranged silver-backed brushes and combs, small bottles of various colours and a shining brass candlestick at either end. A large wardrobe with a full-length door mirror stood to the left of the dressing table. Biddy lit the two candles from the flame of the short piece she had carried upstairs, and threw some sods of turf on the embers of the fire she had lit before going out. The room was warm and comfortable. There were three large armchairs and the bed was the most luxurious Matt had ever laid eyes on; the mattress looked about a foot thick, and over the blankets was a huge red quilted bedspread that must have cost a fortune. A door at the back of the room led to a small kitchen.

It was Biddy's ambition to make enough money while the troubles in the mountains lasted to buy herself a nice little place in a fashionable part of Dublin where she would entertain only the wealthy higher class of person. Some of the more cultured officers who regularly availed of her services told her she was too good to be wasting her time in a God-forsaken place like this. The gentry of Dublin would love her, they said, because she wasn't just a dim-witted whore. She had a mind and could converse intelligently enough with the best of them. She believed them. She knew she was beautiful; knew her power to attract men was almost infallible. It had taken her a long time to acknowledge that fact. At first she had been unsure of her looks and although men would tell her how lovely she was and how they enjoyed her more than their wives or any other women, well, that was what men would say to get their way with a girl, wasn't it? Gradually she had begun to compare herself with the other girls and women of the area. Why did men not give them the hungry eye? What exactly was the difference. She realized as watched them that she was taller than most and that many of them went about with unkempt and unwashed hair, and walked with a sort of ploughman's plod.

While Biddy herself always felt happy and threw friendly smiles at all she met, most of the women she observed, particularly the married ones, wore gloomy and sour expressions, and from this she could only conclude that, incomprehensibly, they did not enjoy making love. She had stood for a long time in her room studying all aspects of her naked image in the long mirror, finally smiling at herself and nodding yes, her body was beautiful, and if as a woman she could now see that, what must its effect be on men? That beauty was going to provide her with all the things she wanted in life.

Looking from the fireplace across at Matt her heart leapt at the thought that the rush of lust she experienced at the sight of him was the same as that felt by men when they looked at her; she understood perfectly now their hunger, their uncontrollable impatience to get at her. She felt her letch-water run on her thigh. Here in the comparatively small room he appeared huge, overpowering, and it had a devastating effect on her. She went and sat on the bed. 'Come and sit beside me, Matt.' She crooked her finger at him, wondering at his shyness; most of the men she brought here would have been all over her by now.

'Tell me,' she asked when he sat down, 'are you stepping out with a girl of your own?'

'No, ma'am... Biddy.' He felt the heat of her body against him again.

'I am surprised! But I don't doubt a handsome fellow like yourself has put dozens of eager young fillies through his hands.'

'Well, you see,' Matt said, his face reddening, 'I had a bit of a farm beyant in Glenmalure and I'm afraid it didn't spare me much time to meet girls, so I've never had a young lady to step out with.'

'Never? Are you telling me, Matt Byrne, that you've never... you know... with a girl?'

'I'll tell you the God's honest truth, now, I've never as much as kissed a girl in my life.'

Biddy shook her head in delighted disbelief; this magnificent giant sitting on her bed was as innocent as a child. As far as she could remember, she had never had a first-timer before.

'Matt,' she took his face in her hands and held his eyes with her own. 'Oh, Matt, I promise you, this is your night.'

She dropped her hand to his thigh and let her fingers travel upwards until her hand covered and caressed the tight, hard protuberance of his crotch. She heard his breath come faster. Kissing him, she forced his teeth apart and he felt her tongue flicking around inside his mouth like a thing with a life of its own. His chest felt about to burst. As his excitement approached crisis point she suddenly stopped her caresses and laughed hoarsely: 'Whoa there, Matt. Easy now. Not yet asthore.'

How could she know such things? How could she tell...?

'Have you ever seen a woman naked, Matt, even in a picture?' she asked, standing up in front of him and undoing the laces that held her dress closed across her shoulders.

'No.'

'But you know what men and women do?'

'Well, I've taken the bull to the cow many a time.'

She laughed. His mouth sagged open as she let the front of the dress fall to her waist exposing her breasts to him, never taking her eyes from his face, relishing his reaction.

'Would you like to touch them, Matt?'

She leaned over and his trembling hands cupped her breasts in childlike wonder. For some reason he had expected breasts to be more solid and their softness surprised him, the only hard thing about them being Biddy's erect nipples. She moaned softly as he weighed her in his hands and he wondered what feelings a woman had in these situations. Could they possibly be as mind-shattering as his own? She reached down and touched him again, teasing, maddening.

'You want to see more, don't you?' she whispered provocatively. 'Go on then, pull it down. Pull the dress down. See everything, Matt, everything.' Her tongue probed his ear.

He fumbled and pushed at the dress. It caught tight at her hips.

'You can do it, Matt. Show me how strong you are.' She wriggled her hips. He took a bunch of dress in either hand, chucked roughly downwards and the dress fell about her ankles. Biddy always thrilled at the gasp of wonder that escaped men's lips at their first sight of her body. The thrill was sweeter this time, knowing she was the first naked woman Matt's eyes had ever feasted upon. Her love of this male reaction was the main reason she preferred entertaining her clients at home to lifting her skirts behind the Flannel Hall. She stepped out of the dress and stood before him, proudly flaunting her beauty. He found it difficult to breathe. He was afraid he would pass out if his heart didn't slow down. When as an innocent young girl Biddy had first noticed pubic hair appearing, she decided she didn't like it and clipped it as it grew. After a year or so she gave up the fight and was soon blessed with the luxuriant red-gold bush through which she now trailed her fingers while Matt watched hypnotised.

'Nicer than your cows, Matt, yes?'

He cringed, recalling his silly remark. He was left speechless by this vision before him. She turned and, laughing wickedly, wiggled her exquisitely rounded bottom at him. Again his shaking hands reached out, this time caressing her buttocks with a wonder that bordered on reverence. He knew he could not take much more of this; if he didn't do something soon he would explode.

She took his hands and stood him up. Again her tongue invaded his mouth. She caught his tongue between her teeth inviting him to explore hers. Her mouth opened to an amazing degree and he probed this strange new world. Extending his tongue he felt the rattling in her throat as her breath rasped through her windpipe restricted by the excessive parting of her jaws.

She pushed him away slightly, still holding his face in her hands 'Now you,' she said, and began unbuttoning his shirt.

'I don't know... I... you'll have to show me.'

'Oh, Matt, I'll show you. I'll teach you everything, don't you fret.'

She tossed his shirt on the bed, then knelt down to undo the buckle of his heavy leather belt. When she dragged his breeches down his freed penis sprung against her face and stood quivering before her eyes. She stood back and looked at him; it was her turn to gasp in wonder. His massive body tapered down from magnificently muscled shoulders and chest to a narrow waist and small hips. Only God knew how many naked men Biddy had seen - she had stopped counting two years ago - but she knew that never before had she gazed on such perfection. And Holy Jesus, he was superbly hung. She had heard from the soldiers stories of tribes in far-off primitive lands where the men were endowed with stallion-like cocks but she reckoned this shy god from Glenmalure would compare favourably with any of them.

She lusted as she had never lusted in her life. Taking him in her hand she drew him to her and, moving her feet apart, placed him between her thighs.

'Now, Matt.'

But Matt knew it was the end; his tortured body could take no more. The touch of her hand as she held him was too much and he began to ejaculate. Sensing what was happening she tightened her grip and masturbated him vigorously until he had spent himself into the golden hair. He was mortified.

'I'm sorry... sorry,' he mumbled.

She was disappointed and frustrated beyond words but the last thing she wanted was to have him feeling bad about himself.

'It's all right, Matt,' she laughed and gave him a hug, 'it often happens like that, asthore, it'll be better the next time. Now come here,' she said, lying back on the bed with her feet still on the floor, 'I want you to see something.'

Lubricating the middle finger of her right hand with some semen she began masturbating herself.

'Watch, Matt. Watch closely what I do. See? You need to know. It's important.'

She closed her eyes then and seemed to leave him, going off into some world of her own, concentrating on some mysterious fantasy as her finger worked in tiny flicking circles. The scent of her womanhood filled his nostrils and he watched fascinated as each exhalation of breath became an increasingly high-pitched whine - until she suddenly brought her thighs together with a slap, trapping her still-working hand between them. Her body bucked and threshed and he was shocked yet excited as she uttered a stream of obscenities interspersed with some of the strangest sounds he had ever heard. With a final guttural blasphemy her body heaved and almost levitated before collapsing back on the bed where she lay breathless and moaning.

'Are you all right?' There was a note of concern in Matt's voice. She opened her eyes.

'I'm grand, Matt. Remember what happened to you a few minutes ago? Well, now you know what happens to girls.'

'Does it feel good?'

'Does yours?'

'God, yes.'

'Tell me, do you do it often?'

'Beg your pardon, Biddy?'

'Ah, come now. You know what I'm talking about, Matt. Do you flog the bishop?'

He shook his head, embarrassed.

'No,' he croaked.

She sat up and putting her hand under his chin raised his eyes to hers.

'Ooh, Matt Byrne, You're the very divil of a liar altogether. Look at you! The biggest, healthiest looking baste that ever crossed the door of this room. You can't fool Biddy.'

Again Matt enquired of Heaven how she could know.

Jumping up and going to the wardrobe she took out a large whiskey jar. Humming to herself she playfully balanced it on top of her head and with outstretched arms glided across the room and placed it at his feet. Curtsying she said: 'Accept my humble offering, my Lord.'

She went skipping into the kitchen as unselfconscious and natural as a baby in her nakedness, reappearing seconds later with two glasses. She sat beside him on the bed and poured.

'Now,' she handed him a full glass, 'we'll just sit and drink and you can tell me all about yourself.'

She suddenly smacked his free hand out of his lap where he had been unsuccessfully trying to hide himself. 'And will you for God's sake relax! Do you think I've never seen a dead one before?'

She had already made up her mind she was not going to betray this young man; it would be madness. His rebel friends would probably kill him if they found out and that, it now seemed to her, would be a loss out of all proportion to any financial reward she might receive, and he certainly didn't appear to her to be the kind of man who would associate with robbers and murderers.

Matt's throat was as dry as an old floorboard. He let the whiskey trickle back slowly and savoured its relaxing warm glow. When the glasses were filled for the second time Biddy spoke.

'Have you ever met the outlaw leader, Dwyer?'

'I have, and thank God for it. I wouldn't be here this night if it wasn't for the man. Saved my life, that he did.'

'Thank God again!' she exclaimed in genuine gratitude, 'I hear he is a desperate murderer.'

'If he is, he hides it well, for I have never heard of him to behave other than honourably.' Matt took a swig from his glass.

'The soldiers tell me different. They say that any rebels still on the loose in the mountains are the lowest villains.' A note of doubt was creeping into Biddy's voice.

'Well, certainly there are some rogues among the rebels who rob and plunder for their own gain, but I know it to be a fact that Dwyer deals with them severely when they are found out. If murder has been committed they are shot or piked, and if they have robbed some gentleman in Dwyer's name they are discharged on the spot with a warning that they will be executed should they betray the rest of the rebels.'

'So you are quite convinced then that Captain Dwyer is not the uncivilized monster he is reputed to be?'

'I know him to be a fair man, and I believe there are those among the soldiery who would say the same of him, for it's known that he has intervened many a time when some hot-head has been bent on piking a prisoner.'

Every now and then as they drank and talked the realization of the fact that he was sitting stark naked and casually chatting with a beautiful young woman who was in the same state struck Matt, and he marvelled at the miracle of it. Maybe it was like the strange hallucinations and dreams he had experienced following his beating by the yeos and he would suddenly wake up to reality. He was drinking too much; his head was light, floating, and everything was all right.

She told him of her hopes for a good future in Dublin.

'Have you ever been to Dublin, Matt?'

'Ay, I have, several times. Went with my father to the big fairs there.'

'I've only been there once myself a couple of years ago, but I can tell you it was an eye-opener. Captain Nethersole-Long of the 89th asked me to travel with him and stay in the city for a few days, just to keep his bed warm like,' she nudged him. 'He introduced me to some important people and as true as God I earned more in three days there than I would in a month here. One of the men, Lord something or other, gave me two sovereigns. He was a withered old thing and hadn't been able to service a woman for over five years. Couldn't get it up at all. But it wasn't the first time Biddy had found herself called upon to raise the dead, so to speak, so I went to work on him and in no time he had a horn on him that would not look misplaced on a fit twenty-year-old. It was a strange sight, looked like it didn't belong on his little wizened body. However, I saw to it that he didn't have to carry the weight for very long. Two sovereigns! Imagine that now, and I not with him half an hour in his plush carriage. Wanted me to visit him once a week at his big house but I wasn't too sure of myself at the time and came back here. Begod I know enough now to take care of myself and make a good living. The old Lord is probably in the soil by now but I believe there are plenty more like him. Does it bother you, Matt, that I like to have a lot of men?'

Matt was not quite sure whether it bothered him or not, but on reflection he did not think it would. After all, he felt, if he were presented with new opportunities by different girls in the future he was sure he would avail of them. He shrugged.

'What business is it of mine, sure?'

'Well, it's a shame and a pity there aren't more the like of yourself in this place. They call me all sorts of names as if it was something terrible I was doing. Have you ever gone for days without a bite passing your lips? Well, that's the way it is with me if I go without a man for any length of time. It's as natural to me as eating and drinking, and I think most women would feel the self-same way only they deny themselves and become bitter old hags.'

Matt was nodding in agreement. 'In truth I would be of a mind that most of what you say is right, for you appear to be as happy a young lady as I've yet laid eyes on, Bid.'

He became hazily aware that he was becoming aroused again and his hand moved to conceal the fact.

'No!' she cried. 'Am I talking to myself or what, Matt Byrne. Come on now, you can be proud of yourself.'

She held onto his hands and watched him.

'Oh, but aren't you the beautiful, beautiful stallion, Oh my Jesus look at you!'

She rolled back on the bed pulling him around on top of her.

'This time,' she breathed, skilfully guiding him. 'No mistakes this time.'

He took her slowly, gently, but such was the overwhelming effect on her of his powerful physique and the way he filled her to capacity that she found herself rising to orgasm almost as soon as he penetrated her. Matt recognized what he had witnessed earlier and was amazed at how her slim body could lift him high off the bed as she bucked under him. He had to fight to stay on her and when her wild movements subsided and died he continued while she whimpered softly and a few minutes later he rode her through a second, even more violent orgasm which precipitated his own and he rolled off her, sweating and exhausted.

'Holy Mother of Christ, Matt,' she threw her arm across his heaving chest, 'I swear to you I've never been fucked by such a weapon before. I thought I was going to split in two like a butchered pig. And to think it has never been used on a woman until now! The years you've wasted! But don't fear, promise you'll come to me every Monday and I'll teach you all there is to know. You have no idea how beautiful you are.'

'Are you telling me, now, that there's more? I thought we had done everything. What more can there be?'

'Oh-ho, my fine brute,' she replied, 'we've only turned the first sod in a field that has no boundaries.'

'And how much will I have to pay you?'

'You've paid me, Matt,' her fingers fondled him, 'by Jesus Christ you've paid me!'

CHAPTER ELEVEN

'What are we to do with you at all?' Michael Dwyer asked as John Mernagh ushered Matt into the room at John Cullen's house. Tired, his head aching from an excessively liberal intake of whiskey, and ignorant of the reason for this unexpected summons, Matt was at a loss for a reply. The best he could muster was an inane 'What do you mean, Captain?' Dwyer gave a long sigh.

'You left the inn at Rathdrum last night in the company of Biddy Dolan and went to her house.'

Matt was astounded that Dwyer should know where he had been, and in such a short space of time. He had awakened early to Biddy's insistent caresses and had taken her once more before stumbling down the stairs and out into the pre-dawn stillness of the sleeping town. First light had found him back in Glenmalure. He had intended flopping down in his barn for a few hours' much-needed sleep, but got there to find John Mernagh waiting for him.

He looked away from Dwyer's eyes, embarrassed at what the Captain obviously knew or guessed.

'Do you know how many good men that young woman has sent to the gallows on her bloody perjured evidence?'

The anger in Dwyer's voice frightened him.

'But you see, Captain, she only did it because they have her convinced we are all murderers. I informed her in strong terms that this was not the case.'

'For the love of Christ, man, she's a whore. She services the whole bloody army and gets paid for any information she can get on us. Do you think a woman like that is going to give up easy money just because you tell her we're not such a bad lot after all?' Dwyer threw his hands up in despair. 'Croppy Biddy! Of all the women in the county you wind up with Croppy Biddy.' He leaned forward, his face close to Matt's. 'Right! I want to know everything you told her about us. Everything. Our lives could depend upon it.'

Matt turned his mind back to the voluptuous maelstrom that was last night. Some parts of it were seared forever on his mind but the later conversation was a bit hazy and fragmented.

'There was nothing of importance.'

What did it matter anyway, he knew in his guts she was not about to betray him. If she did such a thing he would personally strangle her.

'Think, man, was there anything you said in passing that she could have picked upon. Did you, for instance, happen to mention the location of any of the caves?'

Matt dreaded the Captain's reaction, but he had to say it. 'I... think I may have mentioned Keadeen.'

Dwyer slammed his fists into the table.

'Damn!' he shouted, then, burying his face in his hands, he spoke quietly.

'You have just rendered useless our principal hiding place, the only cave large enough to hold meetings in. What others did you talk about?'

'None. I'm sure of it.'

'I declare to Christ,' Dwyer stared hard at him, 'you are having more success against us than the military.' He thought for a moment, then said: 'Two things. Number one, you can spend your days usefully on the mountains searching out a new cave for us, large and well out of the way. Number two, you will never go next or near that prostitute again. Do you understand me?'

'Yes, Captain, I'm sorry.'

'I seem to recall you were sorry yesterday also. Go,' he dismissed Matt.

When they were alone, he addressed John Mernagh.

'Is this known to any of the other men?'

'I don't think so. I went alone to Rathdrum.'

'Good. They might have expected me to shoot him and I don't have the heart for it. The lad bears us no malice. Just seems to be prone to misfortune.'

'I think you may have been a mite too lenient with him myself,' Mernagh said. 'He could be a danger to us out there on the loose with what he knows of us.'

'Not if he stays in the mountains, and he'll be a long time finding a suitable cave in these hills. We've scoured them pretty well ourselves. I will go to Baravore tomorrow night if the coast is clear and ask Pierce Harney to keep an eye on him. You might come yourself and bring Martin. We'll try and work out our next moves.'

On the mountainside a little above Harney's a small fire flickered in the night, the recognized signal to the rebels that it was safe to approach. Michael Dwyer clambered down between the huge rocks to the base of Lugduff, crossed Baravore Ford and climbed the pathway to the cottage. He tapped on the door and let himself in. Pierce sat smoking his pipe beside the fire, his wife and daughter both knitting close by. They nodded to him as he entered. 'God save all here,' he said as he made for the room in which the rebels held meetings from time to time, 'and what has you all so quiet tonight?'

As he opened the door of the room he received his answer in the shape of a neat stack of guns leaning against the wall. He slammed the door shut and ran. Shots splintered the door behind him. Pierce Harney's pipe flew from his mouth as he ducked, showering sparks into the ladies' knitting. Dwyer threw himself out the door and down the path. Not for the first time he was aided by the fact that only the first of the eight soldiers following him could safely fire his gun. Dwyer turned and discharged his musket, grazing the scalp of the leader. He made it across the ford. As his pursuers entered the water they were stopped in their headlong rush by loud cries and shouts from the opposite bank as Burke, Mernagh and Vesty Byrne opened fire. Not knowing how many rebels they faced in the darkness the soldiers turned and splashed their way back from the ford. The four rebels chased them for half a mile in the direction of the Black Banks before turning back towards Harney's, laughing among themselves at the soldiers' panic. Dwyer sounded a note of caution.

'We laugh this time, but there have been so many narrow escapes of late it sets a man to wondering how long this kind of luck can hold out.'

It was to hold for four more long years.

CHAPTER TWELVE

Matt Byrne gazed down from the heights of Lugduff Mountain at the peaceful scene spread before him. Below his feet a great wilderness of dark grey boulders swept down to meet the luxuriant green of the valley floor, bisected by the thin blue line of the Avonbeg. His eyes followed the course of the river as it twinkled across the ford and meandered its way off towards Drumgoff.

Just above the ford a wisp of smoke ascended straight in the still summer air from the chimney of Harney's cottage; even on days like this which made working in the proximity of a fire an unenviable task, the cooking had to be done.

There was no human habitation further up the glen than Harney's, just the magnificent desolation of the Black Banks. Matt had spent most of the past week on the mountains poking sticks into holes and moving rocks in a so far fruitless search for a cave that had been overlooked during previous rebel searches. Several small caves capable of holding one or two people had turned up, giving him encouragement to keep looking. He had spent Friday night in one of these caves, sleeping on a bed of heather after a dinner of hare roasted over a camp-fire.

When he appeared at Harney's the following night Pierce had questioned him closely about his absence and had accompanied him to the cave this morning to satisfy himself as to the veracity of Matt's story. Kicking the bones of the hare before heading back down he remarked that his wife would be greatly flattered to hear that Matt preferred burnt hare to her decent home cooking. Matt sat down on a boulder and rested his back against another. The midday sun beat down on him, only the merest whisper of a mountain breeze tempering its burning rays on his face. Tomorrow was Monday. He had tried not to think of her, to concentrate on finding a suitable cave and re-installing himself in Dwyer's esteem, but it was to less avail than throwing a thimbleful of water on a burning house. As the days passed he became more and more obsessed with her until he was now consumed with an irresistible passion to see her again. No matter what he tried to think about or look at, her body persistently insinuated its beauty onto his mind's eye making anything else impossible to concentrate on for any length of time.

'Come to me every Monday. I'll teach you all there is to know.' Holy God, what could she mean? What mysterious delights did she intend for him? He would go to her.

No fear of Dwyer or anyone else could outweigh or overcome this fierce desire. And the heat didn't help. He would sneak over the mountain to Rathdrum tomorrow night; tell Harney he had slept in the cave again.

He approached her door from the lower end of the street this time not wishing to pass the tavern where somebody might see and recognize him. He walked with head bent, shoulders slumped and affecting a limp. He gave four slow knocks as she had instructed and hoped she had not forgotten. The window overhead was pushed open and her head appeared over the sill. She whispered something he didn't catch and disappeared again. It was several minutes before she opened the door, standing behind it holding the candle-sconce until he was inside.

'What did you say from the window, I couldn't hear?' he enquired.

'I said I'd be a minute or so, I was getting ready for you. See?' She closed the door and he indeed saw; she was stark naked, the flickering candle-light throwing parts of her white body into tantalizing shadow. She climbed the stairs ahead of him and in delicious shock he followed the exquisitely erotic motion of her bottom.

'So,' she said as she closed her room door behind them, 'my proud stallion turned up.'

'Did you not think I would come, Bid?'

'A body can't be certain of anything these times, but I'll tell you this, now you're here I'm about to see to it that you haven't come for the last time this night. No, by God!' She laughed as she undid his clothes. Not being familiar with the expression he failed to see the joke but laughed with her anyway.

She lay on the bed and he made to lie beside her.

'No, Matt. Not that way,' she said.

'Huh...?'

She put her hand to his shoulder and pushed him down until with nostrils flaring he inhaled once again the exciting scent of her. 'The magic spot, Matt, remember?' Her voice shook.

He tentatively probed her with a finger which she pushed aside, at the same time gently nuzzling her golden bush into his face.

'Follow your instinct, Matt.'

He followed his instinct and as he did so he felt her lips encircle him and the engulfing heat of her mouth. It was over in less than one minute for both of them. Matt cried out, his mind reeling and exploding in disbelief as he felt the swallowing action at the back of her throat hungrily draining him. He pulled his face free of her locked thighs and struggled to catch his breath, his body trembling and shocked at the suddenness of it.

'By the living Christ!' Biddy said, half choking, 'you certainly carry an amply loaded weapon. I thought you'd never stop shooting.' She pretended to gag.

'Is it not harmful to you?' he asked.

She assumed a sad expression.

'Oh, yes, I'm afraid it will harm me dreadfully. Just look at me,' she spread her arms. 'Can't you see I'm a poor dying wretch, wasting away to skin and bone after only a few years of it!' and she burst into hearty laughter.

Pierce Harney didn't question his story this time and so for the rest of the year he managed to keep his Monday night trysts undetected. He improved his disguise by wearing an old tall hat and making the limp more pronounced. Monday nights became his whole world, and Croppy Biddy's remarkable ability to startle him with some new delight every time never waned. On New Year's eve, the last day of the eighteenth century, she watched the chiming clock on the mantelpiece - a present from a grateful gentleman - and took delight in timing their love-making so that they exploded into the new century on the crest of an ecstatic wave.

CHAPTER THIRTEEN

'Michael Dwyer, about thirty one years, five feet nine or ten inches high, very straight in the back, short neck, square shoulders, a little in-kneed, rather long-legged with a little rise on the shin bone, very long feet, black hair and complexion, broad across the eyes, which are black, short cocked nose, wide mouth, thin lips, even teeth but stand separate, very long from nose to end of chin, full breasted and rather full faced, born in Imaal. Five hundred guineas for taking him.'

'It seems our worth is increasing,' Martin Burke said, handing Dwyer a copy of the Freeman's Journal, 'a few months back you were only worth three hundred.'

Dwyer smiled as he read the notice.

'Well, isn't it gratifying to know we are appreciated in high places?' He passed the newspaper along for John Mernagh and Vesty Byrne to see. The four men sat on a great rock at the edge of Kelly's Lough, a tiny hidden lake high in the mountains between Glenmalure and Imaal. The prices on the heads of the listed rebels ranged from five hundred for the Captain down to fifty guineas for some of the less notorious outlaws.

'I see I'm only worth a miserable three hundred,' John Mernagh commented, 'maybe I should retire.'

Dwyer laughed. 'With three hundred guineas on your head you might as well retire to Van Dieman's Land, for divil a rest you'd get in these parts.'

'It makes things a deal more difficult for us though,' Vesty said thoughtfully. 'The prospect of gaining a few hundred guineas would be a great temptation to a greedy man who might not otherwise bother himself with us.'

'Or woman,' said Martin Burke, 'which reminds me, what has young Matt Byrne been up to lately? Has anybody seen him?'

'Pierce Harney tells me he still spends most of his time on the mountains looking for caves,' Dwyer answered, 'and seems to be quite happy at his work.
'

'Never tried to get back to Croppy Biddy?' asked Vesty. 'Not that I've had word of, anyway,' said Dwyer.

'You have to admit,' John Mernagh said, stretching his long frame out on the sunny rock, 'the girl would take a man's breath away to look at her, and from what I've heard a night with her would spoil a man for any other woman, and I declare to God I think I believe it. Have you ever seen the way she walks in the street, always laughin' and goin' on as if some great fortune had just come her way? Not at all what you'd expect of a harlot and a perjurer. For a young lady who has sent innocent men to the gallows she appears to have ne'er a conscience at all.'

'Mernagh,' laughed Dwyer, 'you're an animal. I believe you would risk the rope yourself for a taste of whatever it is that Biddy has for sale. As for conscience, maybe what Matt Byrne said is true, that they have her convinced we are common criminals and murderers. Wouldn't you yourself go about with your head high if you had helped rid the world of a murdering villain, even if you had perjured yourself in order to achieve that end?'

'I suppose I would,' Mernagh agreed. 'Don't you think it a mite strange, though, if all they say about her is true, that Matt has not attempted to see her again?'

'I wouldn't be too sure the young scoundrel has not seen her since, but it's over a year now and nothing has occurred to make me think anybody has been giving information. As long as it remains so, we'll let things be.'

The first year of the new century was a sad one for Ireland. William Pitt had earlier proposed uniting the British and Irish parliaments and despite passionately eloquent argument by Henry Grattan and other members the Irish parliament was abolished and the Act of Union with the United Kingdom was passed. Grattan emphasized Ireland's separate identity and the necessity of a separate parliament through which her national individuality could be expressed, but to no avail.

In the first days of the century Dwyer had suffered the loss of Paddy Grant of Glenmalure, one of his most trusted men. Grant had been captured near his farm the previous November and the court had recommended that his body be gibbeted. Viceroy Lord Cornwallis again showed a spark of humanity by forbidding this hideous barbarity. Grant was hanged and his decapitated body thrown in the sea. It was later recovered by his widow and laid to rest among the ruins of the ancient monastery of Glendalough.

'So Grattan has failed and we are to be taken under the kindly wing of Mister Pitt,' Dwyer commented on reading the result of the vote. 'Well, we are not finished yet and if the French would only bestir themselves we might yet regain our own parliament. Grattan served this country well. It is a bitter thing to see the life's work of such a man come to this. I hope they will now allow him to retire in peace at Tinnehinch, I hear he has turned that old inn into a comfortable dwelling house. We can be proud to have him in Wicklow. Some yeos paid a visit there while he was in England and greatly upset his wife. Only Lord Powerscourt intervened God knows what mischief they would have done. As it was they amused themselves by destroying every tree in the orchard. Fine work for a soldier! Now,' he said, getting to his feet, 'let us go down to Harney's and see what the good lady has in the pot. It feels like an age since breakfast and my stomach growls like an old dog.'

The four followed the course of the stream that flowed from the lake until it tumbled over the edge of the mountain to become the Carrawaystick Waterfall. They climbed down through the rocks beside the fall and crossed the Avonbeg. Coming out onto the road they were surprised to find themselves face to face with three yeomen on foot. The yeos were equally taken aback at the sudden appearance of four notorious rebels in their path, and fear quickly replaced the look of surprise in their eyes. The rebels had their muskets drawn with a swiftness born of long experience where life depended upon split second reaction. The yeomen threw up their hands.

'Don't fire! We are unarmed and off duty.'

One of them was close to panic.

'We're dead. We're done for.'

Dwyer laughed.

'Now, now, lads. You will be pleased to hear that you are by no means dead. The day is too pleasant by far for such deeds, don't you think?'

'Oh yes... yes sir!'

'However,' Dwyer continued with a wicked grin, 'we feel that you are somewhat overdressed for the weather, and if you would be so kind as to donate those uniforms to a good cause you may be on your way.'

The yeomen looked at one another and began frantically undressing as if their garments were infested with ants.

'Everything!' Dwyer yelled as the three hesitated in their underdrawers. Embarrassment flushed their faces as they complied. 'Now, Gentlemen, you may be off back the way you came,' Dwyer fought to control his mirth, 'and give our kindest regards to your captain.' He stood erect and saluted them. 'About turn. Quick march!'

The rebels rolled on the grass verge with laughter, watching the unfortunate yeos until they vanished beyond a bend in the road.

✠ ✠ ✠ ✠ ✠

Michael Keogh eyed with distaste the cringing, ragged little individual who stood in the doorway of Keogh's imposing house on the road near Greenane.

'Well? What business have you here, speak up, man?'

The man rubbed his hands together, wringing them as if they were frozen with the cold.

'Michael Dwyer, sir, he plans to visit your house and rob you this very Thursday, your honour, upon my oath he does, the villain.'

'Does he indeed now? And how, may I ask, do you come to be in possession of such information? Am I to believe that the renowned Dwyer makes the tramps of the road privy to his intentions?'

'Ah, sir,' the little man cautioned him, 'you would be wise not to mock me, for things are said in my hearing by them that consider my likes harmless and stupid. There are them that would pay a man handsomely for such useful information.' He showed a mouthful of black teeth in an expectant grin. 'Surely, now, your honour sir, a sovereign would not be excessive in appreciation of a man savin' your property and puttin' a robber with five hundred guineas on his head into your honour's hands.'

Keogh dismissed him with a contemptuous wave.

'If you are not five miles from here by noon I will have you thrown in Wicklow jail.' He called his servant. 'Jackson, see this loathsome creature from my sight.'

Keogh went back inside the house and sat at his writing desk. Ten minutes later he again called Jackson.

'I want you to ride into Rathdrum and deliver this note personally to the captain of the yeomen at the Flannel Hall.'

It would do no harm to take precautions.

Before dawn on Thursday morning a dozen men of the Rathdrum Yeomanry arrived at the house, led by Corporal White. White hid himself in a room off the living room and the others found places of concealment in hedges and behind walls around the outside of the house.

'If there should be any truth in what the tramp said, sir,' White said to Keogh, 'this could be a profitable day's work.'

'You are welcome to your blood-money,' Keogh snapped, 'I want no part of it. Just do your duty and see to it my property is protected.'

It was a long wait; night was falling when three horsemen rode up to the door and dismounted. Keogh opened the door to their knocking and looked out into the barrel of a musket held by the man who was apparently the leader. All three had their faces blackened, but Keogh was too incensed to be intimidated.

'Well, what is it, you scoundrels? It is obvious you are intent upon mischief since you don't have the courage to show your faces.'

'Mister Keogh,' the leader addressed him, 'we have reason to believe you are in a position to contribute to our needs. Allow me to introduce myself. I am Captain Michael Dwyer of the United Irishmen. You may have heard of me.'

'Indeed I have, and I have obviously been sadly misled regarding your reputed intelligence. Only an unmitigated fool would go to the trouble of disguising his face and then introduce himself to his victim.'

The leader laughed.

'My comrades here are Vesty Byrne and John Mernagh, and if you will now kindly invite me in they will see to it we are not interrupted.'

'I will do no such thing,' cried the indignant Keogh. 'If you enter this house it will be by force of arms.'

'Have it as you will.' The muzzle of the musket was pushed into his chest compelling him to walk backwards into the house.

'Now, sir,' the leader said when they were in the living room. 'You will be good enough to bring me whatever money you have about the house, and I might caution you not to stint, for if I am not well pleased with your gift rest assured I will render your handsome pile a heap of ashes.'

Keogh left the room and the leader took a candle and stooped over the fireplace to light it from a burning log as the room was fast becoming dark. White, watching from the partly open door of his hiding place, saw his chance and entered the living room. He got to within a yard of his victim and fired. The ball entered the leader's head at the right temple as he turned from the fire and he fell without uttering a sound. Shots echoed outside as the hidden yeos opened fire, but the two men on guard escaped in the darkness.

Corporal White was ecstatic, almost hysterical.

'I got him! It's Dwyer,' he yelled to nobody in particular. 'The great Dwyer is done at last and I did it! By Christ, I did it!' He kicked the body warily; there was no movement. He rolled it over and looked into the blackened but unmistakable face of a man well known to him - Henry Moody of the Hacketstown Yeomanry.

CHAPTER FOURTEEN

While the rebels were in the dark about Matt's visits to the young prostitute the military were not, and despite Biddy's repeated assurances that the lad knew nothing of value, they were not convinced. As the months passed without any slackening off in the regularity of the visits, they became increasingly worried that her fascination with this fellow might well lead her to divulge things which could be dangerous if they found their way to the ears of the rebels.

Matt Byrne would have to be got rid of. It could not be done officially; he was not on the wanted list. Something had to be arranged without orders from the higher ranks. It should not be difficult; the right gang of yeos would do the job for port.

For all her wealth of experience, this was new to Biddy. She had just soared to the crest of the final unstoppable wave of orgasm when Matt's body suddenly wasn't there anymore. Her body protested violently at the sudden cruel withdrawal. 'Bastard... bastard!' she screamed, thinking it was Matt's idea of a tease to withdraw at the vital moment. She drew her knees up and hugged herself through the intense spasms. As they receded and her mind allowed her to take in her surroundings again, she saw the backs of several soldiers leaving the room and instantly knew what had happened. The bastards had dog-drawn her. They had often told her of how they would sometimes amuse themselves by letting male and female prisoners at it and then hauling the man off. Dog-drawn! Jesus Christ. She leapt from the bed.

'You stupid whore's kitlings! What are you about? Where are you taking him? He has done nothing.'

They laughed, and as she made to follow one of them turned at the door and pointed his gun at her.

'Stay, my pretty bobtail. If you cross this door before dawn the next set of ballocks you feel will be lead ones.'

They pushed and dragged Matt down the stairs and into the street. Biddy fell back on the bed devastated. What had happened? She feared greatly for Matt's life. There was something sinister in the fact that it was yeos rather than the regular militia who had arrested him. Any rebels she had sworn against in the past had been taken by the militia. She beat her fists on the bed as she realized he would think she had betrayed him. What else could he think? And oh God, he had become an incredible lover under her guidance, his confidence growing to such an extent that he now took her as he pleased, and she encouraged him to do so, and to indulge any whim that might enter his head.

'Matt,' she had said one night as he arrived, 'you need no more lessons from me. The teacher is yours now, have your way. I'll refuse you nothing.'

Unsmiling, he had lifted her under the arms, pinned her to the wall and taken her savagely, staring into her eyes while her feet flailed a foot off the ground and both her mind and body were driven to the point where she embraced utter loss of control.

She was proud of the lover she had created and only last week had confided in him that she now had enough money put by to get a place in Dublin. She asked if he would consider going to live with her there; danger was always present for a girl alone in the big city and it would be good to have a strong man to look after her. This had taken him by surprise and while he didn't relish the thought of life without her, he wasn't sure he could adapt to city life. What could a man do with himself all day in the city? He would have to think it over, he told her.

He had come to a decision during the week not to go and live in Dublin but to somehow make it his business to get to her there every week as usual. He had not told her of this decision yet, and now he found himself being man-handled down the steep hill to the open space in front of the Flannel Hall.

There were six yeos in the party that had raided the house and about twenty more had assembled at the Flannel Hall. They were holding another captive and as Matt was brought up to them he heard the young man, who was of slight build and a stranger to Matt, plead tearfully for mercy. They were placing something on top of his head. Matt's heart froze in terror as the pungent smell of pitch assailed his nostrils. He made a violent attempt to free himself from the grips of his captors but there were too many of them. They tied his hands behind his back and pushed him closer to the other man. One of them took a burning stick from a small fire by the roadside and approached the prisoner. The yeomen formed themselves into a circle. 'Now, Croppy!' the man with the burning stick cried as he jabbed it at the unfortunate victim's head. The young man threw himself sideways avoiding the stick, but was quickly hauled upright again and this time the stick made contact and the pitch burst into black-smoking flame. They held him until the pitch was burning steadily, then released him. Screaming, he made a wild run for the river a few hundred yards away but could not break through the circle of cheering yeos. Three times he rushed them and each time was pushed back. Finally, his hideous shrieks rending the night air, he ran to the massive wall of the Flannel Hall and flinging himself in a circular motion with all the strength of a pain-maddened bull he dashed his brains out against the cold stone.

Spiked high on the wall above, the heads of the recently executed Andrew Thomas of Annamoe, Paddy Grant of Glenmalure and the yeoman Henry Moody, shot while impersonating Dwyer in a house robbery, stared blindly down on the barbarism being perpetrated below. The body of the dead man was then bundled into a barrel of tar and set on fire.

They turned their attention to Matt. As a grinning yeo approached him with the cap filled with pitch he made a desperate lunge flooring the four yeos who were holding him. He had run about ten yards when he was brought down by sheer weight of numbers. 'Hold the villain down there,' the man with the pitch cap shouted, 'I'll cap him on the ground if that's the way he wants it.'

They piled on top of Matt and the cap was pressed onto his head, the canvas bursting in the struggle. They pasted the leaking pitch into his scalp and he sobbed helplessly as a yeoman held the burning stick to his head and yelled 'Let him up!' as the pitch ignited. Like the previous victim, Matt knew his one possible hope of getting out of this alive was the river, and he concentrated all the strength of his being into a superhuman dash for survival. As he ran at the circle he saw the yeos in front of him tighten their grips on one another to prevent his breaking through and he suddenly veered to his right bursting into the circle a few yards further along.

His formidable strength coupled with the element of surprise resulted in half a dozen yeos finding themselves on their backs and he scrambled through a hedge and into the field that would take him down to the river. His scalp crackled and an unbearable roaring pain seemed to sear his very brain as he flew madly across the grass. Streams of burning pitch flowed down his face and the back of his neck. He heard his own screams as if they emanated from some separate source and he had just about lost all reason when he stumbled headlong into the river.

Its blessed coldness brought him back to his senses only to realize he was now drowning with his hands tied behind his back. He rolled frantically in an attempt to get his feet under him. For a second he broke the surface and gasped in a mouthful of air before the current pulled him down again. He kicked out and again the upper half of his body came out of the water. He threw himself across the flow and went under again. He repeated this kick and leap, each time taking him a little closer to the other side until at last he flopped like a fish on the far bank. He lay panting and the agony of his head returned. The cooled pitch, welded to his skull, pulled tightly at what was left of the skin of his forehead. He could hear the curses of the yeos up river on the opposite bank, but knew he was safe from detection in the blackness of the night.

'The bloody rascal has drowned.'

'One damned Croppy less in the world.'

The sound of their voices drifted away towards the town. Matt got to his feet; he would have to get as far away as possible before dawn which he reckoned could only be about two hours away. Blood poured from cuts all over him caused mainly by sharp stones on the river-bed as his naked body was rolled by the current.

Stumbling through the darkness he pondered how his life had gone from heaven to hell in a matter of minutes.

Hours later he staggered into his barn. The hay looked inviting but he had only come this way to get some old clothes he kept in the barn. He didn't want anybody to see him in this state.

Having covered his nakedness he crossed the Avonbeg, dipping his agonized head in its cool waters, then continued his way up the side of Lugduff, heading for one of the small caves he had found. He thanked God he had no family; Few victims of pitch-capping survived, the only one known to Matt being Art Kelly who had been so monstrously disfigured that he took to tramping the roads of the country because he could not bear the frightened looks of his own children. Matt knew that where the physical pain would fade with time, the mental agony would torture him to the grave. No woman would want anything to do with him; he had lain for the last time with beautiful Biddy.

When he reached the top of Lugduff he considered taking the old Borenacrow trail to the Glendalough side of the mountain and throwing himself off the cliff into the Upper Lake, but more through exhaustion than self-preservation, he threw himself instead onto the bed of heather in the cave.

Mercifully, he slept through the rest of the day and until the dawn of the following one. He got up and went outside. There was a tightness in his head as if it were being crushed in a vice. Far below in Glenmalure some tiny figures moved along the road. His head began to swim and he had to dive back into the cave and lie down before he fainted. An hour passed and he tried rising again. The sun was up and already warming the mountaintop. Pangs of hunger now added to his misery and he picked his way gingerly through the rocks and heather, each step an explosion inside his head, to a spot where he had set a snare some days before. He was surprised to find a young rabbit in it; rabbits didn't usually venture this high, but so much the better, he thought, rabbit was sweeter than hare. He skinned and cleaned it, gathered some scrub and lit a fire with a flint and tinder-box.

He was ravenous and ate the rabbit half done, unable to resist the mouth-watering aroma as it cooked. He went and checked some other snares but found them empty. Putting his hand to his head he winced as his fingers made contact with the shiny hard surface of the pitch. It would eventually come away leaving his skull red-raw until it healed into the horrible red and blue rippled dome he had seen on Art Kelly. His face too would be dreadfully marked. A line of molten pitch had run down at each side of his nose, spreading across his top lip in a grotesque moustache. A third line had run down his right cheek and dripped onto his chest. Could Biddy have been behind all this? Surely not, he thought, sure hadn't she only last week asked him to go and live in Dublin with her. No, it must be something else. Maybe the yeos were jealous that she favoured him so much; she liked to talk about her adventures so no doubt she boasted about him to the soldiers. Anyway, it didn't matter now, he would probably never lay eyes on her again; he would live out the rest of his life as a revolting freak.

For three weeks he lived on the mountain on a diet of roast hare and water. The pitch loosened after ten days and having spent a further three days painfully moving it about, it came away like a great scab. All that remained of his fine head of hair were some tufts here and there at the back and sides. As time passed and the pain receded he again found his thoughts persistently turning to Biddy. If she hadn't betrayed him then she would be wondering what had become of him. She had probably gone to see if his head was up on the Flannel Hall as soon as day broke. At night on his bed of heather he cried bitter tears. This could not be the end of it all; he felt so alive, and his blood still raced in his veins when he thought of her, but how in the name of God could he face her looking like this? She would surely be revolted at the sight of him.

At the end of his third week on the mountain the long spell of dry weather was broken by a full day and night of torrential thunderstorms. During the night the rain poured into his cave and drove him out. He started down the rock-strewn mountainside to Harney's, pulling an old hat that had belonged to his father down over his head until it covered his nose, so that he had to tilt his head back to see where he was going. He crossed the swollen waters of the ford. No light showed at Harney's. He tapped on the door. He heard shuffling sounds inside and then the voice of Pierce Harney called.

'Who's there?'

'Mister Harney, it's me, Matt Byrne.'

He heard Mrs. Harney take a noisy breath. 'God help us this night!'

'Matt Byrne is dead, rest his soul,' Pierce shouted.

'No, I swear to you, I escaped from them. Let me in for God's sake, I'm half drowned.'

Three heavy bolts were drawn and the door opened a few inches.

'Be Christ, it's himself all right. I'd know the size of him anywhere.' Pierce said, opening the door the rest of the way. 'Come in, avick, come in. Where have you come from at all this foul night?'

'I was in a cave above on the mountain.'

'Are you tellin' me, now, that you've been up there all the time lookin' down at us an' we thinkin' you were dead?'

'Ay.'

'Well, that bates all! The yeos in Rathdrum were boastin' they had drowned you. Get them wet clothes off you, now, an' we'll dry them.'

He uncovered the embers and threw some sticks and turf on top.

'I declare you're a comical sight in that hat, Matt,' Mrs. Harney laughed. 'Take it off and give us a look at you.'

'I won't if you don't mind, Mrs. Harney,' Matt said quickly, holding the hat on with one hand and moving away from her, 'I'm afraid I don't look myself anymore.'

Her hands flew to her shocked face.

'The heartless divil's pitch-capped you! Oh, Mother of God, I'm sorry, Matt. What is the human race coming to at all, at all?'

'We only heard they threw you in the river,' Pierce said.

'I threw myself in the river. That's how I'm here alive.'

'Dwyer will be pleased to hear you are still above ground,' Pierce handed him some dry clothes. 'At first he was in a rage that you had gone to Rathdrum, but when he calmed down he blamed himself, for he reckoned it was your connection with his name that made you a target for the yeos. Ay, This will be a relief to him.'

Matt left the kitchen to change. In the bedroom he caught sight of his reflection in a looking-glass on the wall. He had grown quite a beard in the three weeks. He lifted the hat slightly; no moustache, just a shiny scar above his lip and two similar streaks framing his nose where the pitch had dripped from his forehead. Another streak ran down the length of his right cheek but this one was already almost concealed by his beard. His face, at least, was not quite as horrific as he had feared. Holding his breath, he removed the hat. An involuntary cry escaped him and he recoiled from the mirrored image. He forced himself to look again.

Low across his forehead was an ugly ridge of red and blue burnt skin, and the rest of his scalp looked as if molten glass had been poured over a mottled, angry-looking surface, so that the top of his head resembled a badly glazed jar.

He groaned in a mixture of self-pity and burning hatred for the yeos who had done this to him. He returned to the kitchen. 'I'll not impose myself upon you longer than the duration of the storm. I'll stay on the mountain awhilst the weather permits, and come down to my barn on winter nights, for I don't intend to be a fright to people.'

'Don't be foolish now, Matt asthore,' Mrs. Harney scolded him, 'you know you are welcome in this house anytime.'

'Ay, I know it, and right grateful I am for your hospitality. You have done me more than your share of kindnesses since my father's death, and if you will pardon me for making so bold I would ask one more favour of you, that you knit me some sort of cap that would come down to my eyebrows. The world will have to put up with the rest of my face.' He partly raised the hat.

'That's the spirit!' Mrs. Harney exclaimed. 'Sure, I've seen worse faces on people who never made the acquaintance of a yeo. You just let that fine beard of yours keep on growing and I'll knit you the finest hat in Wicklow, ay, and a spare one for Sundays!'

On the following Monday night Matt crossed the mountains to Rathdrum, still wearing the old farm hat pulled low. Biddy was lying on her bed listening to the peaceful ticking of the clock when she heard the knock only she and Matt knew. Could it be possible? A month had passed since he had been dragged from the room. It had to be him; there was no other explanation. She had stayed home every Monday night, the fact that no body had been recovered keeping her hope alive.

She pushed the window up and looked out.

'Who is it?'

'Matt Byrne,' he replied without looking up.

She flew down the stairs.

'I don't believe it! Oh, thanks be to Jesus Christ but I still don't believe it. Come in here, Matt, and tell me I'm not dreaming.' Up in the room she threw her arms around him and buried her face in his chest still protesting that she didn't believe it.

'How did you get away...? Ooh, you've grown a beard!'

He pulled away as she reached to take his hat off.

'I don't want you to see me, Bid, they pitch-capped me.'

'I know, I heard. They're an evil herd of gets, but just you listen to me, Matt, I've seen to some of the ugliest specimens on earth. You know the tramp Kelly? Ay, well I've had him. He was pitch-capped and must be three score if he's a day. Met him on the Greenane road one morning and took pity on him. Said he hadn't had a woman since the day he'd left his family three years before. They did a far worse job on that poor divil than they did on yourself, from what I can see of you. He hadn't enough skin left on his face to grow a beard, God bless us.'

'I'll be away with myself this minute if it's pity you're handing out, Bid, I couldn't take it.'

'Ah, will you whisht, and don't be taking the foul end of the stick. Oul' Kelly was a sorry sight and a broken man. You look a far cry from broken to me, Matt Byrne. Anyway,' she gave him her mischievous look and suddenly knocked the hat from his head, 'when did I ever give you the notion it was the top of your head I was after?'

She pulled him to the bed.

'Tell me, Bid,' he asked her later, 'do you happen to know of a yeo be the name of Handy?'

'I do. What of him?'

'I want to kill him.'

Shocked, she moved away from him.

'What are you saying at all, Matt? You can't just go killing yeos. They'd hang, draw and quarter you.'

'I can't say I care a rap what they do to me. You told me once that you swore against rebels because you believed them to be murderers. Well, I can tell you with all certainty that this man is indeed a murderer. I saw him with my own eyes pitch-capping a poor fellow the same night they took me from here. He laughed louder than them all when the unfortunate man smashed his skull against the Flannel Hall. I won't rest until he has paid for that night's work. He capped myself as well, and thinks me dead. Help me get him, Bid, do you know where he might be found?'

'I'll help you, but first I have something to tell you. I'm moving to Dublin this week. I've arranged to rent a room while I look around for a place to buy, and the offer I made you still holds good if you're interested.'

Matt shook his head.

'A fellow who has been pitch-capped would stand out like a priest in a whiskey-house. Maybe I'll get to visit you now and then.'

'I want you with me, Matt, and believe me, with a cap on your head you wouldn't stand out at all. Sure the city is alive with freaks, man.'

'Well, I suppose I'll have to get used to being called a freak, and you might as well be the first with it.'

She gave him a dig with her elbow.

'Arrah, now, you know right well I didn't mean it that way.'

He shrugged. 'Well, we'll see. But come now, where can I lay my hands on this Handy wretch?'

'He'll be at the inn this minute,' Biddy replied.

'That won't do. I'd be torn apart if I were to show myself there.' She ran her fingers through his beard and looked him steadily in the eye.

'I'll get him for you. Go now and give me half an hour or so. I'll bring him to the back of the Flannel Hall.'

Matt felt no impatience as he waited in the darkness; she could take all night as long as she got him here. After only twenty minutes he heard voices and recognized Biddy's laughter. He watched the two shadowy figures go behind the dark bulk of the building and followed. The yeo would not have the satisfaction of Biddy before he died. Matt crept to within a couple of feet of them and as the yeo bent to kiss Biddy he was suddenly seized by the collar and lifted off his feet. Matt turned him around so that his face and that of the yeo were almost touching. He shook the old hat from his head.

'Remember me, Mister Handy?' Tears streamed from Matt's eyes as he spoke, 'Remember me? I never harmed you, nor did I harm any of your friends, yet you saw fit to do this to me. My father never harmed you yet your fellow yeos murdered him. No doubt the unfortunate man you put to death before my eyes never harmed you either. You are a disgusting, inhuman murderer and you are about to die for it, so help me God.

The yeo uttered a choked-off 'No' Matt took his throat in his left hand and lifted him into the air, holding him there until his bucking and kicking weakened and died, only thin rattling sounds escaping his throat as his mouth opened grotesquely wide and his tongue protruded stiffly between his bared teeth.

Matt held him for a full minute after the last spasmodic signs of life had finished, then threw the body to the ground with a cry of contempt.

Biddy was standing with her back against the Flannel Hall wall, her breathing heavy.

'Let's be out of this, quickly,' Matt said, taking her arm.

She pulled back.

'Take me, Matt.' Her voice was thick, hoarse.

'Yes. Come on then, back to the room.'

'Here, Matt. I want it here. Now.'

'Damn it, no, Bid, we can't. If someone comes along we'll both hang. For God's sake, come on.'

It was as if he had not spoken. She lifted her skirt.

'Fuck me, Matt.'

The words were spoken quietly, but the passion behind them was almost frighteningly palpable. The sight of her white legs turned lewdly outwards and seeming to glow in the darkness was more than he could endure and he took her against the wall. She worked like a crazed wild animal with him, her cries muffled against his chest. When they finished she fell to the ground beside the dead yeoman. 'God forgive me,' she gasped, 'oh, Jesus forgive me.'

'What?... What's wrong, Bid? Come on now, get up and let's get away from here.'

Great sobs shook her body.

'Bid...' he began.

'All those men, Matt, hundreds of them I've done it with, but this is the first time it's been sinful.'

CHAPTER FIFTEEN

By the late Autumn of 1803 it had become a matter of acute embarrassment to the government of King George III that more than five years after the suppression of the 1798 rebellion a small band of rebels was still outstanding in the Wicklow Mountains despite the best efforts of the military and numerous enticements to surrender. While they remained in the hills their intimate knowledge of the territory rendered it almost impossible for any army to march on them without walking into an ambush.

Dwyer had predicted the failure of Robert Emmet's July attempt at a rising in Dublin. He considered Emmet somewhat naive and lacking in good sense and prudence. Emmet had repeatedly urged Dwyer to muster his Wicklowmen and attack Dublin, assuring him that the Dubliners would be led by men of sterling quality. Through his own intelligence men Dwyer found this not to be the case, and declared that he would not commit his brave men 'upon the faith or good conduct of the rabble of Dublin,' and of Emmet's boast that he would 'free Ireland of the world' he said that if he had known Emmet was depending on the lower orders he would have 'undeceived him,' adding that if Emmet had a brain to match his education he would be a fine man.

Emmet had supplied Dwyer with a colonels uniform, and Vesty Byrne, Mernagh and Burke each with the uniform of a captain. He had also replaced their old muskets with new blunderbusses. Dwyer had eventually agreed that if Emmet succeeded in taking and holding Dublin for twenty four hours or if he, Dwyer, could 'perceive the green flag flying above the King's on the tower of the castle, he would be on hand to cover or second the enterprise.'

During 1802 a new military road had been constructed running from Rathfarnham in Dublin into the very heart of the Wicklow Mountains 'Thro' parts of the country which are infested by insurgent plunderers as a ready means of driving them from those places.' The road would facilitate the speedy movement of large numbers of troops to the hitherto inaccessible reaches of the mountains.

Now, as a further manifestation of the seriousness with which the government viewed the problem of outstanding rebels, a series of massive barracks was under construction along the line of the road, the southernmost one being in the Glen of Imaal. Dwyer cheekily approached workmen on the site of the barracks and assured them they need have no fear of him attacking them or impeding their work in any way, as he would want the barracks for his own people if things turned out well.

Earlier in the year Dwyer had lost his left thumb in a shooting mishap. Walking alone in the mountains he had come upon Thomas Halpin, a former trusted associate who had been arrested in June, 1800, and had turned informer to save his life. Many rebels had been taken and executed on his information in the intervening years and he had now been sent by Major Sirr of Dublin, of whose staff he was a member, back to the hills to see if he could be instrumental in the taking of Dwyer. When the two men came suddenly face to face Halpin fled and there followed a long chase through the mountains. Dwyer pursued his quarry until, realizing Halpin was too far ahead to be caught, he took aim with his blunderbuss and fired. The gun exploded, leaving his thumb hanging by a piece of skin. As he staggered along in extreme pain he met a local tailor, Rogers, and asked him if he had his scissors about him.

'I have,' Rogers replied.

'Well then, you had better cut this loose thumb off me, it can be of no more use.'

Rogers did the necessary and arranged for a relative of his who had studied surgery to visit Dwyer and dress the wound. The tailor took the thumb and buried it in the old graveyard of Leitrim in Imaal, the rest of Dwyer being destined to lie at the other side of the world in far-off Sydney.

Only continuing hope of intervention by the French kept the rebels going through five bitter winters of deprivation and exposure in caves which had adversely affected the health of even the strongest of them, so when word reached Dwyer in early December 1803 that the French had finally decided not to go ahead with any further attempts at assisting the rebels, the prospect of facing yet another winter on their keeping became well-nigh intolerable. On top of this, most of Dwyers family had been arrested along with many neighbours and friends in an effort to coerce him into surrendering, the females being held in Kilmainham jail and the males on small sloops anchored in Dublin Bay. The new barracks in Imaal was now completed and housed a garrison of two hundred men, which greatly restricted movement in the area, and soldiers were free-quartered in every house the authorities suspected might be friendly towards the rebels.

The local Parish Priest, Father John Power, sent messages to Dwyer impressing upon him the hardship his continued obstinacy was causing his imprisoned parents, brothers and sisters, and the great burden placed on local householders forced to support soldiers in their homes. The rebel chief called a meeting in a large cave at Oakwood, near the Wicklow Gap, to discuss the possibility of surrender. 'It would be madness,' John Mernagh argued angrily, 'they would never give us favourable terms, and do you expect me to believe that Hume has forgotten we killed his father?'

Dwyer, Byrne, and Burke had decided to contact William Hume, M.P. for Wicklow, who lived at Humewood, near Imaal.

'Mister Hume is an honourable man,' Dwyer answered, 'and I am perfectly sure he knows we did not order his father's murder. We have always allowed his family to travel these parts unmolested. His father's murder was a stupid act carried out by hot-headed fools. Had we been there it would not have occurred.'

'Nevertheless,' Mernagh said resolutely, 'I think you are throwing your lives away. I'm staying out.'

'Very well, we will not press you, but I think it pointless. What can you achieve alone? You'll probably die of exposure anyway. There isn't a safe house in the parish this winter. We'll see what Mister Hume has to say and if it is favourable maybe you will join us.'

Dwyer went to the house of his old friend, John Cullen, who had for some time been urging him to surrender and save his life for the sake of his growing family; he and Mary now had a daughter and two sons.

'I'm going to surrender, John, if I can get decent terms for the boys and myself. You are on good terms with Billy the Rock Jackson, and he with Mister Hume. Billy could relay my message.' John Cullen threw his arms around Dwyer.

'Thank God, Michael. Thank God you're seein' sense at last. I'm a happy old man this day.'

Dwyer outlined the conditions under which he would surrender and Cullen went straight to his friend Jackson.

William Hume was delighted at this sudden unexpected turn of events and went directly to government where he recommended Dwyer's terms be accepted. Receiving the Lord Lieutenant's consent he hurried back to Humewood and sent word by Billy the Rock that if it was acceptable to Dwyer he would meet him alone outside the gate of Humewood on the following night, December 14th, at ten o'clock. The rest of the men could follow later.

The warmth of the handshake when they met confirmed Dwyer's high opinion of Hume's character. The rebel leader handed his blunderbuss over to the M.P. and the two men walked together up the avenue to Humewood. Hume was full of questions, but there was no hint of triumphalism in his tone. The questions sprang from a genuine enthusiasm and respect for a soldier who had held out against the might of the King's army for five long years. 'Now, Dwyer,' he said, stopping and taking hold of Dwyer's arm, 'you must enlighten me about Mangan's house, for it is something that has puzzled me greatly for years.'

Mangan's cottage was in the vicinity of Humewood and the Humewood yeomen had many times acted on information that Dwyer was there, only to search the place from floor to rafters in vain. Dwyer laughed. 'I will be happy to oblige you with an explanation, sir, if I may have your word that Mangan and his family will not suffer reprisals.'

'You have my word.'

'Very well, but before we go any further I would wish you to know that while I have regrets about certain things that were done in my name over the years, none troubles me more than the murder of your father.'

'I never thought otherwise. If I had you would be long dead, for I would have taken it upon myself to personally track you down, even if it meant my own life. Now, about Mangan's.'

'Well, sir, before the winter of ninety eight Mangan's roof needed re-thatching.' Dwyer was grinning. 'However, you see, he didn't remove the old one, but built the new one a couple of feet above it leaving a comfortable space between the two.'

'Upon my soul!' Hume chuckled. 'The crafty old devil. Whatever will you tell me next?'

'I will compliment you, sir,' Dwyer replied, pointing to a particular part of the house as they approached it, 'on keeping a comfortable and well-stocked kitchen.'

Hume looked at him in astonishment.

'Do you mean to tell me, Dwyer... By God, sir, you are an incorrigible fellow! Now, while we are alone and may speak our minds, tell me if you have ever heard of house-burning carried out by the Humewood Yeomanry.'

'I have not.'

'I am pleased to hear it, for had you heard and, worse, believed such a thing I would now have the task of convincing you it was otherwise, but I feel you are aware, Dwyer, that I am not a man disposed to burning people out of their homes, and my yeomen are strictly supervised.'

The two men shook hands again before entering the house.

'A man such as yourself, sir,' Dwyer said, 'makes surrender seem an honourable thing.'

Dwyer and his companions were held in Kilmainham Jail and although Hume had acted in good faith the government refused to send them to the United States and instead, after twenty months imprisonment, had them transported to Australia along with their families where they were each given some land near Sydney. This included Mernagh, who had surrendered shortly after the others.

William Hume saw to it that Dwyer was paid two hundred pounds and his companions one hundred pounds each in compensation for the governments breach of faith.

CHAPTER SIXTEEN

Matt loosened the wire of the snare from around the neck of the still warm hare and carried the small animal to the spot outside his cave on Lugduff where he regularly cooked his meals on a fire of faggots gathered on the sparsely-clad mountaintop.

He seldom left the mountain now, descending to the barn only in the worst of weather, and still crawled into crevices in the stubborn hope of finding the ideal cave for Dwyer. He had not seen Biddy since she had moved to Dublin more than two years ago, but his obsession with her had not yet died; there were still nights when he lay for long hours tormented by memories of their nights together.

He had made one abortive attempt at going to see her, walking through the mountains, watching from a distance the soldiers and their local helpers working on the new military road. From the heights of the Featherbed Mountain he looked down on the city of Dublin and lost his nerve. He turned back, unable to face the prospect of making his way through the thronged streets with thousands of strange curious eyes on him.

He left the hare beside the ashes of yesterday's fire and set off to gather wood. Having long ago exhausted the supply of scrub in the vicinity of the cave he found himself forced to travel further and further afield to find any. He had gone over a mile from the cave when he spotted a gnarled and windblown holly growing beside a huge boulder. Much of the tree was dead, the rotten boughs still intertwined with the green living wood. On closer inspection he saw that the living part had grown from a shoot put out by the old long-dead tree. He began breaking off pieces of the rotten wood, pleased with himself at finding such an abundance of fuel in one spot. Making several trips to the cave he laid in enough to last him a couple of weeks. On his final trip he gathered some good heavy pieces that had fallen among the roots, and great chunks of the rotten roots themselves came away easily in his hands.

He noticed that some of the dead wood had fallen into some sort of hole at the base of the boulder and began pulling the broken boughs out, reaching through the twisted branches of the living tree. One particular piece had a different feel to it and as he drew it from the hole he flung it away in horror; it was a skeleton foot and shin-bone. Human.

His shock lessened somewhat to be replaced by curiosity as he realized the bones must have been there a very long time, before the older holly had grown there. It would have been impossible for anybody to get into the hole during the lifetimes of those trees. He peered between the stumps and saw a second foot among the dead wood, almost hidden in the mouth of the hole. It looked, Matt thought, smiling at the absurdity of it, as if this monstrous rock had been dropped on some poor fellow as he crossed the mountain. Had he been sheltering? Hiding? Did the hole lead to a cave? If there was a cave it could be the one he had long sought for the rebels. With mounting impatience he raced back to his cave to fetch the small axe he kept there.

He chopped away the upper boughs of the holly easily enough, but the stump and roots, which covered half of the entrance to the hole, were tough and stubborn and after two hours of vigorous hacking he fell back exhausted and sweating despite the bone-chilling December air on the mountain. The hole was still inaccessible. The wood came away in maddeningly small chips. It would take several more hours at this rate. He had no choice but to take a break and went to cook the hare.

He was weak with hunger from his exertion and made short work of the meal, at the same time begrudging every minute it kept him from his task. Back at the boulder, he hacked at the stump until nightfall and still had not gained entry. Frustrated, he climbed down the mountainside to the barn, the cold being too severe to stay in the cave.

The cold grey light of dawn found him back at work, his arms stiff and aching, and in less than an hour he had pulled the remainder of the roots away from the hole. He lay on his belly and inched forward, taking the second foot and shin-bone and placing it behind him. As his eyes became accustomed to the dim light in the hole he could see the white bones of the rest of the skeleton blocking his way ahead. Although he could hardly have expected anything else, he still recoiled at the sight. He gathered his wits and reached forward, taking hold of the pelvic section, then wiggled backwards out of the hole and left it outside. He moved forward again to reach the rest of the bones and more light entered the hole as his body cleared the entrance. There was no skull. The ribcage was now the only obstacle and as he reached for it he saw something that explained the shocking manner in which this unfortunate man had met his end. Lying inside the ribcage was an unusual-looking pike-head pointing straight upwards to where the head would have been. He dragged the bones outside and on his way back in he noticed what he at first took to be some coins lying where the skeleton had been.

On closer examination they proved to be buttons; buttons he instantly recognized. His father had carried an identical button in his pocket for years, and had many times related its history to the young Matt. These buttons came from the uniform of one of Lord Grey's men who fought here in the battle of Glenmalure in the year 1580. Lord Grey, heading an army of one thousand men, had marched on the glen in an attempt to subdue Fiach MacHugh O'Byrne, the Irish chieftain who then held sway in these parts. O'Byrne had intelligence of the impending attack and Grey's army marched into a devastating ambush costing the lives of up to eight hundred men. Among the survivors were Grey's secretary, the poet Edmund Spenser, and the young Walter Raleigh.

The man who had inhabited these dry white bones had obviously been pursued here from the battle below by an alert rebel, and had been overtaken as he tried to crawl into the cave under the rock. The rebel had driven the pike upwards through the length of the soldier's body. Matt wondered if that were the case why the rebel had not retrieved his pike. Perhaps he himself had been followed by some comrades of the soldier and killed on the spot. He moved on and found himself looking down into a fairly large cavern, on one side of which was stacked an incredible array of beautiful objects.

He lay there stunned for some moments then clambered down to examine the treasure. Had this been the last wonderful sight beheld by the eyes of the long-dead soldier before the cruel pike had closed them forever?

Standing among these indescribably beautiful objects, Matt strove for some coherent train of thought. Chalices large and small of silver and gold, studded with coloured stones which he didn't doubt were precious; fabulous crozier tops; things shaped like little cottages; long strands of gold wire; religious pictures etched into solid gold sheets; bells and dozens of smaller objects, all, as far as he could tell, made of precious metals. Staring sightlessly up at him from the midst of these wonders was the missing skull.

The objects had obviously come from the Seven Churches of Glendalough whose ruins lay in the valley on the other side of Lugduff. He had learned at school about the Viking raids and how the monks would take the treasures up into the round tower, pulling the ladder after them until the raiders had gone.

So what had happened that would account for the precious objects being here on the mountain? It didn't matter; it was here and he had found it. He toyed with the idea of going to Dwyer for advice, but thought better of it and decided to wait, to think it all out carefully himself.

Looking around him he saw that he was standing in what would make a perfect replacement cave for the one on Keadeen. He would tell Dwyer about the cave, but not the treasure; not yet. That meant he would have to move it from here. But where to? The barn would be too risky; yeos might come poking about in the hay. Then he slapped his hands together as the thought struck him of how perfectly the old cave on Keadeen would serve his purpose. No rebel or sympathizer would venture there anymore and no others were aware of its existence. It would be difficult. He would have to carry the treasure across the mountain in sacks; there were plenty of them in the barn. It would have to be done by night. He climbed out of the cave and set about making the surrounding area look as undisturbed as possible, carrying the green holly boughs and dumping them a quarter of a mile away. The bones of Lord Grey's man broke and crumbled as he brought them back in and placed them in the lower part of the cave alongside the treasure. He then cleared all the fresh wood chippings into the hole and uprooted some clumps of heather to camouflage the entrance. It would do for now.

When darkness fell that night he made the first journey to and from Keadeen, five miles each way, aided by a full moon and a clear frosty night. He kept off the regular track as much as possible. Boulders and bushes took on the forms of crouching figures ready to spring at him in the ghostly moonlight as he made the lonely trek over the desolate Black Banks with the first sack of objects. He had packed heather between each item to prevent damage, and an extra thick bunch of it in the end of the sack as he would have to drop it part of the way onto the floor of the cave. The entrance to the old hide-out had been sealed by rolling a boulder into it. He moved it back and jammed a stone beneath it to prevent it rolling back into the opening. A pike with a broken handle still stood beside the makeshift ladder as if on guard. He placed the sack in the cavern at the end of the passage, feeling his way in the darkness around the small table with its blobs of candle-grease.

Back at the barn he fell into a deep sleep and woke up at midday to a world of white. It had snowed heavily and he cursed it as he would now be unable to continue transferring the treasure. It held him up for three nights and then the weather quite suddenly became surprisingly mild for December. He climbed Lugduff and found everything as he had left it. There was no moon this time and the journey took twice as long as the first, picking his way carefully to avoid bumping the bag against boulders. His thoughts as he journeyed through the inky blackness settled more and more on the idea of striking some sort of deal with Dwyer about the haul. Dwyer was a fair man and wouldn't cheat him. The proceeds from such treasures would surely equip a small army with the best arms and accoutrement available. A fine Christmas gift indeed! On the morning after he had transported the third sack he decided to call at Harney's to arrange a meeting with the chief. He had not spoken to a soul for a fortnight.

Mrs. Harney welcomed him with a bowl of steaming soup. Pierce was not at home.

'I need to see the Captain,' he said, gratefully spooning the hot liquid into him, 'I'd be obliged if you'd tell him he can find me any morning at dawn in the barn, or if he wishes I can meet him at a place of his choosing.' Mrs. Harney stopped stirring the pot and looked at him.

'Are you serious, Matt Byrne?'

'Why shouldn't I be?' he asked, puzzled.

'Begod, then, you'd better settle yourself down for a long wait, asthore. Where on God's earth have you been that you don't know Michael surrendered to Mr. Hume a week ago?'

Matt spluttered a mouthful of soup back into the bowl. 'Surrendered? Dwyer surrendered?' He was aghast.

'Ay, and Vesty Byrne and Martin Burke along with him. Hume promised to have them and their families sent to the United States. Mernagh is still out, but I don't think it will be for long.'

'Oh, my Jesus,' Matt saw everything falling apart on him. What could he do now about the treasure? He had looked forward to seeing Dwyer's face when he showed it to him. And the new hide-out.

Useless now.

He left Harney's and wandered aimlessly about the glen formulating a plan from the ruins. He would bring the last of the treasure to Keadeen, then marshal enough courage to bring one piece to Dublin and see what he could get for it. If he got a good price he would tell the buyer he had more. Much more. When it was all sold and he was a wealthy man he would track Biddy down and persuade her to come and live in comfort with him. He would build a fine new house for her on his bit of land.

CHAPTER SEVENTEEN

Dawn was breaking over the Wicklow Hills on a crisp Christmas Eve as Matt Byrne rolled the rock from the entrance and went about getting the fourth and last sack of objects into the cave on Keadeen Mountain. Leaning through the opening he lowered the sack as far as he could before letting it fall the last two feet or so to the floor, then turned to descend himself.

There was a sharp crack as his weight pressed on the fourth step down and it disintegrated. He scrabbled madly to save himself but failed to find a grip. He fell down amid a shower of loose stones and earth. There was another sharp crack, this time from his shin-bone as it caught and snapped between the rungs. He just had time to see the jagged bone protruding sideways from his leg before the boulder rolled into the cave entrance plunging the interior into blackness.

Then the pain registered and he screamed; a scream that was as much of terror as it was of pain, for he knew he had little or no hope of getting out of the hole alive. There was a roaring in his head and he lost consciousness.

He came to, still screaming, he knew not how long later. A small chink of light showed above him at the edge of the rock that sealed the entrance. He was lying on his back, his smashed leg still held up and entangled in the rungs of the ladder.

'Oh, dear Jesus, let me die now,' he cried out.

The chink of light faded and he realized he must have been unconscious for many hours. He wanted to dash his brains out like the pitch-capped man at the Flannel Hall, but the slightest movement brought such incredible pain that he passed out each time he tried to swing his head against the wall of the cave.

Cold sweat ran off him and his whole body trembled violently. The chink of light was back. Day. Gone again. His mind was going. At one point he heard voices and somewhere in his confused brain hope stirred. He tried to shout but only a thin squeal escaped from his dried-out throat. The cracked handle of the pike was close to his hand. If he could manage to poke the head of the pike out through the small space above him somebody might see it. He gripped the handle. The pike's eight-foot length swayed crazily as he endeavoured to get the head into the tiny gap of light. He fought to stay conscious. Gripping the handle as high up as he could, he tried again, whining in agony. On his fourth try the tip caught just below the chink more by accident than design and he heaved with what little strength he had left in him.

The point went a few inches through the opening and jammed between the rock and the side of the entrance. He couldn't budge it. The voices were fading and he again tried to call out, the hopelessly pitiful mouse-squeals barely audible even to himself. His head fell back in despair.

He drifted in and out of consciousness, his brain on fire with pain. Sometimes there was light at the chink, sometimes not. He dreamed his leg had magically healed and that he could move it. Coming to, he stared at the leg in the small amount of light afforded by the chink. Sure enough, the leg appeared to be all in one piece again. And there was indeed movement. The whole limb was a seething mass of white maggots.

He shrieked at the unspeakable horror of it. It was a silent shriek.

CHAPTER EIGHTEEN

1980s

Cameras clicked and camcorders whirred among the ancient ruins of the monastic settlement as visitors from all quarters of the earth thronged Glendalough at the height of the tourist season. Most of the visitors conversed in hushed tones; the place still exerted the same tranquil effect on people in the late twentieth century that Kevin had experienced there in the sixth.

Most, but not all.

'Isn't it cute, George!' a lady remarked to her husband who was filming the round tower.

George was a rather large gentleman whose stomach bulged under a floral-patterned shirt that would have been more at home on Waikiki Beach.

'It looks like a goddam rocketship, Betty Lou, just settin' there waitin' to be launched.'

Betty Lou sidled up to him.

'Reminds me of somethin' a hell of a whole lot sweeter'n a silly ol' rocketship.'

They both burst into peals of loud uninhibited laughter which drew contemptuous glances from the more sober souls in their proximity.

Throughout the day, tour buses disgorged and reloaded their clicking cargoes, fitting the glen into its two-hour slot in their itinerary; fourteen hundred years of history to be assimilated in two hours.

Billy Kean drove his old Ford Cortina into the car-park beside the Upper

Lake. The usual tranquillity of the place was jarred by the presence of a fish and chip van with its engine running, discharging black clouds of diesel fumes into the atmosphere. Parking the car he got out and left the car-park, strolling back the way he had come, along the tree-shaded road that led to the graveyard with its cluster of ruined churches and round tower. Away from the noise of the car-park the great serenity he experienced whenever he came to the glen descended upon him and he was at peace with world.

Not that he was religious in the accepted sense, but he touched the stones of the old ruins with an awe and reverence that would put the more orthodox to shame. He believed in God all right. That was only common sense; he just had to look around him to know some great Intelligence was behind it all. The nature of that Intelligence was the big question, and he didn't think any of the religions had the answer. The idea that God, a super-intelligence, required human beings to repeatedly perform primitive rituals and sacrifices was, he believed, an insult to that Intelligence.

He pushed open a small wooden gate with the name Camaderry Cottage carved into it and walked up a path barely wide enough for the purpose between luxuriant masses of flowering shrubbery alive with the hypnotic hum of countless bees. The whitewashed walls of the cottage were dazzling and the heat rose in shimmering waves from its galvanized roof. The door was open and outside it, seated in a cane chair, a man sat reading a book and smoking his pipe.

'Hello there, me lad! ' he said, closing the book and standing up as Billy approached. 'Are you lost?'

He looked in his seventies, but was tall and straight with a great bald dome of a head. He exuded the air of a man who was, like Billy himself at that moment, at peace with himself and the universe.

'No, no, I'm not lost. Are you Mister Byrne?'

'Ay, that I am,' the man replied, 'but then, you could knock on any door in these parts and have a fair to middlin' chance of being speaking to a Mister Byrne. I go be the title of Cam.'

'Ah! I'm in the right place, then. They told me at the hotel that you know more about this place than anyone alive. I'm Billy Kean. I wonder if you could spare me a few minutes?'

'A man should always have time for conversation,' Cam said, wagging the stem of his pipe to emphasize his point, 'and if the conversation is good he'll be the richer for it be the minute. And where does Billy Kean hail from?' He extended a big hand and gave Billy's a knuckle-crushing shake.

'Bray.'

'Ah, Bray be the sea. Gone a big place now. Used to go there a lot as a lad, but at my age I appreciate the gentleness of the lakes. The sea can get very angry betimes. Now, come on in and I'll make a pot of gossip-water.'

Billy followed him inside. It took some moments for his eyes to get used to the dim interior after the brilliance of the sunshine on the whitewashed walls. The windows were tiny, four small panes in each, set in walls that looked to be four feet thick. As his surroundings gradually materialized out of the gloom he saw that all the walls were shelved from floor to ceiling and packed with books. Everywhere he looked there were books and more books; on the mantelpiece above the huge open fireplace; on two small tables and on a big old writing desk, but far from making the room appear untidy, all were packed and stacked neatly.

'I see you're fond of a book, Mister Byrne.'

'Ay,' he replied, holding a match to a small gas cooker and sitting a kettle over the blue flame, 'if a man's bookshelf is empty, you can't expect his noddle to be otherwise,' he tapped his head with the tip of his finger, 'and besides, as some wise man once said, there's no furniture as charming as books. Sit yourself down there, now,' he indicated a bentwood chair by a round table in the centre of the room, the only table free of books.

'Yes,' he went on, finger raised, ' "a good book is the precious lifeblood of a master spirit..." Milton... now there was a man!' He shook his great head in admiration. 'Now, what can I do to help you, Billy Kean?'

'Well, it's to do with the history of Glendalough, Mister Byrne...'

'Ah, would you for God's sake call me Cam. That Mister stuff makes me feel old.'

'Sorry. All right. Cam.'

'And in case you're wonderin' what sort of a quare name that is, my great-grandfather, who built this place, was known as Camaderry Byrne on account of living at the foot of Camaderry Mountain, to distinguish him from all the other Byrnes around here. The nickname stuck and came down to me pruned a bit. Believe it or not, I was christened Kevin in a brilliant flash of originality on the part of me parents.'

Billy laughed, 'Well, if they'd told me at the hotel to go and ask Kevin I'd have driven straight home. Anyway, I wondered if you had ever heard any stories or legends about the treasure of Glendalough. I read recently that no precious vessels or objects connected with the Seven Churches have ever been found.'

'That's a fact, but most folks would say the reason for that is the Vikings got everything.'

'D'you think they did?'

Cam shrugged.

'I suppose it's as likely an explanation as any, but there again, me father used to say there was an old tradition that the monks hid their treasures somewhere near the Prison Rock, up there on Lugduff near the old Borenacrow track across the mountain to Glenmalure, and he had it from his grandfather.'

'And has nobody ever searched for it?'

'Not that I've heard tell of, but I'll tell you this, if it is up there they didn't bury it with a shovel. Too rocky.'

They were interrupted by the whistle of the kettle and Cam spooned some tea from an old tin caddy with its design almost completely worn away, then poured the boiling water over it in a big brown teapot.

'There's only one thing to beat the cuppa tay, and that's a good mug of it,' he observed, filling two huge blue-ringed mugs that looked like ancient treasures themselves.

'And what would you do, tell me, if you found this treasure?'

'I'd hand it over to the National Museum.'

'Would you now?' Cam sounded mildly surprised. 'Well, well, it's a refreshing thing in this day and age to come across somebody not motivated by greed.'

'I'm sure there would be a reward of some kind,' Billy said, embarrassed, 'but can you imagine the satisfaction of discovering something as important as that?'

'Oh, I can surely, but there's many a one wouldn't be content with that kind of reward. What put this treasure idea into your head, anyway?'

'Well, for twenty years I worked in a factory, and always found Glendalough the perfect place to come and unwind after a week of noisy machines...'

'Ay,' Cam put in, ' "Far from the madding crowd's ignoble strife..." Tom Grey... now there was a man! But go on.'

'So, to cut a long story short, when the factory folded a while back I didn't fancy the idea of hanging around the street corner or becoming a slave to the box, so I bought myself a metal detector. I thought detecting would be an interesting hobby.'

'Right you are. Nothing worse than an idle mind. I'm amazed when I hear people say they're bored. I mean, just look around you, for God's sake. Boredom can only be attributed to a lazy mind, and, as me father impressed upon me more than half a century ago, doing nothing is the most direct route to being nothing. But you weren't contemplating using the detector here in the glen, surely? You'd be run out of it like a fox out of a fowl-farm. '

'God, no. I was thinking about searching up in the mountains, well away from any monuments. I can't see any harm in that.'

'Maybe not, but even so, I still think you'd be wasting your time up there among the rocks. Are you married, be the way, if you don't think me too forward in asking?'

'Not at all. Yes, I am. Five years.'

'Little ones?'

'Two girls.'

'Ah, bless them. It must be the divil being made redundant when there's a family depending on you.'

Billy saw genuine sympathy in Cam's intelligent eyes.

'It could be worse. We've survived the first year anyway, but there doesn't seem to be much hope of a job turning up. I've spent a fortune on postage and phone calls. Most places don't even bother to reply.'

'Isn't that sad, now. When common courtesy becomes too much to ask of a firm then things must be bad indeed, and maybe you're as well off out of such a place. But don't you fear, the bad times will pass. I remember the thirties and people thinking things would never improve, but improve they did, and if I may quote me old father again, he said there was no better friend to see you through hard times than a good book, and you could go to bed each night a little more knowledgeable than the night before. I can tell you're not averse to turning a page yourself, Billy.'

'You can? How?'

'You're relaxed here. People who don't like books tend to be uneasy in a bookish atmosphere, and feel obliged to pass inane remarks about readers. I'm sure you know the sort of thing I mean.' Billy nodded.

'Like "Bookworms don't know a thing about real life".'

'Exactly, and unfortunately there is seldom anything one can do or say to alter their attitude.'

Billy surveyed the packed shelves around him.

'I've collected a few books, all right, but nothing compared to this.'

'Ah, but what you see around you here is the lifetime collection of three generations. I've made me humble contribution but most of these are me father's friends, ay, and his father's.'

Billy shook his head.

'Wonderful. That's just wonderful.'

'And when I join them over beyant at the tower, I have a son in England who wants to come and live here, keep the old place going.'

'I envy you that, Cam.'

'Come again?'

'Being buried in the old graveyard among the ruins, it brings a sort of comforting assurance to the idea of resting in peace.'

'Ay, it's a restful spot, sure enough, most of the time. It can be like O'Connell Street at this time of year.'

'Don't I know it! It was murder trying to drive past the hotel on the way here. Have you lived in the glen all your life, Cam?'

'Sadly, no. I was born here. Went away when I was twenty and worked first in England, then in the States. Was away thirty years in all. Always had a longing on me to come back here and get stuck into reading all the old books. I came home when my father took bad twenty five years ago and I have to say I was never as contented as I have been since then. If I have any bit of regret about my life it's that I stayed away so long. I belong here. Jack, me son in England is of the same mind. There are four others, you know, three lads and a daughter, but Jack is the only one with the feel for the old place. Their mother died ten years ago.'

He refilled the mugs and they talked on, Billy becoming more and more fond of the old man with his seemingly boundless wisdom on all topics ancient and modern.

When Billy was leaving, Cam walked down the path to the wooden gate with him.

'Anytime you need to do a bit of research, you're very welcome to come and make use of the books. I don't loan them because I feel they are only on loan to me during my time above ground and it's up to me to pass them on safely to their next custodian, but I'll be happy to share them, certainly, with another friend.'

'Thanks. That's very kind of you and I'll more than likely take you up on the offer. I'll call in whenever I'm passing and let you know if I find anything. All the best.'

'Good luck, now, Billy Kean. Good luck.'

Cam stood awhile, leaning on the gate smoking his pipe and listening to the bees in the shrubbery, then, muttering contentedly, made his way back up the path.

' "... And live alone in the bee-loud glade..." Willie Yeats... now there was a man!'

CHAPTER NINETEEN

Back at the car-park Billy took his metal detector, trowel and a small rucksack containing his lunch from the boot of the car, then walked along the path skirting the eastern end of the Upper Lake. In a grove of trees close to the water's edge a big old row-boat lay abandoned, its timbers crumbling. Over many long years it had ferried countless tourists across the lake to the otherwise inaccessible St. Kevin's Bed and the ruined Templenaskellig. The Bed, hacked out of the beetling cliff of Lugduff thirty feet above the water in prehistoric times, was reputed in legend to be the cave to which the amorous maiden Kathleen had pursued the young hermit Kevin only to have him fling her into the lake for her trouble. Research into ancient writings had shown that the saint's crime was the much lesser one of stinging the young lady with a bunch of nettles in his efforts to avoid seduction. No boat had plied the lake since the seventies and visitors now had to content themselves with viewing the Bed and church through binoculars.

Passing close to the ruin of Refeart Church where ancient local chiefs were laid to rest Billy climbed the steep mountain path that rose alongside Poulanass Waterfall whose roaring torrent plunged into the cool depths of the green pool at its base. At the top he rested and took in the breathtaking view of the sunspangled Upper Lake, with picnickers looking like little groups of ants on the green space by the shore. Across the valley he caught the glint of sunlight on a corner of Cam's roof where it peeped through the foliage.

Continuing out onto the open mountaintop he saw that Cam had been right; there wasn't much scope for a metal detector up here. Boulders everywhere. There was no way anybody had dug a hole deep enough to bury even a modest hoard of objects. Still, if the tradition went back as far as Cam's great-grandfather. The only solution that made sense if there was any substance to the story was some sort of cave, which again rendered a metal detector next to useless. On ordinary soil it could only penetrate to a depth of a foot or so, and at that the target would need to be fairly large.

Having come this far he decided to have a go anyway. He tuned the detector and began searching between the rocks, holding back clumps of heather with one hand. It was awkward, tiring and unrewarding. At least, he thought, there aren't any pull-tabs. Too far up for the average litter-bug. The ubiquitous pull-tab was the bane of the detectorist's life. Wherever humankind had congregated in recent times, pull-tabs were to be found in abundance, and the bleep caused by a pull-tab was just as sweet and pretty as that produced by a twenty two carat gold ring. An enthusiast could spend a whole back-breaking day searching and end up hobbling home with a bulging pocketful of the frustrating little demons. Deeply buried horseshoes came second in the frustration stakes. It could take a half-hour's digging down through hard-packed soil to a long-lost horseshoe. Most detectors could discriminate against iron but it could be risky to use this facility because something as big as a horseshoe could mask the signal of a valuable coin.

After an hour and a half without as much as a single bleep, Billy laid the detector gently on the heath and sat on a warm rock for a break. He took some well-filled salad sandwiches Jenny had prepared that morning and a can of Coke from the rucksack. When he had eaten he lay back on the heather and scanned the cloudless blue for the lark that had serenaded him throughout his meal. The enchanting notes continued to grace the air, piping and trilling as if their composer believed this to be the last day, but Billy's squinting eyes failed to spot the feathered minstrel. Must tell Cam about this, he thought, anticipating some entertaining comment from the old man concerning Thomas Moore's lines about the dearth of skylarks over Glendalough.

He lay for some time, savouring the solitude, then wandered around in a haphazard fashion probing with the head of the detector in any spaces he could find between heather and rock. When the bleep came it startled him with its suddenness after the long lulling silence. Bending to investigate, he pulled a clump of heather out of the ground and ran the detector over the space. There was no signal. He held it over the roots of the clump and there was a loud bleep. Holding the heather over a flat rock he teased out the small amount of turf that clung to the roots and heard a tiny metallic 'ding' as a small button fell out onto the stone. It was some sort of old military button by the look of it, obviously nothing to do with the Seven Churches. Dropping it into his trousers pocket he commenced a thorough search of the immediate vicinity; if there was a button there could be something else. Almost at once the detector bleeped again. He pulled out another clump of heather and this time he didn't need the detector to pin-point the target. It was lying there in the hole left by the roots; a fragment of what looked like a tiny grid, and it was gold. Less than half an inch across, two of the sides were straight as if it had been part of a strap or band of some kind. He put it in his pocket with the button and resumed his search enthusiastically, but, two more hours yielding nothing, his enthusiasm waned and he decided to call it a day, flopping down exhausted near the spot where he had found the button. He checked his watch. Half past four. He would have to leave soon; Jenny would have the dinner ready at six. There would be time to give Cam a shout and show him the finds. He took the button out to have another look at it.

'Shit!' he exclaimed as it slipped from his fingers and vanished between the heather and a large boulder. The heather here was growing about two feet high and didn't pull out as easily as the smaller clumps. He bent the bushes away from the boulder and found himself gazing in dismay into a gaping hole beneath it; if the button had gone down there he would never get it.

He jumped on the heather to flatten it as much as possible and reached into the hole. He could feel that it sloped downwards, not too steeply, but could not locate the button. Getting the detector he moved the head around inside the hole, gradually going deeper until almost at the limit of his reach he got a signal. Damn! How was he supposed to get in there after it?

He moved the detector from side to side.

Bleep! Bleep! Bleep! Bleep! Bleep!

He thought he was hearing things.

He checked again. No, there were definitely five separate signals. What on earth could be in there?

He withdrew the detector and tried wriggling into the hole on his stomach. With his head and shoulders in the entrance there was only blackness ahead. Stretching his arms out in front of him he felt around until he had located five coin-like objects. A bit like winning on the slots at Bray seafront; pop one in, win five. He smiled to himself at the analogy.

Getting out was difficult. He found it almost impossible to move backwards against the springy heather at the entrance and became suddenly claustrophobic, nearly panicking. Deep breaths. Deep breaths, he told himself. Taking it inch by inch he got himself back out into the sunshine.

He examined the objects. Three were identical to his original find - one was probably the same button - and the other two were about half the size. He cursed himself for not thinking of bringing a torch along; God knew what else was down that hole. He would have to come back. Better see if he could get somebody to come with him too, it would be bad news to get stuck down there with nobody to raise the alarm. He could contact Teddy Brien. Teddy lived in Dublin and had worked at the factory with Billy, both being made redundant at the same time. Billy had waxed so enthusiastic about getting a detector that Teddy had bought one as well, not because he was deeply into history but because he was certainly into unearthing a sudden fortune. Billy didn't know him all that well, they had worked in separate areas of the factory, but he was the only one he knew who owned a detector and might be interested in accompanying him.

Cam's door was closed and there was no reply to Billy's knock, so he drove home along the road he liked to travel more than any other. Through the village of Laragh, known as the gateway to Glendalough; over the quaint humpbacked bridge at Annamoe; through Roundwood, the highest village in Ireland; across the desolate expanse of Calary Bog and down the Long Hill into Kilmacanogue village a few miles outside Bray.

As a youngster he had often cycled the twenty miles to Glendalough and to this day his heart leapt as he descended the hill into Laragh with the wooded valley of the Seven Churches spread below him and the conical top of the round tower visible above the trees.

'Daddeee!'

Dawn, the older of the two girls ran into his arms as he opened the door of their terraced home at St. Kevin's Place, just off Main Street.

'How's my favourite six-year-old?' he said, hugging her to him.

'Fine, Daddy. Dinner's just ready.'

'Ah, lovely!'

'Hiya, Hon!' Little Susie came scampering from the kitchen with her endearing imitation of her mother's usual greeting. 'Hiya, yourself, angel, and what's my favourite four-year-old been up to today, eh?'

'I drawed a picture for you.'

'You did? Oh, thank you. We'll have to have a decko at that. '

He picked her up and carried her to the kitchen.

'H'mm, that smells delicious!'

'Good timing, Love.' Jenny turned from the table and he kissed her.

'You're a wonder, Jen, you really are.'

'Well,' she said, tossing back her long dark hair, 'any luck? Are we rich?'

'Of course we're rich. Just look at this pair of gorgeous imps. Look at that mouth-watering spread. And look at you!'

'D'you know what, that tongue of yours would get you anywhere.'

'Oh yes?' he said, eyes widening.

'Get lost,' she swiped at him playfully with the tea towel. 'Ooh, you're rotten.'

'And aren't you just glad!'

They laughed and sat to attack the dinner.

'I found some old buttons in a cave on top of Lugduff. Don't know what they are yet, but there's this interesting old character I spoke to, should be able to tell me about them. His cottage is stacked with books, hundreds of them. The thing is, the buttons were a few feet inside the entrance to the cave and I couldn't see what was further in. Have to go back with a torch.'

'Jesus, Billy, be careful. If anything happened to you up there you'd never be found. Where is this Lugduff anyway?'

'It's over the Upper Lake, you know, the mountain with Kevin's Bed in the side. And don't worry, I'll bring somebody with me next time. No kidding, Jen, it's like heaven up there, you'll have to climb it with me someday.'

'Right. Let me know when they build a chairlift.'

'God forbid that day ever dawns.'

He watched Jenny as she ate. God, he loved her; her every little move and mannerism was a joy to him. They still held hands in the street and friends sometimes ribbed him about it, boasting that they had passed that sloppy stage after the first year. It didn't bother him; many of the ones who sneered were experiencing trouble in their relationships, some had already separated. Anyway, he was just so proud of Jenny and the girls that he couldn't conceive of the time coming when he wouldn't want to hold her hand.

She looked up from her meal, caught him looking at her, and flushed.

He loved that too.

'Would you ever feck off, Billy, and eat your dinner.'

'Look, Daddy!' Susie held up her masterpiece for inspection. A matchstick Mammy and Daddy, a smaller matchstick Dawn, and a tiny matchstick Susie, all holding hands.

'Well, would you look at that, now, and signed by the artist and all!' he said, pointing to a small jammy handprint.

Later he phoned Teddy Brien, put him in the picture, and asked him if he wanted to come along.

'Fuckin' sure!' Teddy said. 'There might be somethin' worth a few quid down there.'

Billy winced. It wasn't exactly the sort of enthusiasm he had in mind.

'Can't make it till the weekend, though,' Teddy continued, 'doin' a bit of a nixer at the moment on the buildin's.'

'How about Saturday morning then?'

'Yeah, great. I'll be at the Divil around eleven, right? I'll bus it out. No sense bringin' two cars.'

'O.K. See you then.'

CHAPTER TWENTY

Billy was impatient to show Cam his finds and on Wednesday left the car with Jenny and caught the midday St. Kevin's bus at the Divil, a fierce-looking stone statue of the mythical wyvern which stood in front of the Town Hall surrounded by stone horse troughs and seats. It had once been a fountain, but the water had ceased to flow with the passing of the horse. The wyvern was part of the family crest of the Earl of Meath who had built the Town Hall for the people of Bray, and for more than a hundred years now the Divil had vented his stony silent roar at all and sundry as they passed on either side of him where the road forked left for Greystones and right for Wicklow and Glendalough. The bus route to Glendalough was the only one in the country remaining in private hands, all others having been taken over decades ago by C.I.E.

The bus was crammed to capacity and Billy had to stand. Day trippers and back-packers swelled the regular quota of country folk. Baskets of day-old chicks chirped in the overhead luggage racks, bound for their free-ranging life in the Wicklow uplands. The passengers sweltered as the sun streamed baking hot through the windows, but there was much good-humoured banter between farmer and foreigner.

Leaving the bus at the Royal, Glendalough's only hotel since the closure of Richardson's at the Upper Lake, he took his time along the last mile or so to Camaderry Cottage. Cam was leaning on his gate, rings of his pipe-smoke ascending in the summer air.

'Aha, begod it's the treasure-hunter!' he said, pipe clenched between his teeth. 'Find anything exciting above?' he jerked his head in the direction of Lugduff.

'Hello, Cam. I don't know about exciting, but I found these,' he handed Cam the buttons.

'Well, well, isn't that interesting, now,' Cam said, scrutinising them.

'D'you know what they are?'

'I've a fair idea, but come on inside and we'll find out for sure.'

Billy followed him up the path where the scent of honeysuckle was heavy on the air. Inside, Cam took a large book from a shelf and flicked through the pages.

'Yes!' he exclaimed, slapping the book down on the table and stabbing at it with the stem of his pipe, 'There you are, Billy Kean, sixteenth century English army buttons, and being from that period I'll bet you the Taj Mahal to a tent they've been there since the battle of Glenmalure in fifteen eighty, though what they were doing on top of the mountain is a bit of a puzzle. Have you read about that battle?'

'Only what I learned at school, and I've forgotten most of that.

'Well, the bould Lord Grey led his men into Glenmalure against the O'Byrnes, but walked into an ambush and lost the best part of his army, and here's a thought to ponder on: We might not have had the Great Famine had Walter Raleigh not survived that ambush. He introduced the spud and we became over-dependent on it. The rest is history, ay, sad history. And of course the poet Spenser was there too,' he paused, pipe in hand, and gazed at the ceiling, ' "and he that strives to touch the stars oft stumbles at a straw..." now there was a man! And you tell me you got them in the mouth of a cave. Was there anything else down there?'

'Don't know. It was black dark and I didn't want to risk getting stuck down there. I'm going back this week with another chap.'

'That's sensible. If I were a younger man I'd go with you myself, but I haven't been up old 'Duff this two years. A lad would see a fair bit of the world before he'd come across anything that could compete with the view of the lakes from up there. I always came back down feeling as if I'd been on a fortnight's holidays after just a few hours. Anyway, back to the buttons. I think you're on to something. They didn't just happen to fall there all at once. They were on a uniform that rotted away, so the question is, what happened to the owner of the uniform? No sign of any bones?'

'No.'

'I suppose animals could have dragged them away over the years. Well, it may not be treasure but you've certainly got me interested. The mountains around here are full of caves. I used to ramble about looking for them years ago because many of them were rebel hide-outs after the '98 rebellion.' He went to the mantelpiece.

'I found this in a cave over towards the Wicklow Gap.'

He handed Billy the remains of an old gun, its wooden butt almost rotted away but most of the metal parts intact.

'It's a '98 musket, and who's to say it didn't belong to Michael Dwyer himself?'

'Oh yes, Dwyer. We learned a song about him at school, about his escape from a burning house.'

'Ay, that'll be the cottage at Derrynamuck beyant in Imaal. It's a tourist attraction these days. Turned it into a little museum they have. But there's a lot more to Dwyer's story than that. I've a few books about him here you could do worse than bury your beak in for a while. So, anyhow, the buttons were all you found?'

'That's all...oh,' Billy rooted in his pocket, 'except for this. Looks like it might have come from an officers cap or something like that.'

He handed Cam the little piece of gold filigree. Cam examined it with a magnifying glass.

'Holy God!' he exclaimed, 'I can tell you here and now, Billy me lad, that this never graced any soldier's cap. Where did you find it?'

'Same place as the buttons. Well, almost. It was just outside the cave, inches from the first button.'

'Well, well, a nice little mystery. This, Billy Kean,' he held up the tiny piece, 'is treasure, and more than likely Glendalough treasure at that, but the fact that it was among those buttons is not a good sign, there's something decidedly piscatorial about that.'

'Piscawhat?'

Cam turned his head so that his face was within an inch of Billy's.

'Fishy, avick, fishy!'

He took a heavy-looking tome from the shelf and opened it at a section on ancient church treasures.

125

'Take a good look at that,' he said, pointing to a colour photograph of the Ardagh Chalice.

Billy saw it straight away; a band of gold filigree circling the chalice. The band was divided into short sections by coloured glass studs, each section of filigree of a different incredibly intricate design, but unmistakably similar to the fragment found on the mountain.

'Whew!' Billy whistled. 'This is fantastic, Cam. Good God, the whole treasure is probably up there in that...'

'Whoa, whoa there! Easy now! Don't be jumping the hedge before you come to the stile. What you found up there almost certainly came from the Glendalough treasure, but I think it unlikely you'll find it in that cave.'

'Why is that?' Billy asked, disappointment in his voice.

'Two good reasons. One,' Cam crossed his forefinger with the stem of his pipe, 'the presence of those buttons means somebody was in the cave four hundred years ago. Two, you found that fragment outside the cave. The monks would never have been so careless as to damage their precious objects, and they would have had plenty of time to hide them knowing the Vikings wouldn't follow them up the mountain. No, that fragment was broken off during the removal of the treasure by less conscientious hands. I'm afraid, Billy, it looks like you've been beaten to it by several centuries.'

Billy slumped in his chair.

'Ah well, I'll take a look in there anyway, just in case.'

'Oh, begod yes! Certainly, I'd examine the place. Never know what might have been left behind by somebody in a hurry to get it out, and even if there's divil a thing in there I wouldn't give up hope entirely of finding it.'

'Oh?' Billy looked surprised. 'Why not, if somebody's already found it?'

'Aha, yes, somebody found it all right, but think, Billy Kean,' he stabbed his pipe in Billy's direction to emphasize his point, 'where is it? If it had stayed found it would be well known in museums and the like here or in England if the English had found it, but there's no trace of it anywhere. That kind of treasure doesn't just disappear again. Even if the hoard had been broken up into private collections, some pieces at least would be known today, all of which suggests to my humble intellect that it was taken from one hiding place and deposited in another. Now!'

He sat down and puffed on his pipe, resting his case.

'There was one more thing I found up there I thought unusual,' Billy said.

'By the Lord Harry, you're slower than a dripping tap,' Cam sat back expectantly. 'Come on, then, out with it!'

'A skylark, singing away good-oh.' Cam whipped the pipe from his mouth and, to Billy's delight, began reciting to the ceiling, his great bald head slowly shaking in admiration.

' "By that lake whose gloomy shore, skylark never warbles o'er..." Tom Moore... now there was a man! But you're right, he was wrong about that. Oh, ay, wrong about the lark. Heard it myself, I did. Moore must have been unfortunate with the weather when he called. Gloomy shore? Ah, no. Still and all, there was a man.'

He got up suddenly.

'There you are, now, with all this treasure talk I forgot to put the kettle on. We'll have a nice cuppa tay.'

Having lit the gas he went again to the book shelves.

'Here,' he said, handing Billy a green-covered hardback book, 'if you're going cave-hunting I'd recommend you read this first and save yourself a lot of wasted time.'

Billy glanced at the title page. The Life of Michael Dwyer, with some account of his Companions, by Charles Dickson.

'You'll find caves galore described in there which were used by the rebels around here. You can eliminate them from your search. Had any treasure been hidden in them it would have been discovered in '98 and would certainly be known to us. There's a story that Dwyer hid in St. Kevin's bed one time, and somebody informed the military. They climbed down the cliff and were all around the entrance, then called on him to come out. He did, in one flying leap, and swam to the far side of the lake where the soldiers had neglected to leave any men, and he got clean away. The man was a regular Houdini when it came to getting out of tight spots. I doubt if he used the Bed very often, though, it was too well known. Ay, too well known. So tell me, when do you propose to check the cave out?'

'Saturday. Seems like years away. I'm itching to get in there.'

'And why wouldn't you be? I'm curious myself, and didn't somebody say that curiosity is the lifeblood of civilization? Who was it, now? Anyway, there was a man, whoever he was.'

CHAPTER TWENTY ONE

'Bones ! You can't sell fuckin' bones, for Jaysus sake.'

'I know that, Teddy, but for God's sake, they're human bones. Look at the skull. Where's your sense of history?'

Billy squatted beside the pile of mouldering bones on the floor of the cave while Teddy lay on his belly looking down from the sloping ledge inside the entrance.

'History me hole. If you can't make a few quid on it, it's not worth a shite. That's my motto.'

'Hey, what's this?' Billy's flashlight had picked out something among the bones. He picked up the badly rusted object.

'It's a pike-head!' he exclaimed.

'Oh, yeah, an' what's a pike-head when it's at home?'

'It's the point of a long sort of spear. They used them in '98, but these bones are from 1580, so...' he shrugged, 'I'll bring it down to Cam, he'll know.'

'Would it be worth anything?'

'I doubt it. Not much anyway.'

'Ah, fuck it, then.'

Billy threw his eyes heavenwards. He carefully searched the interior of the cave and found six more buttons and an even tinier piece of gold filigree decoration, convincing evidence that the treasure had indeed been in the cave.

'What about them buttons? They must be worth a few bob,' Teddy asked.

'I suppose if you knew somebody who collected that sort of thing they might fetch something all right.'

'Giz a few, then.'

'I will, I will! Just wait till I get out of here. Jesus, you're an awful man, Teddy.'

'What the fuck are you on about?'

'Look, the important thing is the treasure was here. It was taken out and hidden somewhere else. It's up to us to find out where.'

'An' how do we know they didn't just lug it over to the edge of the cliff there and chuck it in the shaggin' lake?'

'We don't, but I can't see anybody being stupid enough to do something like that with a load of treasure.'

'Ah, they were all mad back in them days anyway. Seen them on telly. An' the stupid clothes they wore! Jaysus!'

Billy was now seriously questioning the wisdom of having Teddy along.

'Teddy,' he sighed, 'I really think you should take in a few history books.'

'Yeah? Loada crap. I know all the history I need to know. The English attacked us an' we've been tryin' to get rid of them for seven hundred years.'

'Well, you've got the first bit wrong for a start. They didn't invade us, we invited them in because we were doing what we still excel at, fighting among ourselves, and when it comes to invading, we were raiding Britain long before the Normans set foot here.'

'Bollix!'

'I'm telling you, Teddy, get a good history book. Don't take my word for it.'

'That crap was probably wrote by some Brit, tryin' to get them off the hook, an' anyway they woulda told us in school if that was the way it happened.'

'They did, Teddy, they did. They just didn't push it the way they did most of what followed. Now back out there and let me up, there's nothing more here.'

They ate their lunches, then stretched out on the heather in the sun.

'Beautiful, isn't it?' Billy said, his voice dozy.

'What is?'

'Up here. The mountains. The silence. The peace. I could live up here.'

'You must be bloody jokin'! There's fuck-all for miles only rocks an' shaggin' heather. There's nothin' to do, not a house in sight.'

'That's the beauty of it,' Billy said.

Teddy snorted in disgust.

'An' how far is it to the nearest pub?'

'I suppose it's about three miles to the Royal, but there's a hell of a lot more to life than the pub.'

'Oh, yeah, that's what all the begrudgers say, but I say a few pints each night is all a workin' man's got, especially if he's not workin'.'

Billy laughed. 'So I suppose you'll be off out tonight, then?'

'Fuckin' sure! But we can stop for a few jars on the way home at that Royal place, can't we? Just to keep us goin', like.'

'If you want.'

'You goin' out yourself later?'

'If we can get a babysitter. If not we'll stay in.'

'Would you not just leave her there an' go for a few yourself?'

'I could, I mean Jenny wouldn't object, but I'm just not that pushed about drink, and as well as that the money's a bit tight so we tend to go out only when both of us can, which isn't very often.'

'Bejaysus, I can tell you no woman would come between me an' me pint, an' the one at home knows that, too. If the cow ever opened her mouth about it I'd soon fuckin' shut it for her, uh,' he grunted, punching the air with a white-knuckled fist.

Billy winced again, now heartily regretting his bad judgement. The more Teddy Brien revealed of his character, the more Billy realized he did not want this relationship to continue, but on the way up in the car they had already more or less agreed to go exploring each Saturday on a regular basis; he would have to get out of it some way.

Teddy jumped to his feet.

'Right, then, let's get down from here an' get a few scoops in. I suppose we'll have to call in on this oul' fella you told me about.'

Billy wondered if that was a good idea, but was itching to show Cam the pike-head.

'Yes. We won't stay long.'

'Good.'

Arriving at Camaderry Cottage, Billy introduced his partner.

'This is Teddy Brien, Cam, we've been up to the cave on Lugduff.'

Cam took his pipe from his mouth and offered Teddy his hand.

Teddy grinned and took it.

'I'm pleased to meet you, Teddy Brien. Now, lads, don't keep me in suspense. What did you find up there?'

Billy produced the pike-head.

'We found this among some old human bones.'

'Did you now, begod? Well, it's not a '98 pike anyway, so it's a safe bet it's a 1580 one, and no doubt the bones are those of the soldier who wore the uniform the buttons belonged to.'

'Yes, we found more buttons inside the cave, and another piece of the gold decoration.'

'If those sad bones could only speak,' Cam wistfully shook his head. 'We'll never know what went on in that cave all those years ago.'

Billy could see that Teddy was close to sniggering.

'Teddy wondered if maybe the treasure had been dumped in the lake, probably with the intention of diving for it later,' he said by way of keeping the conversation moving.

'Possible, ay, possible,' Cam looked thoughtful. "Full many a gem of purest ray serene the dark unfathomed caves of ocean bear..." he recited, 'not, of course, an ocean in this case, but...'

He was interrupted by a ragged snort as Teddy lost what little control he had been exerting over his urge to snigger. Billy was mortified and furious at the ignorant outburst. Not so Cam; he turned smiling to Teddy, puffed on his pipe a couple of times and said: 'Son, most folk have passed that stage at your age, others take a little longer, and some never grow up at all, God love them. With a bit of luck you'll find yourself in the middle category, for there can be no more shameful waste than to spend one's entire life a giggling teenager, fond and all as my own memories are of those years.'

'What's the oul' bastard on about,' Teddy sneered, getting up and going to the door, kicking at table legs and door jamb as he went. 'What a spa! What a fuckin' spa!'

Shocked, Billy tried to apologize.

'I... I don't know what to say. I'm so sorry. I...'

Don't you fret about it, lad,' Cam was completely unruffled, 'I can tell you didn't know him very well before you signed him up.'

'No, I most certainly did not. Listen, Cam, I'll call again by myself if that's still all right with you.' Billy made to follow Teddy.

'Of course, of course.'

Teddy was at the gate, still chuckling, and knocking heads off flowers with a piece of stick.

'Just what in the name of Christ did you think you were at in there?' Billy hissed.

'Jaysus, Kean, you were right, he's brilliant. Haven't had such crack since me an' Dommo threw that queer in the canal last Christmas.'

'It was bloody-well unforgivable. I brought you into the man's home and you laughed in his face. Jesus, I just can't believe it!'

Teddy remained unmoved.

'But he's so fuckin' stupid, did you not hear him? Sayin' bloody poems, he was. A genuine fuckin' looney spa. An' no wonder, all them shaggin' books!'

'And did you understand what he meant by the poetry?'

'No, an' I don't give a shite either.'

'Then who's stupid, eh? The man knows what he's talking about and you don't, but you have the neck to call him stupid. He told me last week that the only thing in this world that really terrified him was ignorance. I see what he meant.'

'Hey, watch your mouth now, Kean, whose side are you on anyway, takin' up for that oul' bollix? We're mates, Right?'

'Wrong. Now, I'm going home. If you want a lift to Bray, get in.' He opened the car door.

'What about them few pints we were goin' to have?' Teddy said as they drove past the Hotel.

Billy slowed the car.

'If you want to get out, go ahead. I'm going on home.'

'Ah, shag it, then, I'll get a boozer in Bray. Might never get a lift out of this hole.'

On the journey down he behaved as if nothing unusual had happened, chuckling to himself every now and then about the antics of the crazy old man.

Billy pulled in opposite the Town Hall.

'Are you goin' to ask me in for a sambo or somethin'? I'm starvin'.'

'No'.

'Come on for a few pints then. We can get a toasted sambo in the pub.'

'No, thanks.'

Teddy shrugged.

'Right, then, I'll go meself. See you next Saturday,' he said, getting out of the car.

'No, you won't,' Billy shouted after him. 'You must be joking!'

'An' what about all this treasure huntin' an' stuff we were goin' to do?'

'Forget it.'

'Like fuck, I will! No way, pal. Next thing we'd be seein' Mr. Kean on the telly after findin' a million quid's worth of treasure. If you're on to somethin' I'm goin' to be in on it. You invited me, 'member?'

'I didn't know you. You're pathetic.'

'Ooh, will you listen to him with his fancy words like the oul' fuck up the mountains,' he stuck his head in the car window. 'See you Saturday,' he almost spat the words, then went swaggering down Main Street. Billy again cursed his rotten judgement. He decided not to trouble Jenny with the unsavoury details of the day.

CHAPTER TWENTY TWO

Jenny Kean hummed contentedly as she stepped from the shower and dried herself. She shrugged into her dressing gown and went into the kitchen. Scrambled eggs on toast. That'll do the job. Sit down and have it in peace. The girls were out playing with their friends at the top of the square. She turned the radio on, then off again in disgust. Saturday. No Gay Byrne Show. She listened to Gaybo most mornings; reckoned he had done more for women over the years than all the fanatical libbers put together. She popped a Kris Kristofferson tape into the player and sang along. She felt good; vaguely horny, if it was possible to be vague about something like that. She and Billy had made love early that morning before he had gone off to Glendalough. He was a good lover and she could count on one hand the number of times she had failed to have an orgasm with him. Whenever they made love in the morning, the glow always stayed with her throughout the day. They were good together. Only once in their five years of marriage had she been unfaithful to Billy. That was when she had worked part-time in the evenings at the local supermarket. The good-looking assistant manager had asked her to stay back late to stack shelves, and before she left that night she had discovered for herself the derivation of the term knee-trembler.

Tormented by guilt, she had handed in her notice and quit the job. Billy had sensed something was amiss and assured her she could tell him anything. Eventually she confessed. He was devastated, and they went through two months of hell until at his cousin's wedding Billy, having downed more than his usual quota of drink, disappeared into a bedroom with one of the hotel waitresses.

Jenny had opened the bedroom door to find the waitress, who looked about seventeen, climbing out of the bed and Billy snoring his head off.

Jenny, although gob-smacked, couldn't help smiling at the situation.

'I'm his wife,' she said calmly as the waitress tried frantically to get into her clothes. The girl's eyes widened in horror.

'It's OK, it's OK,' Jenny whispered, 'just go and leave us.'

'Yes... yes... Oh, shit... sorry,' she stuttered gratefully, unable to believe her luck as she struggled into her tights and straightened herself up. 'You'd better lock the door if you're staying here,' she advised.

'Something you didn't think of yourself, isn't it?'

The girl, her expression a comical mixture of embarrassment and gratitude, nodded and left.

Jenny locked the door, undressed and got into bed beside Billy. She tossed and turned, jabbing him with elbows and knees to make him wake, but it was a good half hour before he rolled over and let his hand rest on her breast. He groaned and opened his eyes as she responded and the look on his face was beyond description as his alcohol-dulled brain struggled to comprehend how he came to be gazing into the eyes of his Jenny. Stranger still, what possible explanation could there be for the fact that those eyes, far from being on fire with an understandable fury, were laughing! She hugged him to her.

'Jen, what...? Oh, God, I'm sorry, Jen...'

She laughed out loud.

'What are you laughing at, Jen?' he asked, mystified.

'You,' she chuckled. 'You've just screwed that waitress, or are you going to tell me you fell asleep and did nothing?'

'No, no. Ah, Jesus Jenny, what's so funny?'

'Do you love her?'

'Oh, for God's sake, no.'

'Are you going to leave me for her?'

'No! Jenny... Jen, I love you so much.'

He sounded close to tears.

'And this doesn't make you feel any different towards me?'

'Nobody could do that.'

'Well?' She raised her eyebrows.

'Well what?'

'Well, what have we been doing to ourselves for the last two months? That quickie I had with the assistant manager means the same to me as your romp with little Miss Hornibody means to you. We both just happened to be tempted at the wrong, or should I say right, moment. Now, please, Love, no more torturing ourselves. Just look on it as a bit of passing fun. Anyway,' she giggled mischievously, 'tell us, what was she like?'

They both laughed, then cried and laughed again, and it was all right. They promised that should either of them ever yield to temptation again they would tell the other immediately, thus eliminating the necessity for deceit and the cruel sense of betrayal which could wound so much more deeply than the act itself. They had grown closer and closer, and were constantly moved to tell each other how much they were loved. In the three years since Billy's trip upstairs with the waitress neither of them had had any reason to confess anything. Until now.

The doorbell rang.

Kids! Who'd have them? Too good to be true, breakfast in peace. She left her fork down with a piece of toast and scrambled egg impaled on it, and opened the door. A tall, fairly good-looking young man with black curly hair stood there.

'Ah, you must be the famous Jenny. I'm Teddy Brien. Is Billy there?'

He looked her up and down and she was acutely aware of her nakedness under the dressing gown.

'No,' she told him, 'I'm afraid he's out at the moment.'

'Gone to Glendalough?'

'Yes,' she said it without thinking.

'Well, would you believe that, now? Must've forgotten he was to pick me up. I've been waitin' at the Divil for the best part of an hour. Ah, well,' he shrugged resignedly, then said: 'D'you know what, I'd murder for a cuppa tea. I'm as dry as Good Friday, as true as God I am!'

She hesitated. Something told her he was not to be trusted. But if he was a friend of Billy's there was no point in causing any awkwardness.

'Come on in, then, there's a cup on the pot.'

'Billy often mentions you,' he said as she poured the tea, 'but the crafty bugger never let on you were so good-lookin'.'

Jenny said nothing, feeling distinctly uncomfortable and already regretting her foolishness in asking him in. She was surprised at Billy, this was certainly not the type of person she could imagine him being friends with. Teddy's eyes followed her every move.

'Can't say I blame him, though, if I'd a mot like you I'd be keepin' her tucked away for meself too.' Jenny continued eating her scrambled eggs.

'Do you and your wife go out much?'

'Nah, I go out most nights meself. She doesn't drink so it'd be a waste bringin' her out with me an' spendin' good money on shaggin' minerals. Anyway,' he laughed, 'if you saw the state of her you'd see why a lad wouldn't be too keen on showin' her off in company. Now if she looked like you...'

'Maybe if she was brought out for a nice meal now and then she'd have some reason to take care of herself a bit more.'

'Ah, now, you're havin' me on. The only meal I'll pay for outside the house is a feed of Guinness,' he leered across the table at her. 'Listen, will you be here all on your ownio now for the rest of the day?'

She looked at him, wondering how God could have afflicted with a cretinous mind an otherwise quite attractive person.

'No, I will not be alone. The children are playing outside.'

'Ah, sure, on a fine mornin' like this I wouldn't say they'll be knockin' the door down to get in for a while yet,' he winked, 'an' I'm sure the bould Billy wouldn't miss a slice off a cut loaf, now, would he?'

'You'd better go now,' she said, getting up suddenly from the table. Her action caused the dressing gown to fall open, and although she whipped it closed again in a fraction of a second it wasn't quick enough to prevent his catching a fleeting glimpse of her nakedness.

'Aw, wow! Jaysus Christ, Jenny, you're bleedin' gorgeous. You can't make me go after flashin' the ace a' spades at me like that.'

He stood up and came towards her.

She put out her hand to fend him off but he caught it and held it firmly against his crotch. She freed herself with a violent yank, her disgust tinged with excitement at his obvious need of her. 'Aw, come on, Jenny, please. If you make me leave in this state I won't be able to bloody walk. Hey, come on outa that, now, I know you're tempted, right? An' nobody'll know a thing, I swear.'

She looked him in the eyes and slowly, angrily, hissed: 'Brain-dead subhuman yobs do not turn me on. Get out of my home.'

'Think you're a clever bitch, don't you? Well, I'm tellin' you here an' now I'm not movin' outa here till you do somethin' about this,' he unzipped his jeans as he spoke and waved his penis at her. 'You don't want me here when the kids come in, now, do you? An' if I don't leave happy I'll see to it that the neighbours get an earful on me way out. I can be a noisy bastard when I like.' Jenny was trying not to panic. Jesus, what can I do? Would I get rid of him by giving him a wank? Mightn't be enough for the bastard. 'An' if what the neighbours think doesn't bother you, I can think up a nice steamy story for Billy about how you seduced me.'

'He wouldn't believe you.'

'Oh, no? An' just how else could he explain me knowin' his pretty Jenny wasn't a natural brunette?'

'You filthy bastard,' Jenny cried, 'You scum!'

He grinned at her.

'That's it, love, talk dirty. Now, what's it to be? Do I have a cosy chat with ol' Billy or are you goin' to be nice to me?'

Eyes filled with contempt, she began masturbating him where he stood, averting her gaze to the window. He roughly grasped the hair at the back of her head and pulled her around to face him.

'Look at it, you cunt,' he demanded hoarsely. 'Keep your eyes on the fuckin' job.'

She could see the bread knife on the table. It was within easy reach. She wanted to use it. Oh, dear God she wanted so much to use it. Destroy him. She resisted the temptation. Wouldn't be worth it. Be in the papers. The girls. No, but she would cut him in another way. When she sensed he was about to ejaculate she moved her stroking fingers back towards his scrotum to avoid getting him on her hand. She tightened her grip as his body jerked and jets of semen arced into the air and fell with tiny thuds on the lino. She felt him dying in her hand and flung him contemptuously from her. She suddenly felt powerfully in control, having rendered him powerless to sexually harm her.

She looked at him and smiled.

'You're bigger than Billy,' she said.

He looked pleased with himself.

'Ah, well, we can't all be perfect, right?'

'I'd say now,' she continued, 'I'd say you're about three inches taller and about a stone heavier.'

'A bloody good three inches taller,' he said, pulling himself up to his full height.

'Strange, then,' Jenny said, mock puzzlement on her brow, 'strange that your cock's a bloody good three inches shorter!'

That hit home. He became flustered as he tucked himself away and zipped up, mumbling unintelligibly, only the expletives discernible. It was Jenny's turn to laugh and she took it with a vengeance, pulling out all the stops to make him feel ridiculous.

'What the fuck are you titterin' about, you stupid bitch?'

She just pointed at him and went into a helpless kink.

'Right!' he roared, furious, 'I'm goin' up there after him to tell him I fucked you.'

'I couldn't care less what you do, you pathetic excuse for a human being.'

He slammed the door violently behind him and she winced, visualizing the neighbours peering out to see a strange man stamping angrily from her door. What the hell. She had done nothing wrong, and in fact was feeling quite good about the way she had defused the situation. She did care, though, about him talking to Billy before she could explain. She would tell Billy the whole story when he got home, whether Teddy had got to him first or not. Her immediate problem now was that she was no longer vaguely horny; she was intensely excited and delicious tremors shook her body. She climbed the stairs and lay on the bed.

CHAPTER TWENTY THREE

'Any luck, partner?'

Billy was loading his detecting gear into his car when he heard the voice of Teddy Brien behind him.

'Look,' Billy said, turning, 'I told you it was a mistake the two of us getting together, so where's the point in following me around?'

'An' I told you, partner, that if you come up with this treasure you reckon is up in them mountains it's fifty-fifty between us. I'll sort of tag along and be your bodyguard, see that nothin' happens to you, like.'

'You can get lost. Even if I did find something I'd hand it over to the museum. You'd be wasting your time.'

'Like shite you'd give it to the museum. You couldn't be that thick.'

'Think what you like,' Billy said, slamming the boot-lid down.

'By the way,' Teddy called after him as he got into the car, 'that mot of yours is a fine bird.'

Billy turned to face him.

'What the hell are you talking about?'

'I dropped in this mornin' for a cuppa when I didn't see you at the Divil. Oh, yeah, she's one great looker all right. Very obligin', too,' he grinned.

'Just shut your filthy mouth about my wife, and don't go near my home again. Jenny wouldn't be into a low-life like you, anyway.'

'You don't think so? Well, I can tell you mister goody-goody, I was into her, then. No bother. What do you have to say about that, now?'

'I'd say you're a liar, and a lunatic with it.'

'Now, now, Billy boy, that's no way to talk to your partner. You know, that little Jenny of yours is full of surprises. I didn't expect to find myself looking into a little blonde bush an' her with a head of hair on her as black as the arsehole of midnight.'

Stunned, Billy lashed out with his right arm, pushing Teddy away from the car, and drove out of the car-park. He sped recklessly towards home. His mind raced and chased after all kinds of explanations and possibilities, grasping and rejecting them one after another. Surely not. Oh, God, surely not Jenny. Not with that obnoxious bastard. No, he wouldn't believe it. She couldn't have. Tears kept welling up in his eyes. The car hurtled along the road, tyres squealing as he threw it into bends at alarmingly excessive speeds.

What if Teddy had played the nice guy, come on all charming and gentle to Jenny? She didn't know him; wouldn't have a clue about what he was really like if he decided to put on an act. And he was good-looking, Billy supposed. But no, Jenny would see through him. She was good at sussing people out. Then what had happened? How could he possibly...

He wrenched the steering wheel to the left, narrowly avoiding a head-on collision with a tour bus as he careered down the Long Hill. Easy, easy, Billy. No sense killing yourself.

Jenny knew as soon as he walked in that Teddy Brien had carried out his threat. Billy just stood there looking at her, swallowing hard, trying to find the words with which to open this awful conversation.

'Jenny...'

'Billy, please, before you say anything just listen to me. Whatever he told you, it's not as bad as it sounds. I didn't know what he was like when I let him in. How on earth did you get involved with a creep like him?'

'Just tell me what happened, Jenny, I'm feeling pretty sick this minute.'

She put her arms around his neck.

'Oh, my poor Love, I'm so sorry. That bastard! You must be in bits.'

She told him the whole story.

'It was the only way to get rid of him without a fuss. I thought it the best thing at the time. I'm really sorry if you're upset about that part of it.'

'And that was it?'

'That was it.'

'But, Jesus, Jenny, he knew...'

'I know,' she interrupted him, holding her hand up, 'I know what you're wondering about. That was just an accident. My dressing gown fell open when I stood up to tell him to get out. I'd just had a shower.'

'Shit, Jen, I hate the thought of him looking at you. It's my fault. I should have told you about him last week. Brought him to see Cam and he laughed at him, into his face. He has to be the most ignorant person I've ever met.'

He took her in his arms.

'Sorry I came in in such a state, Jen, I love you so much. I was nearly going crazy trying to figure out what could have happened. Thought maybe he'd raped you or something. I'd have killed him.'

'I love you too. Remember what we agreed? No secrets. Didn't think I'd forget it all that easily, did you?'

'No. I didn't know what to think. I'm just glad you're OK.'

Billy brightened up a bit.

'Christ, Jen, you must have made him feel small.'

'That's a good choice of words. I couldn't resist saying something when he was being so obnoxious, even though I knew it would probably drive him to tell you. He couldn't know I'd have told you anyway.'

'Jen,' he said quietly.

'Yes, Love?'

'I think you handled it pretty well.'

They both laughed and hugged each other.

'Oh, Billy Kean,' she said, 'you certainly have the knack of coming up with the right words.'

'And you really are a dirty rip, Jennifer Kean.'

'There's one more thing, Billy.'

'Oh, what's that?'

'Well, when I got rid of him I was shaking with relief, but I was also as horny as hell. Can you believe that?'

Billy shrugged.

'I suppose I'll have to. You mean you wanted him?'

'No, God, no. It was just... I don't know... the whole situation, I suppose it excited me, especially when I got control of it. If you'd walked in the door after he walked out I'd have shown you who I wanted.'

'Well, I'm here now,' Billy raised a questioning eyebrow.

Jenny grinned and shook her head.

'Too late, me oul' stallion, you weren't here when the meal was hot so I dined alone. Anyway, I have to get the dinner on now. The kids'll be screaming for it any minute.'

'Like I said, you're a dirty rip. Ah, well, as long as everything is all right.

They held each other again.

'I think we've cracked it, Billy,' she said.

'Cracked what?'

'The secret of a great relationship. What happened today could have destroyed some other couples. Do you think he'll come here again?'

'Probably not, especially when he sees he hasn't caused any problems between us.'

'How will he know that?'

'He says he's not going to give up tailing me into the mountains. Thinks I'm going to find the treasure and wants to be there to claim his share. '

'You're not serious!'

'I am. Wish I had his confidence. There's an awful lot of wild country up there and no guarantee that there's any treasure at all, but Cam says the whole area is dotted with caves used by the '98 rebels, so there's always a chance of coming across something interesting other than treasure. He found an old musket himself once.'

Jenny smiled and shook her head.

'You're really hooked, aren't you?' she said.

'You could say that, I suppose. But then, it's better than hanging about the street corner moaning, or wasting good time sitting at a bar drinking all day. Couldn't afford to do that anyway, even if I wanted to. I see some of the lads every week heading straight from the dole office to the pub. Don't know how they can do it on the miserable few bob they get. Somebody has to be going short. Anyway, to get back to the subject, even if I did find anything Teddy reckons it would be crazy to hand it over to the museum. Can't seem to get his stone-age mind round that way of thinking at all.'

'Be careful up there, Billy,' Jenny cautioned, genuine concern softening her eyes and tone of voice, 'I wouldn't put anything past that lad.'

'Don't worry, Love, I'll keep my eyes open.'

There was a sudden confusion of knockings on the hall door. 'Uh-oh, battle stations!' Jenny declared. 'Here come the hungry heroines.'

While on balance things had turned out better than he had dared hope, Billy had difficulty in coming to terms with the fact that Jenny had actually touched Teddy Brien, and for the rest of the evening he struggled to reconcile his confused feelings until in bed that night Jenny's almost frighteningly wild love-making helped him forget.

Teddy Brien drove home late, having spent the evening drinking at the hotel in Glendalough. His mood was ugly. Who did mister Billy fuckin' Kean think he was, anyway? Gettin' on his high horse just 'cause I laughed at an oul' loony that only a shaggin' loony wouldn't laugh at. Wouldn't last pissin' time in our estate, Mister Kean. Fuckin' sure! Soon show him what's what. Kick his stupid fuckin' head in, a few of the lads. Smack! Thump! Against the wall, heh-heh. Nice mot, though. Jaysus, I wouldn't mind slippin' a length into that one. Yeah. Knows all about it, too. Best hand job I ever had. Wasted on that soft bollix, she is. Needs a bit of a hidin' maybe, to show her the man is boss. Make her show a bit of respect.

Driving through Bray he pounded on the horn and roared: 'Be seein' you, Jenny. Soon. Whoo-ee, ride the arse off you. Ride, ride, ride!'

CHAPTER TWENTY FOUR

Billy gazed from the heights of Lugduff across the rolling summits to the north-west where an ominous-looking blue-black cloud was rapidly filling the sky. Better get down out of here quickish. He switched the detector off and headed back towards the point of descent. It was now mid-September and the weather had held beautifully throughout a long, blisteringly hot summer when the only complaints were of water shortages. Twice a week he had searched the mountain without any further discoveries and had just about exhausted all the possibilities in that area.

He climbed downwards in warm sunshine, but far below on the grassy space beside the lake people were running for their cars as the shadow of the great rolling cloud moved across the floor of the glen transforming the day from laughter-filled brightness to silent gloom in a matter of minutes. A strange sensual delight welled up in him as he beheld the awesome power of nature, and he felt humbled and grateful that he should be in this place at this time. The shadow rolled over him as he neared the bottom and he stood still savouring the sheer magic of the moment when the very air seemed to crackle with anticipation before the first big drops spattered on the rocks about him.

Then it teemed, drenching him to the skin. He didn't run for the car; the rain was pleasantly cooling after his exertions, and he strode along the lakeshore smiling broadly and blowing the streaming rain from his face, while the waters of the lake danced in the downpour and drops beat a tattoo into hastily abandoned plastic cups on wooden picnic tables. He grinned back at incredulous faces that peered from steamed-up car windows as he squelched his way through the car-park, only stopping to lock the detector in the boot of his own car before stepping on down the shining road to Cam's house.

The door was open as usual and Cam was seated just inside looking out at the rain.

'Oho, begod, will you look what's come down in the shower!' he exclaimed, pipe clenched between his teeth, when Billy appeared in the doorway. 'Come in and don't be standing there blocking my view. It isn't every day we get a decent downpour.'

'Have you an old towel or something I can stand on?' Billy asked, 'I don't want to be dripping all over your floor.'

Cam whipped the pipe from his mouth.

'Would you come in out of that and don't be talking tripe. Isn't that the beauty of the oul' flagged floor, a drop of water won't do it a ha'p'orth of harm. Put a carpet in a living room and you're afraid to live in it.'

Billy stepped inside. The rain drummed loudly on the roof and they had to raise their voices to be heard above the din.

'You're lucky,' Cam said, 'this is the first day I've had a fire going since May. I'll get you an old dressing gown of mine and you can drape your wet things over the back of a chair at the fireplace.' Billy changed in a small room with shelved walls full of all kinds of odds and ends: A storm lantern; Wellington boots; coils of rope and twine; a cobblers last; glass jars full of nails, screws and staples of all sizes; old cracked delph; buckets and cans, and tools of every description. A small workbench with a vice occupied one end of the room and, looking incongruous in this setting, a state-of-the-art Sony television set perched on top of a high stool in one corner. A wooden kitchen chair was the only other piece of furniture in the room.

'I'd never have taken you as a man for the telly, Cam,' Billy said as he hung his shirt and trousers before the fire, 'but I see you have one in the little workroom there.'

'Bedad, I have, but as you've observed, I keep it in its place. A comfortable room is no place for a television, where it can tempt a body to sit and goggle at any oul' twaddle. If there's something of particular interest on the news I go in there and watch it, but most of the time I just listen to the radio. Now and then I'll watch a good documentary if it's something I might learn from. When a man stops learning he's dead, whether he decides to lie down or not.'

A thoughtful look came into Cam's eyes.

'All those thousands of people, their lives taken away from them by the box in the corner. Hour after hour staring at other people play-acting. Meanwhile life outside goes on all around them.'

Billy laughed.

'Have you found a giggle's nest, Billy Kean, or have I said something amusing unbeknownst to myself?'

'No, no, Cam, it's just that the last line you used there paraphrases a line written by... ah, you wouldn't know him, wouldn't be your kind of music. Well, I doubt it, anyway...'

Cam had walked to a bookshelf. He came back and dropped a large pink-covered volume on the chair beside Billy.

'Writings and drawings by Bob Dylan! Cam, you amaze me!'

'My son sent that from England a few years ago and I've dipped into it occasionally. Not everything in there would be to my liking, but there are some gems, and there's no doubt the man is a poet. Just don't ask me to listen to the unfortunate noise he makes when he sings. Saw him on television once, looks like an owl in an ivy bush with all that hair. Now, where was I? Ah, yes, the box. For some people their whole existence revolves around it, and it's even come to the point where, if they have to leave it for any reason, they must have the bits they miss recorded so they can gape at them later! Now, I ask you, what will they have to say to their grandchildren? Regale them with tales of programmes watched in their young days, I suppose. A sad legacy, oh, a sad, sad legacy. I tell you, Billy, avick, the only thing television has contributed to conversation is a massive upsurge in the use of the word sshh!' He stopped and lit his pipe, then continued:

'Saw recently where somebody described television as sedation for the retarded. Now, there's a man who knows what he's talking about. I wonder do these soap-addicts realize the deprivation they are inflicting on their own children by never having a worthwhile conversation with them. How can an unfortunate child learn to care and behave responsibly in the world if all it gets is the odd grunt from its parents during the commercials? And it's a telling fact that many parents use the evening news as an opportunity to get their children to bed. Ay, a telling fact! And the result is the sort of mindless yob that comes into a place like Glendalough with one of those ghetto-blasters on his shoulder and that vacant stare in his eyes like a corpse, God bless us. The only time the eyes show a sign of life is when they glare at anybody who might happen to glance in his direction. The new Vikings, I call them. The Vikings of old came here and destroyed the peace and harmony of the glen, and these fellows do the same thing. Only the useless is sacred to them. Learning, art, caring — anything remotely connected with the good of the human race is anathema to them. A decent man, to their way of thinking — and I use that word loosely — is a gobshite. The irony of it is that they themselves eminently qualify for that noble title. Only yesterday I was having a smoke at the gate when one of them came swaggering along. I remarked as he passed that it was a lovely afternoon, thank God, and his response was a sneer and a spit on the ground.'

The great head shook sadly.

'Ignorance. Oh, terrifying ignorance. Don't get me wrong now, I have no great fear of any individual. The worst he can do is kill me and I'm long past the stage of fearing death. No, my fear is for all decent folk in the face of widespread ignorance. Can you imagine a world dominated by the type of person who spits at a friendly greeting? My father and those before him could go off rambling in these hills and leave the key in the door. Today a man's afraid to leave the place even if it's locked up. I've been burgled five times in the last three years. Usually it's the television that goes, which adds weight to my point. That's how I come to have the latest model in there. Not once has a book been stolen. They just throw them all over the place. Maybe they think I might be using fivers as bookmarks.'

'Have the police ever caught anybody?'

'Sure they haven't a chance. These boyos come out here over the Sally Gap from Dublin in stolen cars and they're gone like cats out a skylight long before the guards can get here. By the way, have you seen anything of your refined friend lately?'

'God, don't remind me, Cam. Yes, he turns up in the car-park now and then, and I saw him on the mountain a couple of weeks ago. Haven't spoken to him, though. I'm afraid I was the gobshite in that little arrangement.'

Billy looked apologetically at Cam.

'Not at all. Not at all, avick. It's only right to take a man as decent until he shows himself to be otherwise. I've made many a sad mistake myself. Begod ay, many a one, and to tell the truth, as soon as that chap walked in here I thought by the cut of his jib the poor divil wasn't too well furnished upstairs,' he tapped his temple with his forefinger, 'but then, I have more years on me than yourself.'

'You're going very easy on him, Cam. I'm afraid I wouldn't be inclined to refer to him as a poor divil.'

'But, sure, isn't it his loss, his deficiency. The chap can't know any contentment. There now, I haven't shut my gob since you came in, and never asked if you had one on you at all. I'll brew a cuppa scaldy for us.'

They had tea to the almost hypnotic accompaniment of rain on the roof.

'I'm sorry I didn't meet you a whole lot earlier, Cam, I always go out that door wiser than when I came in.'

'Get away out of that with you,' Cam roared with laughter. 'Sure, any oul' prate you'd hear out of me would be no more than common sense, there for anyone to see if they had a mind to.'

'Ah, now, I think there's a bit more to it than that.'

Cam shrugged.

'Well, it's seldom someone comes along who will bother to listen, if I may return the compliment. Some folk pretend to listen, and they're as transparent as the water in the lakes out there, all over-polite and condescending, not to offend this poor senile old native, and of course the poor senile old native usually goes along with it to avoid offending them! It's a curious old world and that's a fact. Oh, ay, curious,' he tamped his pipe with a matchbox. 'The art of conversation has gone to the bow-wows.'

Billy changed the subject.

'I think I may give up on the treasure, Cam.'

'Ah, no. And why is that, now, tell me?'

'I've scoured the whole mountain. Not a sign of anything more up there. Maybe it's at the bottom of the lake like Teddy Brien says.'

'Or down one of the old mine-shafts,' Cam put in. 'The upper glen here is honeycombed with them. Many have been sealed up for years and any that are still open would be dangerous to go poking about in by yourself. I climbed up to one of them myself years ago. Dickson describes it in his book on Dwyer as being used by the rebels. It has a vertical shaft going down a few yards in from the entrance, a death-trap if a lad was to fall down with nobody to raise the alarm. Dickson says there was a piece of rope still hanging from a beam over the hole in his day, back in the nineteen forties. There was no sign of a rope when I was there, and I have no idea how deep the shaft goes. Might even be full of water. A lot of the old mine-shafts are flooded.'

151

He stood up, took some books from the shelves and left them in a pile on the table in front of Billy.

'Why don't you amuse yourself going through that lot while your clothes are drying? I'm going to make a dash for the shed out the back. I have some bulbs and corms to sort out for planting. God, will you listen to that rain. Wonderful. And yet this minute there are people cursing it.'

Through the open door they could see the rain slanting down in bright silver streaks, bouncing off the mica schist slabs of the pathway and running along a little channel before gurgling down a drain. Cam watched with that endearing idiosyncratic shaking of his head in wonder.

'Is that not a moment to be preserved?' he said. 'If I were a poet this rainy afternoon would be enshrined forever. Can't you feel the great calmness over everything?'

It was true; the rain on the roof, the splashing and gurgling outside the door, all contributed to a soul-healing natural serenity.

'Yes, I know what you mean, Cam. Almost inexpressible, but very real. Beautiful. If psychiatrists could bottle it they'd make a fortune. I wouldn't have thought you'd have much trouble capturing it in a poem, though. You seem to have a ready supply of poetic quotes for every situation.'

'Ah, yes, but all created for me by great civilized minds. As for myself, I thank God for the soul even if he forgot to give me the talent. Oh, well, here goes!'

With a wild shout he plunged out into the teeming rain, an oilskin coat held over his head and a trail of pipe-smoke behind him. Billy resolved to examine his own values closely, to root out the silly little things that had been allowed to assume major importance in his life. People ranted about others not living in the real world when in fact they themselves, cocooned in their manufactured world and surrounded by every modern convenience, were the ones who hadn't a clue about reality. It was out here, away from the mind-crushing mill of the cities, that the real world could be found, and God too, if it came to that. Wise men had known this from time immemorial and although Billy had long ago stopped attending Mass, every time he crossed a field, climbed a mountain or beheld some new natural wonder, he found himself thanking God from the bottom of his dancing heart.

He already knew that in years to come he would be telling his children and grandchildren about Kevin 'Camaderry' Byrne, quoting him as he quoted the great poets, holding him up as an example of a good human being. Now, there was a man!

More than two hours later Billy was still engrossed in the books and had acquired a healthy respect for the exploits of Michael Dwyer. He made a list of any caves mentioned and rough ideas of their locations. He was pleased to find detailed directions to the cave Cam had described earlier; it was only half an hour away on foot, cut into the southern slopes of Camaderry.

Cam came in, shaking the rain from his clothes like a big dog.

'Tell me, Cam, was the old beam still across the perpendicular shaft in that cave you were telling me about?'

'It was.'

'How did it seem — any sign of rot?'

'Well, I put the weight of one foot on it and it held. I wasn't about to try the two, though, and if you're thinking what I think you're thinking, don't.'

Billy thought about it.

CHAPTER TWENTY FIVE

The following Saturday morning was fine, the sun already high over the mountains as Billy walked along the Miners' Road, the Upper Lake glinting through the trees down to his left. The freshness of morning still tinged the air with a balmy sweetness. He didn't meet a soul along the way, but it was only half past ten and most trippers tended to arrive in the afternoon.

The unmetalled road, closed to vehicular traffic, ran the two miles or so from the car-park along the length of the lake and beyond to the ruins of an old miners' village at the head of the glen where the Glenealo River rushed down the mountain, coming within a splash or two of qualifying as a waterfall. Beyond the village a path zig-zagged up out of the glen beside the river and petered out before reaching the ancient spoil heaps from the workings known because of their isolation as Van Dieman's Mines. Billy's destination was close to the village. He rested on a window-sill of one of the long-abandoned cottages and checked his notes. Gazing high among the great jumble of grey boulders he spotted his target — the remains of an old mule house directly above the ruined village.

He began climbing, the coil of strong nylon rope he had brought with him slung over his shoulder bandolier-fashion, a heavy-duty flashlight hanging from his belt. He had called to Cam's on his way up and had been duly scolded with an appropriate quote on the subject of foolhardiness. He assured the old man he would be cautious in the extreme and Cam warned him that if he didn't get back to the cottage by tea-time he would call in the mountain rescue team.

The climb was a lot steeper and longer than it had appeared from ground level and he gratefully flopped down on a rock when he finally reached the mule house. He looked about him for a brownish-yellow boulder the book said should be about a hundred yards due east of his position. Taking the direction of the round tower as roughly east, he easily identified the boulder and scrambled across the rocks to it. There beside it, as the book had said, was the opening. He unhooked his torch, flicked it on and carefully entered the cavity. Nine yards, the directions said, to the top of the shaft. He inched forward. The old beam still lay across the opening in the floor as Dickson and Cam had described it. He directed the beam of his flashlight into the shaft, and although it was a long way down, twenty feet at least, he was pleased he could see the bottom, which appeared to be strewn with debris of some kind. He eagerly anticipated a good root among that lot.

The beam certainly looked strong enough and like Cam he brought his right foot down on it as hard as he could and as far out as he dared. Not a budge out of it. Looks as if it could support an elephant. As a precaution he took his brightly-coloured jacket off and spread it on the boulder outside. Looping the rope around the beam, he started down, feet scraping the sides of the shaft to slow him down and lessen the effects of the burning rope on his hands. Should have thought of bringing gloves. Was John Harman, the rebel reputed to have used this cavern regularly, the last person to have shimmied down this shaft? Probably not; a rope from that period would surely have rotted away by the nineteen forties when Dickson was here, and anyway, as Dickson suggested, Harman probably only utilized the upper chamber where he could keep watch from the opening. He would have been a sitting target at the bottom of the shaft. The place was surprisingly dry and didn't have the dank atmosphere usually associated with caves, but then, until last week it had been an exceptionally dry summer. His feet touched the bottom and he swung the light round the wall of the shaft. Another surprise. A passage led off deeper into the mountainside.

He contented himself for the moment with carefully sifting through the rubble at the bottom of the shaft. He found a couple of what had at one time no doubt been strong iron spikes about six inches long, but which now crumbled in his hands with the rust of centuries. He picked up a small heavy marble-sized ball which he guessed straight away must be a musket-ball, and he pictured John Harman dropping it into the darkness and listening for the thud that would give him an idea of the depth of the shaft. The little thud echoed down almost two hundred years.

Apart from some more shapeless pieces of iron there was nothing else among the debris. He stood up and shone the light into the passage. He was not a little scared yet fascinated at the thought of what might lie hidden in the blackness, and worried that the slightest movement in there after so many years might bring half the mountain down on top of him. He inched forward, shining the light on the roof. It seemed solid enough, no cracks or loose material. He moved on in, careful to cause the minimum of disturbance. When he had ventured about ten feet he could see the end of the passage another fifteen feet ahead. Dickson had been right in his guess that it was only a trial shaft. Moving on, he found the floor close to the dead end covered in stone chippings and debris similar to that at the bottom of the shaft. He hunkered down to go through it and had soon come up with an old buckle, several more pieces of unidentifiable iron and what looked like the remains of a leather belt, probably that to which the buckle had once been attached. There were also some pieces of broken stoneware but none with any identifying marks. Examining the end wall he was delighted to see some initials cut into the stone: LB '52, J.O'T '57, JH '99 and several others undated. They surely had to be eighteenth century, and if so did JH mean that Harman had after all ventured down the shaft? The date was right.

Fascinated, Billy scanned the rest of the wall. One wit had carved the words THE END below his initials. Abandoning as vandalism the temptation to add his own, he scribbled all the initials into his notebook so he could check them out later with Cam and his books. Moving slowly back along the passage he scrutinized the side walls for more signs left by men long gone but found none. Faint though it was, the light that penetrated down as he approached the perpendicular shaft was reassuring and he set about examining the wall at the shaft-bottom. He had almost finished when his blood suddenly froze with the realization that something was very wrong. He had been back and forth across the floor several times; he should have felt the rope brushing against him. Oh, Jesus, the rope. Somebody's cut it. He swung the light beam around the floor. No, it's been pulled up. A sudden claustrophobic panic seized him for a moment until he remembered that Cam knew where he was and would get him out.

It had to be Teddy Brien's doing. Too much of a coincidence that somebody should just happen to come upon the cave at the moment he was down there. And even if they did, why should they pull the rope up? Looking up he could see the beam with the rope stretched across to the floor of the upper chamber. Was Teddy up there chuckling to himself, waiting for Billy to break down and start screaming for help? Calming himself, he shouted in a steady voice: 'OK Teddy, a joke's a Joke, now throw down that rope.' His words haunted the cavern for some moments, then complete silence. He began throwing some of the bigger chunks of rubble up through the shaft, hoping to get one to go above the rope and fall back on it, thus dragging it down. When, after dozens of tries, a chunk found its target it only caused the rope to sag a few inches lower. It was exhausting work heaving the stones, then dodging into the passage after each throw to avoid being struck on its return journey, and eventually he gave up and sank to the floor with his back against the wall.

'Aw, now, Billy-boy, you're not giving up already, are you?'

He looked up into the grinning face of Teddy Brien. So, the lousy creep had been up there gloating all the time. Billy said nothing.

'Hey, Billy, let's have a little chat before I head off. Right?' His words were interspersed with the same uncontrolled giggling he had exhibited at Cam's place.

He's bloody insane, Billy thought, how the hell did I let myself get mixed up with such a lunatic.

'See, Billy me oul' mate, there's somethin' on me mind, or should I say someone. I fancy another go at that little Jenny of yours.' The very sound of Jenny's name on his lips angered and sickened Billy.

'You can forget it. You never had a go in the first place. I know all about what happened.'

'Oh, do you now? Well, in that case we'll have to make sure the fuckin' job gets done proper this time, won't we?'

'Jenny will never give in to you.'

'She's a right stuck-up little bitch all right, I'll give you that, but she'll give in, trust ol' Teddy, she'll give in,' his semi-hysterical laughter echoed round the old mine. 'Anyway, I just wanted you to know, bein' her husband you have a right to know that she'll be well taken care of while you're away, an' if all goes well I'll come up here sometime tomorrow an' drop you the rope. If things don't go the way I want of course you could be here a bit longer. Oh, an' before I go you might as well have a look at what she'll be gettin'.'

He unzipped and took his penis out.

'Get a loada that, Billy-boy, feast your eyes on that weapon, cause before you see your precious Jenny again she'll have had it in her up to the roots.'

Before Billy realized what was happening he found himself spluttering in disgust as a stream of hot urine hit him full in the face. Teddy disappeared from above the shaft, his laughter fading towards the entrance.

'Up to the roots, Billy-boy, up to the roots.'

'It won't work, you stupid mad bastard,' Billy shouted after him. 'Somebody knows where I am.'

Immediately he wanted to bite his tongue off for his own stupidity.

'Is that so, now?' Teddy appeared above him again. 'That oul' fuck down the valley, I suppose. Well, I'll just have to make sure he can't pass on that bit of information. No bother to Teddy.'

He disappeared again and the laughter faded to silence.

Billy kicked the wall with rage. He had just ruined his only chance of getting out of there and making it to Jenny in time, and in the process had placed Cam in danger, for he had no doubt Teddy would carry out his threat, tie the old man up or something. He checked his watch. Nearly one o'clock. Christ, even if Cam were free to get help, he would still be here for another five or six hours.

CHAPTER TWENTY SIX

As she tucked Dawn and Susie into bed Jenny was almost frantic with anxiety. It was eight o'clock, nearly dark, and no sign of Billy. This is it. He may give up his treasure hunting. Her nerves wouldn't stand it. She had been worried at six o'clock when he hadn't turned up for dinner. Most unlike him. He was usually so considerate and appreciative of her culinary efforts, never once before failing to show for a meal. Something was wrong; she just knew it. At seven o'clock and several times since then she had dialled Cam Byrne's number but there was no reply. She tiptoed down the stairs and tried again without success. As she replaced the receiver the doorbell rang and she recognized Billy's jacket through the small pane of glass in the door. Overjoyed with relief she flung the door open and threw her arms around Teddy Brien. His arms went around her and he pushed her into the hallway. A cold fear struck her heart as she realized her mistake and she struggled away from him. He closed the door behind him.

'What have you done, you bastard,' she hissed at him. 'Where did you get Billy's coat? I'm calling the police.'

She picked up the receiver.

'Put...it...down,' he stood over her menacingly and said the words slowly.

Something in his tone made her do as he said.

'Now,' he leered at her, 'Billy-boy has checked himself into a little place in the mountains, an' I don't think it's right that a fine mot like yourself should be without a man overnight. Never know what kind of weird characters might be knockin' round.'

'If you think for one minute...'

'Oh, but I don't think at all, pretty Jenny,' he cut in, holding her by the chin and glaring into her eyes, 'I know, I fuckin' well know. You laughed at me the last time I was here, so now I'm here to show you that nobody laughs at Teddy Brien, least of all a fuckin' woman. The only thing I regret is that you're goin' to enjoy it.'

'You're mad.'

'Am I? Oh, dear. Oh, golly-fuckin'-gosh. Then you'll understand I'm not responsible for me actions. Right?' He giggled. 'Now, let's go.'

'Where?'

'To the bedroom, cunt.'

Jenny felt sick with disgust.

'No! No, I won't.'

'Yes you will, cunt,' he grinned confidently at her. 'You see, at the little place Billy's checked into they hate guests to leave unless a certain fella signs them out, namely Teddy Brien. Now, you play ball with me tonight an' I'll be up there tomorrow bright an' early to do the necessary. I'm warnin' you,' he grabbed her chin again, 'we can do it the hard way or the easy way. Either way, we do it. Now, make up your mind, I'm not arguin' with you much longer.'

'No. I don't care what you say, I'm going to call the police,' she jerked away from him.

He squeezed her hand until she let go of the receiver and he replaced it gently in its cradle, then pinned her arms to the wall, digging his fingers painfully into her flesh. 'Listen to me, you stupid bitch, if the cops come near me I'll just lose my memory and that little shit of a husband of yours can stay up there till he rots for all I care.'

Jenny's mind raced, searching for something, anything to get her out of this situation. If she resisted he would rape her; if she fought him all out the girls would be wakened and terrified, and he would probably overpower her in the end anyway. Worst of all, he had Billy trapped in God knew what kind of place and how could she risk him being imprisoned indefinitely? There was no way out.

'Let me go,' she said quietly.

He released her arms and without another word she started up the stairs. He followed, his hands mauling her as she climbed. Her skin crawled. She was determined he would not have the satisfaction of any response from her. When they reached the landing she indicated the bedroom door.

'In there,' she said, 'I need to use the bathroom.'

'Be quick about it or I'll be in there after you.'

She squeezed some KY jelly from the tube and applied it liberally; that bastard wasn't going to hurt her. When she entered the bedroom he had dropped his trousers and was waving his penis about like a schoolboy behind the playground shed. Christ, she thought, what an immature moron. She took a packet of condoms from the bedside locker. He laughed and slapped them from her hand.

'Bareback, Jenny, bareback.'

In what she hoped was the least erotic manner she removed her clothes and lay back on the bed. As she might have guessed, he mounted her without the slightest nod in the direction of foreplay and commenced his crude pounding of her body. She willed herself to lie there totally detached from what was taking place.

'Move,' he growled in her ear. 'Move your arse, fuck you.'

She stared blankly into his face. Dead meat, you scum, that's all you're going to get. After less than two minutes of hissed obscenities he rolled off her.

'Is that it?' her eyes mocked him. 'Is that what all your crowing and cursing was about?'

'What the hell do you mean. That was a good fuck an' if you weren't a frigid bitch you'd know it.'

'Bullshit. Any dog can fuck. It takes a man to make love, but you wouldn't know anything about that. Now, you've got what you came for, so you can get out of here, and if Billy's not home safe by lunchtime tomorrow I'll be down to the police station.'

'You just keep your mouth shut an' lie there. I'll go when I'm good an' ready. I haven't finished with you yet.'

Oh, God, what now?

He lay with his hands behind his head for more than half an hour, and just grinned at her when she asked what he was waiting for, then his hands moved over her body and he ordered her to watch him become aroused again.

'Don't you want to touch it, Jenny baby?' he said when fully erect.

'No.'

He shrugged.

'OK, roll over.' '

What?'

'Roll fucking over and give us a look at that tight little arse of yours.'

'No, you can't...' she began, shocked, realizing what he wanted.

'Yes I can. Don't try an' tell me Billy-boy doesn't use the tradesman's entrance now an' then.'

'You're not fit to mention his name, you filthy bastard. Get out. Go.'

'Look,' he grabbed her right breast and squeezed cruelly, 'the job gets done. If you want to make a whole lotta noise an' have the kids in to watch, that's fine with me. I don't give a shit.' Jenny Kean was not the hating type, but when Teddy Brien dared to speak of her children with his foul mouth, raging hatred filled her heart. She wanted to tear his eyes out, kill him with her bare hands. But the girls; her first thoughts had to be for them. She was strong enough to handle this somehow, but the innocent girls could be scarred for life.

'Again! Jaysus, do you ever stop goin'?' he complained when she said she needed to visit the bathroom. 'Hurry up, then, for fuck sake.'

He hurt her, making no attempt whatever to be gentle. Her cries were muffled as his heavy hand on the back of her head crushed her face into the pillow. Mercifully, it was over even quicker than the first time and she gritted her teeth as he roughly withdrew. She rolled over and drew the covers over her, saying quietly :

'You are useless.'

'Shut up.'

'Completely useless,' she repeated, her voice full of contempt, 'and you probably think you're a great lad for the ladies. Well, I can tell you, you know nothing about sex and nothing about women. You are less than scum. You are nothing. Nothing.'

As he mumbled obscenities at her and began to get his clothes on, Jenny again felt the surge of power she had felt at the end of his first visit; the feeling that she was somehow coming out on top of the situation again, having the last word, and she enjoyed his humiliation after what he had done to her. She followed him downstairs and as he left warned him again: 'I'll swear you into ten years jail if Billy's not here on time tomorrow.'

He turned and spat at her, missing as she stepped to one side. 'Completely useless,' she said, and closed the door. She went to the bathroom and showered and washed over and over again. She was still under the shower when the phone rang half an hour later.

CHAPTER TWENTY SEVEN

As the dim light from the top of the shaft faded Billy gave up hope that Cam might somehow have evaded Teddy Brien. He had worn himself out with sessions of rock-heaving that had only succeeded in bringing the rope down another foot or so. At intervals he had yelled for help, all the time aware that the likelihood of anybody hearing him was remote, and had attempted to hack footholds in the wall with pieces of stone to no avail.

He was worried to distraction about Jenny. Although he had every confidence in her ability to deal with a situation in the way she thought best, he feared Teddy might turn nasty to the point of violence. If he harmed Jenny or the girls he would regret it. Billy began to doze from sheer exhaustion, then jumped suddenly when a voice called 'Hello!' from outside the entrance.

The light was almost completely gone now and he switched on his flashlight.

'Hello! Who's that? Give me a hand out of here.'

'Holy God Almighty, Billy Kean, what happened to you? Are you hurt, avick.'

'Cam! It's good to hear you. No, I'm OK. Listen, can you get into the tunnel. Teddy pulled up the rope and left me here.'

'Isn't that the divil, now! Maybe you'll listen to the advice of your elders in future, me lad.'

There was scuffling and scraping as Cam edged his way to the top of the shaft holding a flickering storm lantern.

'The oul' bones are getting a mite stiff for this game. Look out below!'

In his fatigued state the climb up the shaft nearly finished him. He collapsed on his back in the tunnel.

'Take it easy there for a while, now, and get your wind back. There's no rush,' Cam said sympathetically.

'There is a rush, Cam, did you see Teddy?'

'I did not. After you left this morning I decided to take a run into Bray in the van to fetch a few things, and halfway up the Long Hill on the way back the oul' jalopy let me down, failed to proceed, as they say. Had to get a fellow out from Bray to get me going, and when I got back and there was no message from you I decided to check the car-park. Your car was the only one still there, so I knew something must have gone awry.'

'Christ, Cam, you shouldn't have come up here alone, you should have called somebody. If you'd broken an ankle or something we'd both have been here for God knows how long.'

'To tell you the truth, Billy lad, I didn't think I'd ever be this high up any mountain again, and I'm feeling right pleased with myself.'

The air was chilly when they emerged from the tunnel, and Billy saw that his jacket was missing.

'Look, Cam, I'm going to hurry on ahead of you, go carefully, for God's sake.' He explained about Teddy's threats.

'So I'm in debt to that oul' van. Had I arrived home earlier I might have had more to contend with than a dirty carburettor. You go on, now, don't worry about me. I've been prowling around these parts since before you were born, ay, and maybe before your daddy was born.'

There was an eerie beauty about the mountain in the dark of night, the flashlight and lantern creating moving shadows among the boulders, while the still shadows thrown by the moon stood like sentries outside their circles of light. Billy gradually moved ahead and when he reached the ruined village glanced back at the swinging lantern still high on the mountainside. Be safe, Cam. The lake was a sheet of silver under the full moon as Billy ran and walked alternate stretches of the Miners' Road. As he approached the car-park he stopped suddenly and slapped at his trouser pockets.

'No! Oh, shit, no!'

His keys must have been in the pocket of his jacket. He turned and sprinted back along the lakeside road until he saw Cam's lantern waving in the darkness.

'Billy, What's wrong.'

'No keys,' he wheezed breathlessly, 'listen, can I phone Jenny from your place and impose on you to drive me home?'

'Of course. Of course you can. Here, take my key and go ahead. I'll be there shortly.'

'Thanks.'

Billy sprinted off again.

His hands trembled as he dialled his number. Jenny answered.

'Jen, It's me, love. Are you all right?'

'Billy! Oh, Billy, thank God. Where are you? He said you wouldn't be let out until tomorrow.'

He could hear her voice breaking into sobs.

'I'm out, Jen, I'm at Cam's. Are you sure you're all right, love? Has he left?'

'Yes, I'm OK. He's gone.'

'And the girls?'

'They're fine. Just come home, Billy.'

'Cam's going to run me home. Brien took my jacket with the car keys in the pocket.'

'I know. It's here. I never thought of looking in the pockets. Oh, Billy, please don't be long. I love you.'

'Here comes Cam now, love, we'll leave straight away.'

The Town Hall clock chimed eleven as they entered Bray.

'Will you come in and have a cuppa tea?' Billy asked Cam.

'Some other time, thanks. You'll have a lot of talking to do and you won't need an oul' fella like me around, but I promise I'll drop in and meet this wonderful family of yours before long.'

They pulled in at Billy's door.

'I'm really grateful to you, Cam, coming all the way down here at this hour of the night.'

'Get away with you! Anyone would have done the same. And besides, at my age I can't afford to be wasting too much precious time in Sheet Alley. Goodnight now, and I hope things turn out all right for you all.'

Billy waited while Cam turned the van and drove out of the square, then knocked gently on the door; the bell sometimes woke the girls.

'Just hold me,' was all Jenny said when he closed the door behind him. They stood there in the hallway for a full ten minutes in a silence that was full of gentle reassurance, and when she finally started to say something he hushed her and told her there was no need for her to say anything about it unless she wanted to, he knew she had done what she thought best. Nothing more was said between them that night. They climbed the stairs to bed and fell asleep clinging to each other.

After breakfast next morning when Dawn and Susie had gone out to play, Billy said: 'I think we should go to the police, Jen love, and so does Cam. How do you feel about it yourself?' She reached across the table and took his hands in hers.

'I'd like to see him locked up for life. I think I would have killed him last night only for the girls, but I don't know. What could we have him charged with? He didn't rape me, I went along with it to spare the kids. Billy, I don't want to have to stand up in court and describe it all in public. If he had raped me, yes, but I'll be all right if you're with me. He's not worth all the trouble and the hurtful publicity it would bring down on us.'

'God, Jen, it kills me to think of him getting away with the like of that. He terrorized you. That sounds close enough to rape for me.'

'He's not exactly getting away scott free, I sent him off with a pretty low opinion of himself. His self esteem must be lower than a slug's.' She squeezed his hands and her eyes pleaded with him. 'Please, Billy, let it go, for me. Don't put me through all that.'

'All right, love, we'll leave it, But I want you to promise that if he tries to push his way in here once more we'll report it, even if we just tell the police he's been making a nuisance of himself.'

'Promise. I love you, Billy.'

'Love you, too, Jen. Now, I have to go up there to collect the car. Why don't we all hop on the St. Kevin's bus and we can call on old Cam? He's dying to meet you and the kids. You can thank him personally for rescuing your beloved husband?'

'That'd be nice. I'll get dressed and stick a bit of make-up on. Will you call the girls, they're probably manky dirty.'

With the girls, Cam was a revelation, tirelessly keeping them entertained with a seemingly endless fund of yarns, giving them guided tours of the house and garden, and showing them all kinds of games that were played when he was a boy.

'Now, girleens,' he said, winking at Billy and Jenny, 'I'm going to bring you for a nice walk beside the lake.' An excuse to buy them ice-cream cones from the mobile shop in the car-park. 'We'll let Mammy and Daddy mind the house for a while.'

'You were right,' Jenny said when Dawn and Susie had trotted off, a little hand held in each of Cam's big ones, 'he really is something else.'

'Honest to God, Jen, the man's a cross between Solomon and Santa Claus. I'd never have guessed he'd be so great with the kids. He's full of surprises.'

He surprised them again at teatime with delicious chunks of his own soda-bread, spread thickly with butter and home-made blackberry jam.

'I make about half a dozen different jams every summer. Never buy a pot of shop jam from one year end to the other.'

'It's delicious,' Jenny said. 'We'll have to start making our own.' The girls echoed her appreciation.

'I don't think you can beat the wild blackberry for flavour. It's a pity you weren't here a month ago, you could have tried some of my fraughan pie.'

'What's fraughan pie?' Dawn asked, saving her parents the embarrassment of showing their ignorance.

'Fraughans, alanna, are little berries that grow wild on the mountains. That's their Irish name. They're known in English as bilberries.'

'Could we come and pick them with you next year, me and Susie?'

'Of course you could, and you can come and help me pick the garden bushes too. I have blackcurrants, gooseberries, raspberries and the divil knows what out there.'

'Yay!'

CHAPTER TWENTY EIGHT

'Well, that settles that, then,' Billy said, putting down a copy of the Irish Independent, 'the Glendalough treasure, if it exists, will have to remain lost as far as Billy Kean is concerned.'

He had just finished reading an article Cam had pointed out to him on his return from a fruitless search. A new bill was to be passed banning the use of metal detectors for the purpose of discovering buried archeological objects.

'A bit over the top, don't you think, Cam? I mean, you'd understand them not wanting untrained people digging around ancient monuments and the like, but this,' he indicated the paper, 'this rules out detecting in your own back garden.'

'If you're looking for archeological objects,' Cam nodded.

'Yes, but if I'm out in an open field that has no known connection whatever with any ancient settlement, I'm not searching for anything in particular. I'd have no idea what might turn up, a ring lost yesterday or one dropped by Finn McCool. Whether I'm guilty of an offence or not depends on what I'm thinking at the time of the find!' Cam puffed on his pipe and looked thoughtful.

'It's a tough one all right, but you see, it seems there have been some go-boys recently digging up ancient artifacts and selling them abroad. Not right at all, that. Selling their own country's heritage.'

'I agree completely. But there's always a minority of cowboys in all walks of life. Hundreds of people use metal detectors these days, and to ban the hobby because of a few unscrupulous criminal types seems unfair to say the least. A bit like banning fishing because of a few poachers.'

'A good argument,' said Cam, 'but it looks like it's too late for anybody to protest now. The bill is about to be ratified.'

'Yes, but I wonder did any of the people involved in drawing it up really think it through thoroughly? The thing could backfire on them in regard to keeping treasures here in Ireland because detectorists who happen to turn up something worthwhile, even if they weren't looking for it, will now be afraid to hand it over for fear of prosecution. Then there'll be the temptation to sell it abroad and the people of this country will be the losers. In England, according to the article, a coroners court decides whether a find is treasure trove or not. If it is, and the state wants it, the finder is given the value of the find. If not, the finder keeps his treasure. Sounds like a fair system, and it almost guarantees that any treasures found will stay in the country to which they belong. OK, I can appreciate a small country like Ireland might not have the resources to pay huge rewards, but I don't think any reasonable person would expect it anyway.'

'Begod, you should have gone into politics! You're a great man to argue a point.'

'Look at it another way,' Billy went on, 'a fabulous chalice lies buried in the middle of farmer Murphy's field. Someday there is a chance that a detectorist will ask farmer Murphy's permission to search his field and the chalice is found and goes on display at the National Museum. Now because there was no known ancient settlement in farmer Murphy's field, the chances of the chalice being found otherwise than with a detector are virtually nil as it lies below ploughing depth and archeologists would have no reason to dig there. This new law will ensure it is never found.'

'True, true,' said Cam, 'and who's to say that it will survive indefinitely with all the modern chemicals going into the ground these days? I heard on the radio recently somebody from the museum saying he would rather see these treasures rot in the ground than have them found by metal detector. Now, there's a man with a sad attitude.'

'As I said, the whole thing sounds completely over the top, but I suppose there's no use crying over spilt milk. I may stick to searching for rebel caves. I shouldn't think anything from Dwyer's time would have attained archeological status yet, so I suppose it'd be all right to use the detector if I needed to.'

'Oh, I should imagine so,' Cam grinned, 'but just be careful not to think about anything older while you're searching. If they're intent on passing this kind of legislation they have obviously figured out some way of monitoring a body's thoughts!'

'Well, it won't matter until the spring, anyway, the weather is becoming too unpredictable and I can't be dragging Jenny and the kids out in the cold.'

The girls and their mother had gone for a walk along the green road. This was their fourth visit in as many weeks to Glendalough, and Cam had become their adopted Grandad.

'Don't be strangers over the winter, now, drop in anytime,' Cam said as they piled into the car, 'and make sure to call at Christmas. Jack will be home. It's been a long time since there were children in this oul' place for Christmas.'

On Christmas Eve the girls were given the choice of their traditional trip to Dublin or a visit to Cam, and without a moment's hesitation chose Glendalough. Billy phoned Cam to let him know they were coming. The day was cold but fine and midwinter and all as it was, Cam's door was wide open when they arrived.

'Hello! Anybody home?' Billy shouted in the doorway.

'Are you there, Cammy?' added little Susie.

There was no reply and they went on in.

A huge log fire blazed in the grate and the living room was adorned with richly-berried holly. Long, trailing strands of ivy climbed all over the bookshelves and a Christmas tree stood in the ingle nook. Billy went outside and checked around the back.

'The van's not there, I'd say he's just slipped to the shop in Laragh for something.'

The girls stood staring into the great fireplace, their faces aglow in the flickering of the flames.

'Now that's what I call a fire!' Billy exclaimed. 'It'd take us a week at home to burn what Cam has on there. Just look at the size of those logs!'

'It's so-oo cosy, Dad, with just the big fire and no light on,' Dawn observed.

The tiny windows didn't allow much daylight into the room and their shadows thrown by the firelight danced on the book-lined walls.

'Cam won't mind us making ourselves at home,' Billy said, and, fetching some chairs, he found his words confirmed in a note they hadn't seen on the table: 'Merry Christmas! Make yourselves comfortable. Back soon. Cam.'

Ten minutes later they heard the van pull in through what Cam called the back gate, although it was to the front of the house just fifty yards along the road from the smaller front gate. A gravelled driveway led to the back of the cottage and moments after the wheels of the van had crunched to a halt, Cam came in laden with bags and parcels which he piled onto the table. He stood back and beamed at the little group gathered round the fire.

'Ah, my friends! My good friends. What a pleasant scene you make in my humble abode. It warms my old heart to see you here on this day... "of all the good days in the year, on Christmas Eve"...,' he wagged a finger at the girls, 'Charles Dickens... now there was a man... there was a man... Well, now, first things first, the kettle!'

'You took a bit of a chance leaving the door open, Cam,' Billy remarked.

'It's not so chancy this time of the year. Any strange faces we see around here over Christmas are usually here to savour the peace of the place. Genuine folk, and after all, it is the season of peace. I suppose the yobs are too busy robbing the unfortunate shoppers in Dublin to bother venturing out this far. I always throw the door open at Christmas time, even when I'm out. Never know who'll be sitting at the fire when I come home, neighbours in the glen, mostly, but sometimes total strangers. I call it my conversation trap. Ay, next to a good book, there's nothing like good conversation. Last Christmas I found a retired American drying himself off at the fire. Threw his hands in the air when I walked in, all apologetic and assuring me he wasn't here to rob me. I told him to sit down out of that and tell me about himself. From Boston, he was, here to trace his roots. His wife had passed on and his children had their own families so he figured it was a good time to go and see where his great-grandfather had come from. All he knew was that he had emigrated from County Wicklow, asked me if the name Byrne meant anything to me! Well begod, says I, you're in the right county, sir, but you'll need to be a mite more specific, for the Byrnes are as plentiful as platitudes in parliament around here. He had a few names and dates to start with and I gave him some addresses I thought might be useful to him. We talked for a good two hours and when he was putting on his coat to leave didn't a small hand-gun fall out of it. Well, needless to say I was a bit taken aback because the man had seemed to me anything but the gun-toting type. I told him I was aware that in the States many people owned guns but I didn't think anybody would feel it necessary to bring a gun to Ireland with them.

I didn't bring it, he says, I bought it here. Went on to tell me how he had overheard a conversation in a hotel, somebody saying there were lots of hostiles in the Wicklow Hills — you know how Yanks pronounce hostile — and he wasn't taking any chances. Well, I couldn't help chuckling, and the man looked at me as if I'd suddenly taken leave of my senses. What the hell's so funny, he wanted to know, and when I explained that it was hostels they were talking about he saw the funny side and laughed himself, which was nice, because laughing at themselves is not a common trait in Americans. Now girls! While we are having our tea I think it would be nice to light up the Christmas tree.'

Dawn and Susie, and indeed their parents, were surprised to see Cam, instead of putting the expected plug in the socket, strike a match and commence lighting several dozen small white candles held on the branches of the tree by little crocodile clips.

'And we won't forget the traveller,' he said, going to the window and lighting a large red candle there.

'Speaking of travellers,' Billy said, 'you said your son was coming home for Christmas.'

'Yes. Jack'll be here around midnight. Flight gets into Dublin shortly before ten, so I'm afraid you'll miss him. I don't think old Santa Claus would be too pleased to find certain little girls missing from their beds in the middle of the night. Right, ladies?'

'Right!'

'Now!' Cam said, handing each of them a parcel. 'You just sit there and open these, and I'll be back in a jiffy.'

He went into the back room rattling a box of matches in his hand.

'This weighs a ton!' Jenny cried, unwrapping a huge old volume of Mrs. Beeton's Home Management.

'You won't find much use for the section on how to treat servants, but there are some good old recipes in there,' Cam shouted from the other room. 'Sorry it's second-hand,' he laughed.

'Would you go way out of that,' Jenny answered, 'God, it'll take me years to get through this!'

Billy's present was second-hand, too, a copy of Dickson's Life of Michael Dwyer. A quick glance at the bookshelf told him that Cam had gone to the trouble of locating a second copy somewhere. The girls gifts were beautiful new volumes on Irish wildlife and flowers. They heard the scraping of match against matchbox, and then Cam re-entered the room like Mrs. Cratchit, but bearing a much larger cannonball of a Christmas pudding than that poor Dickensian lady could afford.

'It's on fire!' screamed Dawn, jumping up.

'Don't fear, alanna, it's all right. Just a little brandy.'

He left it on the smaller table and fetched some plates.

'It's not even heated,' he said, 'because it isn't usually eaten until the day itself, but for my special friends I'll make an exception this year.'

'How do you make it so roundy?' Dawn enquired.

'Oh, that's no big secret. I cook it the way me mother did, in a cloth. All Christmas puddings were roundy when I was your age. Most people nowadays cook them in bowls. You ask your Grandma about it.'

'Which one?' Susie asked.

'I beg your pardon, little honey.'

'Which Grandma, we have two.'

Cam laughed.

'And long may you continue to have two. Ask either of them. I can tell you it's long time since oul' Cam had a granny, and if she were here today eating a slice of my Christmas pudding she'd be over a hundred and fifty years old.'

The girls giggled.

'This is magic!' Dawn exclaimed as they sat with hot cups of tea and thick slices of pudding in the dancing light of fire and candles listening to Cam's tales of long-ago Christmases in the glen.

CHAPTER TWENTY NINE

'Bleeep!'

'Oh...Shit!'

Billy jumped as the first signal in two hours of silent searching suddenly blasted his ears. He had turned his attention to Keadeen Mountain in the spring having studied everything he could lay his hands on about Dwyer and his men over the winter months. It appeared the important hide-out on Keadeen had been abandoned for some reason long before Dwyer's surrender and Billy figured that if the abandonment had been sudden then some items of interest might have been left behind. It was now early June and he had spent many days on Keadeen searching in vain for the entrance to the subterranean headquarters of the rebels.

He had brought the detector today hoping it might succeed where hand and eye had failed, maybe by locating a coin or some other metal object that might have been dropped close to the cave-mouth. He bent to examine the ground, uprooting some small clumps of heather, and recognized the tip of a pike-head sticking upwards between the turf and a fairly large stone. He was puzzled; if it had been dropped it would never have fallen in that position. It looked as if it had been left standing against the stone.

He tugged at it with his free hand but could not pry it loose. He left the metal detector down and when he went to try with both hands he was astonished to find the pike-head had disappeared, his astonishment quickly turning to excitement as he realized it must have fallen into some sort of opening under the stone. He went to his rucksack which was lying some distance away and took a small trowel and his flashlight from it. The turf came away from around the base of the stone without much effort, and when he had cleared it all the way round he pushed at the stone and it moved aside quite easily to reveal an opening just large enough to admit a human being.

He saw that the hole went straight down and he switched on his flashlight. The sightless eye-sockets of a human skull glared their hollow blackness into the beam of light and he cried out and jumped backwards, losing his balance and falling over in the heather. He picked himself up and scrambled back to the hole. The pike-head had fallen into the open mouth of the skull giving the hideous impression that it had been the instrument of death. He cried out again, this time in disbelief, as he saw that the bones lay among dust- and turf-covered objects that had very obviously nothing to do with Michael Dwyer or his time. He judged it was about nine feet to the bottom and could see that the cave continued off to one side of the shaft.

It's it! Exactly as Ann Devlin describes it in her Jail Journal. Ann was a first cousin of Dwyer's, imprisoned for many years for her involvement with Robert Emmet and the Wicklow rebels. She had visited the cave once with Dwyer and had described it in detail. Billy wanted to get down there. Now. But his means of descent, or more importantly, ascent, the nylon rope he had used at the old mine-shaft, was a mile and a half away in the boot of his car down on the road. He looked about him. A pillar-like stone protruding from the ground a few feet from the entrance would do to secure the rope. No sign of another human being caught his attention as he scanned the Glen of Imaal below him and the green hills rolling away in all directions. He pushed the stone back into place over the entrance and started down the mountain.

An exhausting ninety minutes later he was tying the rope around the protruding stone. Avoiding as far as possible disturbing the bones, he set his feet on the floor of the cave at either side of the skull and bent to examine the objects strewn about. Some of them he recognized from photographs in books and visits to the National Museum. Book shrines, crozier tops, chalices of various sizes, bell-shaped objects, brooches, pins and dozens of small objects, most of which appeared to be fashioned in gold and silver and decorated in an incredibly beautiful manner.

It could only be the Glendalough treasure. But how on earth had it ended up here, and when? Did the former tenant of these bones have something to do with it being here? No way of knowing. It was certain that it only arrived here after Dwyer's time; The rebels would never have taken a secret like that with them to their graves. There's enough here to make the Derrynaflan hoard look paltry.

As he was about to move on into the passage the flashlight picked out the reason why the skeleton was lying here at the bottom of the entry shaft; the left foot and about six inches of shin lay separated from the rest of the leg, the splintered bone clearly indicating a violent break of some kind. Horrible way to go, God rest the poor devil, whoever he was. Wonder how the stone came to be in place?

The passageway was empty and when he swung the light on the interior of the chamber at the end Billy's breath stopped in utter stupefaction. Wonderful objects, piles of them, heaped around the floor as if somebody had heaved them out of sacks like a coalman. He understood how Carter must have felt when he gazed on the fabulous treasures of Tutankhamun. He stood there, stunned, unable to take it all in. Large chalices, lying on their sides, poured heaps of smaller precious objects from them in glittering cascades. More beautiful shrines of all sizes and shapes. There was less dust in the inner chamber to dull the brightness of the marvellously worked gold decoration.

He climbed out into the sunlight, trembling like someone who has just experienced a sudden intensely-exciting sexual encounter. What should he do? He felt dizzy as he tried to think coherently of the best way to deal with the situation. He pulled the rope up and replaced the stone over the entrance.

'You wouldn't be pulling an old man's leg, now, would you?' Cam cast a sceptical eye at him when he had finished breathlessly relating his story.

'Cam, look at me, for God's sake, I'm in bits! It's all there in the cave on Keadeen. Don't ask me how, but it's there. I'm telling you, Cam, you've never seen anything like it. They'll have to build a new wing onto the bloody museum for this lot!'

'Sorry, Billy, I believe you. Congratulations! I'm delighted for you. What'll you do now?'

'I'll phone the museum from here, if you don't mind, see what they have to say.'

'Help yourself,' Cam invited, taking up the phone directory, 'I'll get the number for you. Take you a week to find it in that state. '

Billy dialled the number.

'National Museum of Ireland, can I help you?' a male voice answered the phone.

'Yes, I want to report an important discovery. Can you put me onto the person in charge of that sort of thing.'

'Hold on, please.

'Presently a different voice said: 'Hello, George Murphy here. To whom am I speaking?'

'Mister Murphy, my name is Billy Kean.'

'You've found something, Mister Kean?'

'Yes, I have, and I believe it to be a very important find.'

'Well, maybe the museum should be the judge of that. What exactly have you found?'

'Dozens, maybe hundreds, of ancient sacred church objects. I'm almost certain they belonged to the monastic city of Glendalough. '

'What?...' Billy could almost see the look of shocked amazement on Murphy's face. 'Are you serious, Mister Kean? I trust you are aware it is a serious offence to go digging on a National Monument like Glendalough.'

'I am aware, and I am serious. There was no digging involved and I didn't find it in Glendalough. I'll take you to it if you can come out here or send somebody. '

'Hundreds of objects, you say?'

'Probably, I didn't want to disturb the heaps.'

'Good God! Well, you did right not to disturb them, if this is a genuine call. Can you come in to the museum tomorrow yourself?'

'Of course it's genuine, for God's sake. Why would anyone want to make up something like that?'

'You'd be surprised at the amount of wild goose chases we've been called out on, Mister Kean, and the valuable time that has been wasted on hoaxes, so if you would just come in for a chat tomorrow, we may be able to treat this thing with the seriousness you say it deserves. You must admit your story sounds a bit fantastic.'

'I suppose so. All right, I'll be in tomorrow. Any particular time?'

'Around eleven will be fine.'

'Right, I'll be there. Goodbye.'

He hung up.

'Can you believe that, Cam, they think it could be a hoax!'

'Well, I suppose they must have their reasons. Looks like Billy Kean is going to be a household name before too long.'

'Hadn't thought of that part of it. Not so sure I like the idea, either.'

'And very probably a rich household name at that. There should be a handsome reward for the finder of something this big.'

'I'll believe that when I see it. Listen, Cam, thanks for everything. I'll head off now. Can't wait to see Jenny's face when she hears this.'

'Can we move to the country now?' Jenny asked, wide-eyed.

'What? Ah, come on, Jen, you're laughing at me. I swear to God, this is huge. Nothing like it has ever been found in a single hoard before, not that I've heard of, anyway.'

'I'm not laughing. I mean it. If we get a big reward wouldn't it be lovely to move to the country? It would be great for the girls.'

'Look, Jen, let's take one thing at a time. We can't be certain about anything yet. But yes, it's a nice thought.' In the morning he drove to Dublin, parked the car in Mount Street and walked between the richly blooming flowerbeds of Merrion Square to the museum.

George Murphy was a tall thin man with a shock of jet black hair showing a little grey at the temples. He wore thick-lensed spectacles and his handshake was of the dead fish variety. 'Well, Mister Kean,' he eyed billy across his desk, 'tell me your story.'

'I was searching in the mountains for rebels' caves from the ninety eight period, didn't have any success until yesterday when I got a signal and...'

Murphy jerked forward in his chair and interrupted, his eyes glaring into Billy's.

'A signal, Mister Kean? Are you telling me you were using a metal detector?'

'Yes, but...'

'That's an offence, Mister Kean, searching for archeological objects with a metal detector is a serious offence,' his face was red and his tone furious.

'I told you,' Billy countered indignantly, 'I was searching for a cave. Surely a cave can't be considered an archeological object in itself. And I rang you straight away. Why are you treating me like some sort of criminal?'

'I'll tell you why — because I hear the same story from so-called treasure hunters all the time. They come in here when they find something pretending they weren't looking for it, expecting to be rewarded for breaking the law.'

'And that's what you think of me?'

'Unless you can convince me otherwise I have no reason to think of you any differently from anyone else.'

Billy was disgusted.

'This is ridiculous. Look, I've been searching on that mountain for weeks and yesterday was the first time I used the detector, and then only because I thought it might locate something accidentally dropped in the vicinity of the cave entrance. It was a last resort, and I was not searching for an archeological object. As it happened there was a pike-head sticking from the entrance and that's how I found it.'

'A pike-head?'

'Yes, there were human bones at the bottom of the shaft leading into the cave. It looks as if someone got trapped there and died.'

'The objects. What did you see?' Murphy seemed to be relaxing a little.

'Well, the largest would be chalices similar to the Ardagh and Derrynaflan, there must be at least six of them, and many more smaller ones.'

'Six!' incredulity distorted Murphy's face.

'Yes. Crucifixes and small statues which look to be solid gold, but I'm no expert. Patens, croziers, book shrines, bells, brooches, lots of small pins, rings, goblets. Piles of small stuff. And tangles of what looks like very fine gold wire.'

'Probably decorative gold threads from vestments which would have rotted away long ago,' Murphy's voice was now an awe-stricken whisper.

'God knows what else is there that I didn't see, hidden under the heaps and the larger objects.'

'Mister Kean, if all you tell me is true, this will be world news. The international media will descend on us like vultures. How many people have you talked to?'

'My wife, yourself and a friend of mine, an old man in Glendalough.'

'Will they have told anybody else?'

'No, I'm certain of it.'

'Then I would advise you to keep it that way. I'm inclined to give you the benefit of the doubt about the detector. It will be better if we can co-operate on this and show a united front to the press when the time comes, and believe me, when this breaks they will be at your door like hungry wolves day and night, so enjoy these few days.'

Billy nodded, wondering what exactly had brought about the softening of attitude.

'So when do we go and check the cave out?' he asked.

'Tomorrow afternoon. I'm full up today and in the morning. I'll pick you up in Bray at half past two if that suits.'

'Yes, fine.'

At precisely two thirty the following afternoon a maroon Ford Granada rolled up to the Divil and Billy got into the back seat. Murphy introduced the heavy-set man who occupied the passenger seat beside him as Charles Mason, an 'eminent archeologist'.

Neither man spoke on the journey other than to acknowledge Billy's directions.

'You can pull in just here,' he said as they came to his usual parking place below Keadeen.

They had climbed for about ten minutes when Mason stopped and sat down gasping on a boulder.

'Wait... wait a minute, there's no rush. God, I'm not fit for this. Is it much further?'

'Over a mile,' Billy replied.

'A mile?... Over a mile!' Mason wheezed, 'No, no I can't do it. I'd have a heart attack. You two go ahead. Sorry, George, I didn't realize what was involved.'

They left him fighting for breath and continued the climb.

'We're here,' Billy said, setting about tying the rope to the jutting rock. 'Will you be able to go down the rope?'

'I'll manage. For this I'll manage.'

Billy removed the stone from the opening.

'Whoever brought it to this place went to a lot of trouble,' Murphy remarked.

'Yes,' Billy agreed, 'especially if he did it alone. Would you like to go first?'

'No, thanks, I'll follow you. Go ahead.'

Billy reached the floor and moved aside to allow Murphy descend.

'My God! ' Murphy said, shining his light on the skull and bones. Billy didn't reply and Murphy shone the light on his face.

'Something wrong, Mister Kean?' he asked, seeing a look of shocked dismay on Billy's features.

'Somebody's been here. Part of the treasure was here among the bones. It's gone.'

'And where was the rest?'

'Most of it was in the chamber at the end of that passage.'

'Well, go on, man, look and see.'

The flashlight revealed an empty chamber. 'Mister Kean,' Murphy's words came in a hiss over Billy's shoulder, 'I don't know what you hope to gain from this, but I don't find it in the least amusing.'

'It's not a joke, Mister Murphy, I assure you,' Billy said, dropping to his knees and searching through pieces of rotted wood and dust.

'Look, he didn't get everything.'

He handed Murphy a small decorated pin.

'And here,' he picked up a beautifully crafted brooch and some strands of gold thread.

'Yes... yes. Right,' Murphy examined the items. 'You said 'he', Mister Kean, are you talking about your friend in Glendalough?'

'No, when I was searching on Lugduff last year I had some trouble with a man following me.'

'You knew him?'

'Yes. Well, I thought I did. Worked with him for a while. Asked him along with me on a few searches and when he turned out to be a nasty piece of work I dropped him. He didn't take kindly to that and began shadowing me. I thought he had become bored and given up, but it looks like I was wrong. It's the only possible explanation. He must have been watching me.'

They sifted through the debris and found several more small objects, mainly pins, but also a gold buckle and some silver buttons which at first glance looked like hammered coins. On the way out they searched among the bones and Murphy uncovered another brooch, similar but larger than the one from the chamber.

'Just look at that craftsmanship!' he breathed. 'Beautiful! Absolutely wonderful!'

Billy picked up a flat oval-shaped object about the size of his hand. He brushed the dirt away and it gleamed golden in the beam of sunlight that penetrated the shaft. The figure of a monk holding a crozier in his left hand while his right pointed a finger towards a small church was incised on the front, and the back was decorated with a cross similar to that cut in the great sanctuary stone at the gateway to the monastic city. Murphy turned it over and over, his finger tracing the lines of the ancient craftsman, his face a mask of wonder.

'Probably meant to be Kevin himself,' he said. 'Can you remember anything in particular about the shrines you saw? I mean was there one that stood out from the rest or anything like that?'

'Yes, now you mention it, one of them was much bigger and looked to be more elaborately decorated than the others. It wasn't a book shrine, more of a cottage shape. Why do you ask?'

'Oh, dear God. Some very early writings tell of the relics of Kevin being kept in a special shrine at the monastery, but there's no mention of them being there after the ninth century. From what I've seen here, this hoard dates from the eighth or early ninth century. To hold that shrine in one's hand! To touch...' he was overcome with emotion. 'We have to find these things, Mister Kean, you can't conceive of their importance.'

They divided the items they had found, twenty in all, among their various pockets, and started back to the car.

'You can give me this person's name and address,' Murphy said as they sped along the country roads. 'Much as I dislike the idea, we'll have to let the police follow it up from here.'

Next morning Billy jumped from the bed to answer the phone before eight o'clock.

'Hello,' he croaked, still half asleep.

'Hello, Mister Kean, George Murphy here. Your friend Teddy Brien, He's in intensive care at Beaumont Hospital. Traffic accident.'

CHAPTER THIRTY

'He's onto somethin',' Teddy Brien muttered, lowering his binoculars, 'as sure as fuck he is.'

From his vantage point in a thicket in the valley below Keadeen he had watched Billy scramble down the mountain and return with a rope. He saw him vanish into the mountain and re-emerge some time later. He carefully noted some rocks in the area as landmarks and when the sound of Billy's car had faded into the distance he climbed up to the spot and rolled back the stone. He had brought his own rope.

He let a yelp of delight out of him when he saw the objects scattered among the bones.

'Yes! Yes! Yes! Yee-haaa.' His crude cowboy yells shattered the stillness of the lonely mountainside as he picked up one piece after another and brushed the dust away to reveal the bright gold and the sparkle of precious stones.

'Oh, thank you, Mister bloody smart-arse Kean. There's a right few quids' worth here. Bejaysus there is!'

The yells streamed forth with renewed vigour as he negotiated the passageway and discovered the bulk of the treasure. He went back to his car and took a roll of old coalbags from the boot. Only this morning he had tied them up and put them there with the intention of dumping them somewhere along the way. His luck was in in more ways than one.

Although he didn't suppose Kean would be back this evening, he had no intention of taking any chances. The place would probably be crawling with all sorts of weirdos tomorrow if that stupid fucker did as he said he would and went to the museum. Jaysus, there really is one born every minute.

By dusk he was heaving the last of seven bags from the cave. The journeys up and down the mountain had been heavy going, but fuck it, he would probably never have to do a day's work again. He pushed the stone back into place. Give the bastard no warning. Oh, shit, I'd love to see his face when he gets down there. Teddy stood the last bag on the floor in front of the passenger seat, the boot and back seat having taken three apiece. He knew the ideal place to hide the stuff until he found a buyer. There was a piece of heavily overgrown waste ground a few hundred yards from the hotel in Glendalough and he had discovered when he needed to relieve himself one day last autumn a huge hole where the roots of an enormous old tree had rotted away. He had been able to climb down into it and at the time reckoned it would make a good hide-out. A lot of the old root was still there, but as soft as sponge and could easily be removed to make even more room if necessary.

It was dark and had started to rain before he got to Glendalough. That was good. Discourage any late evening strollers. He stopped at an old wooden gate that opened onto the waste ground and got out of the car. Ahead he could see the lights of the hotel and music faintly reached his ears on the night air. The rain was steady but not too heavy. No sign of anyone about.

He took the bag from the front of the car and got it over the gate. The lush undergrowth and bushes drenched him as he pushed his way through them to his destination. It was perfect. The great roots had stretched out almost horizontally away from the central trunk preventing the rain from falling directly into the hollowed-out cavern. He placed the bag at the deepest point which was about six feet underground and when all of them had been carried in he got another coalbag from the boot and filled it with stones from the nearby Glendasan River; no sense running the risk of somebody accidentally finding the stuff. He laid the stones carefully over the bags of treasure and went to collect some more.

He worked for two hours, dumping bag after bag into the hole until it was filled to within a few inches of the surface, then covered the stones with earth and leaves which he kicked in from around the entrance. He collapsed into the car and lay there, soaked to the skin, for half an hour to recover his strength.

He checked his watch; almost two in the morning.

Right, let's go.

As he drove he thumped the steering wheel and yelled. When the possibility of finding something had arisen he had made enquiries at his local pub and had heard about an American who was in the business of buying ancient Irish treasures and shipping them out to collectors in the States. Somebody had found an old bell of some kind and the yank had coughed up twenty grand for it. Twenty grand for one lousy bell! Jaysus Christ! He thumped the wheel again.

He was rich. Bloody stinkin' rich.

He saw his life ahead as a never-ending world-wide pub-crawl, with dozens of gorgeous mots clamouring to be screwed by the rich Irishman and his pals. Oh, yeah, he would bring his two best mates along. Dommo and Biller couldn't half down the pints! Always stood their rounds, too. Genuine lads, the pair of them. Only snag was, all three of them were married. One thing was sure, the cow at home would have to be got rid of. How the fuck could a lad have a decent bit of fun with a naggin' bitch like her hangin' out of him? Give the ugly cunt a few grand to shut her up an' let her go an' fuck herself. Heh-heh.

At a wooded area outside Laragh he spotted an unusual-looking stone gatepost with steps set into it. The gate itself and the other post had long disappeared. It would do as a landmark. He stopped the car and wrapped a small chalice-like goblet he had kept back as a sample in several plastic bags. He climbed into the wood and hid it behind the boundary wall close to the stone post.

He drove off again. The rain fell heavier now, thundering on the roof and sloshing before the wipers. The road shone in the headlights. He stepped on the accelerator as he sped through Annamoe village and approached the humpback bridge. The sudden lifting of the car beneath him and the leap over the hump as the wheels left the ground always gave him a kick. His foot was to the floor. The car swooped upwards and he gripped the steering wheel tightly.

'Yee-haa! Lift-off!' he roared.

All he saw as he rose into the rain-lashed air was a pair of glaring headlights before the car embedded itself in the cab of the oncoming truck above them like a bullet going into a forehead.

CHAPTER THIRTY ONE

'Where did it happen?'

'Annamoe Bridge, early hours of yesterday morning. He was coming from the mountains.'

'The treasure, had he got it with him?'

'No, no sign of it. The car hasn't been thoroughly examined yet. I'm going with the police to have a look at it later today, see if there are any clues as to where he might have gone with it. He had obviously spent the intervening hours from the time you left the cave transporting the hoard to a new hiding place and was on his way home. Unless the car tells us something we'll be looking for a needle in a haystack, it could be anywhere out there. If he doesn't recover — and from what I've been told, his chances are almost non-existent — then the treasure will probably stay lost again unless somebody stumbles upon it by accident, and that's only likely to happen if he hasn't actually buried it.'

'I don't think he has buried it, Mister Murphy, he would have had to dig a hole as big as a grave. He has more than likely left it in one of the caves or mine-shafts he saw while following me, and if that's the case the haystack won't be such a big one.'

'Yes, of course, you're right. Listen, would you be willing to accompany me on a search of the caves you already know? I'm talking about now, today. I'll leave the car to the police. Should we find the hoard the rewards all round would be great, Mister Kean.'

Within the hour Billy was climbing into Murphy's car at the Divil.

They located Teddy Brien's parking spot without difficulty, less than a quarter of a mile farther along the road than Billy's. The path he had trampled through the undergrowth at the roadside in his journeys to and from the cave was easily identifiable in the luxuriant summer growth of the valley. They searched the trampled area around where the car had been but found nothing, and then drove to Glendalough and climbed to the cave on Lugduff. It was empty. They checked the old mine-shaft on Camaderry where Billy had been trapped, and some other old shafts in the vicinity, then called empty-handed to Cam's cottage in the late afternoon. Over tea the conversation came around to the new law on metal detecting.

'In my humble opinion, Mister Murphy,' Cam commented, 'it's a bit like knocking your house down to get rid of a bat in the attic.' Billy winced at Cam's directness.

'An amusing analogy, Mister Byrne, and maybe to some extent you are right, but the fact is that important Irish artefacts were being lost to this country almost daily, sold to buyers in America and elsewhere by people who care nothing for their own heritage. Something drastic had to be done to stem that flow, surely you can see that?'

'Yes, yes, but maybe a more vigilant scrutiny of what people were bringing or sending out of the country would have been a better option, because from what I know of human nature the ordinary honest person like Billy Kean here, who would hand over anything he happened to find, will be forced to give up his hobby, while the criminal types will merely be more careful not to be caught. In other words, this law will work against the innocent rather than the guilty.'

'Oh, now, I think that's a bit harsh, Mister Byrne.'

'Well, then,' Cam smiled, 'I suppose the best answer for the moment, one I'm sure all present will agree on, is another cuppa tea!' For the rest of the summer and until the weather became too inclement in October, Billy and Murphy went into the hills every Monday but failed to find a clue as to where the hoard might be hidden, while Teddy Brien lay in Beaumont Hospital in a coma from which he wasn't expected to recover.

'There will, of course, be a reward for the items we found on Keadeen,' Murphy said as he dropped Billy off at the Divil, 'but I'm afraid it won't make you a rich man, and I'll arrange for you to be paid for the days you accompanied me.'

'So much for our house in the country,' Jenny remarked good-humouredly when Billy arrived in from the final search wet, miserable and discouraged, 'but not to worry, there's a nice hot casserole in the oven, and better still, Christmas is coming!'

'Did I ever tell you, Jen, that you have a warped sense of humour?'

'You're not without the odd little warp yourself, thank God,' she grinned knowingly at him. 'What about last night?'

'Ah, Jen, lay off, I'm wringing wet right through. I'm going to have a shower.' He dropped his wet clothes on the bathroom floor and the hot shower was easing his aching muscles when the door opened and closed again.

'Need a hand?' Jenny asked.

CHAPTER THIRTY TWO

There were voices. Low murmurings. Coming and fading. Meaningless. Long period of silence. Voices again. Shadows. Think. Think!. What...? Something wrong... bad wrong. Sick, sick feeling. Dizzy. Shadows moving.

Voices.

Gone again. Nothing...

The shadow leaning over him said one word: 'Nothing.'

Who? Please... what?

Think... Oh, think. Why this... nothing?

Thoughts, half formed, reeling, coming close, then reeling off into infinity again.

Teddy Brien... me. Who?

Hate getting up. Can't wake in the mornings. Can't open me eyes.

Where was I last night? What's wrong?

Treasure. Found it. Rich.

Where is this? Something up me bloody nose. Oh, God!

Open me eyes. Must open... see. Open...

His left eyelid shot suddenly upwards and the first thing he saw was a young nurse sitting engrossed in a book on a chair across from the bed on which he was lying.

Hospital!

Tubes up his nose. More in other parts of him. Jaysus, what's wrong with me? What happened?

The nurse glanced up, then jumped up and ran wide-eyed from the room, the book landing with a slap on the floor.

'He's awake!' he heard her call echo in the corridor. 'Quickly, he's come to.'

Feet pattering, running.

Teddy closed his eye again.

'Are you certain?' Male voice.

'He was looking straight at me, doctor.'

'Mister Brien, I'm Doctor John Moore. Can you hear me?' Teddy heard, but made no effort to communicate the fact.

Doctor Moore shook his head.

'Obviously not with us now, but if he did regain consciousness momentarily it could mean that he's close to waking up permanently, even after all this time. What his mental capabilities would be in that event is impossible to predict. From now on I want him watched constantly and any more signs of recovery reported to me straight away. And that means no Maeve Binchy, nurse,' he added, spotting the book on the floor.

The doctor left.

What did he mean, after all this time? Surely something had happened to him last night on the way home and he wound up here? He remembered everything about yesterday now, if it was yesterday. Christ, he had gone head-on into something going over the bridge. He winced as he recalled the split second of unparalleled horror in the blaze of headlights before everything went black. Wonder how bad I'm hurt? No pain, anyway. Maybe I should open me eyes again, the doctor might say somethin'. Sing dumb meself. Shit, what's up with the right one? Again only the left eye opened and he stared at the ceiling. The nurse left the room again and returned in a matter of seconds with the doctor.

'Teddy,' he said softly.

Teddy turned his eye to him but showed no sign of emotion.

'Do you understand me, Teddy?' Teddy stared as if looking through him.

'Doesn't look great,' Moore shook his head, 'but still, he can hear me, and that's more than we've hoped for. Better phone his wife, nurse, she should be here.'

The nurse went out.

Jaysus, no. Could do without the quare one whingin' over me. Why the hell did they have to send for her, for Christ's sake?

Doctor Moore pulled the chair to the side of the bed and sat.

'Now, Teddy, I don't know whether you will understand what I'm saying, but in case you do I'm going to bring you up to date on what has happened to you. You were involved in a very serious road traffic accident back in June, nineteen eighty six, and you've been here at Beaumont Hospital in a deep coma ever since.'

What the fuck's he talkin' about, back in eighty six? This is eighty six.

'Your injuries were severe. I'm afraid you've lost your right eye.'

Teddy tried to hold his stare on the ceiling.

'Both your arms were smashed but as far as we can tell they have healed all right. We couldn't save your lower right leg, but the knee is still intact and that makes things a lot less complicated when it comes to getting you walking again. You had head injuries the long-term effects of which we cannot yet fully ascertain, and of course you will have no idea how long you have been here. I must warn you, if you do understand what I'm saying, this will come as quite a shock to you. Today's date is,' he glanced at his watch, 'the twenty ninth of September, nineteen ninety.'

With a superhuman effort Teddy held himself still and kept his eye fixed on the ceiling. Surely the wave of shock that passed through him must have been noticed by the doctor? But no, he continued talking. Nothing he said after that registered with Teddy Brien.

Ninety! Nineteen ninety! That's four years. Oh, mother of fuck! Four years out of my life. Gone in one bloody night. Shit!

'Teddy.'

The doctor had finished and left unnoticed by Teddy and now he heard his name called by a voice he knew and hated so well. It was the cow.

'It's your wife, Mister Brien,' the nurse offered helpfully.

Patsy moved round into his line of vision. If there was any grain of doubt lingering in his mind regarding the doctor's revelations it was gone now. He hardly recognized the woman before him. Her hair was dyed a deep auburn, beautifully styled and shining with health. Perfectly applied make-up enhanced her sensuous face and tremulously smiling lips, and her shape bore no resemblance to the one he remembered. Also gone was the cowering, threatened look which before had been characteristic of her. She stood before him now with a confident dignity.

Fuckin' hell, he thought, she's actually bloody attractive! Now what could have brought on a change like... Oh, Jaysus Christ, some bastard's fuckin' her! That's it. The lousy bitch went out cock-huntin' an' me lyin' in bits in me hospital bed. Look at her! You can nearly smell it off the whore. Easy, Teddy, easy, he fought not to show emotion. Whoever he is, he's dead when I get outa here. I'll kick the shite outa her too. Nobody screws around on Teddy Brien.

'How are you feeling, Teddy?' Patsy enquired.

He stared at the ceiling. The neck of her to ask me somethin' like that, as if she gave a fuck one way or the other. Probably sorry I didn't kick the bucket. Well, I'll tell you how I feel, you fuckin' bike, I feel like fuckin' you on account of the way you look, an' I feel like stranglin' you for fuckin' someone else. Maybe I'll do both together. Yeah, I'd enjoy that. I'd come while you'd go, heh-heh. Careful, Teddy, no smiles, now. Oh, just wait till I get outa this kip.

'Can he understand me?' Patsy asked the nurse.

'We don't know yet. He responds to voices sometimes but shows no signs of understanding or speaking himself. That's not to say he doesn't understand, of course.'

Patsy looked closely at him.

Oh, I understand you, all right. You're like all women. Give them a taste of a bit of whorin' around an' they'll open their legs for anything with a stiff dick.

Patsy interrupted his thoughts.

'I wonder, nurse, would it be possible for me to have a few words with him in private? I'd like to talk to him about some family matters, just in case he can hear me.'

'Certainly, I'll leave you alone. Just press the bell over the bed if you need me.'

'Teddy,' Patsy began when the nurse was gone, 'the doctor has told you how long you've been here, and some things have happened in that time that you have a right to know about. The first thing is I'm living with somebody else, have been for three years. At first just being free of the beatings was enough, but then I met Peter.'

Peter, is it? Fuckin' Peter!

'And do you know, Teddy, I came to realize that not only did you never love me, but you never made love to me. Thought you were a great man, didn't you? Roughing me up and then satisfying yourself on me like an animal. Well, all I can feel for you now is pity and contempt, because you never had a clue. You're not worth the effort of hating. Your Social Welfare money has been going into your bank account each week. I didn't touch a penny of it after the first year, and what I used then I put back the following year, and in case you're wondering about the house and if I'm doing it in your bed, I'm not. I let the house to some friends of mine so it would be kept in order. It's yours whenever you need it. I want nothing more to do with it. I live with Peter in his house in Foxrock.'

Foxrock! The bastard must be loaded. An' that rigout she's wearin' didn't come outa Dunnes Stores.

'We have two children. If they're lucky they'll never know about you.'

The bitch! The rotten bitch!

Rage coursed through Teddy's veins. He had always blamed their childless state on her being 'no fuckin' good as a woman' and had often emphasized his accusation with a well-aimed kick.

'I just want it to be clear to you,' Patsy continued, 'that no law, no religion, no threat or bribe on this earth could persuade me to go back to living with you again. I hope you recover, but I want absolutely nothing more to do with you. Any legalities can be sorted out through solicitors. Goodbye.'

She got up and walked away.

He wanted to shout after her, ask her who the fuck she thought she was, but he resisted the temptation, merely letting his eye follow her incredibly transformed figure until it vanished into the corridor.

'Shit!' he hissed.

An hour later his tubes were removed by the nurse.

'I'm sure you'll be glad to get some real food into you, Teddy.'

The real food turned out to be some sort of gooey soup.

'Take my word for it,' the nurse said, 'there are all kinds of goodies in there. It has to be liquidized until we see how you can handle it.'

She fed him like a baby from a small spoon. It tasted good but swallowing felt odd found he had to concentrate to get each mouthful down.

'There, you did fine,' she said when the bowl was empty.

Next day they propped him in a sitting position and kept him that way for several hours. God, he felt weak. He couldn't hold his arms up off the bed for more than a few seconds at a time. Gradually as the days passed his food intake was increased until he was eating more or less normally, and with the help of a pretty physiotherapist he felt his strength returning. Then one day she arrived with a pair of crutches.

'Time to try standing on the leg, Teddy. Give me a hand, nurse.'

They caught him under the arms and lifted him into a standing position. At no time did he give them any sign that he had anything more than a modicum of understanding, letting them show him where to place his hands or make any movement they wished him to. On this occasion he didn't have to put on an act; as soon as they placed the crutches under his armpits the room began to swim and he passed out. It took days before he could stand with the crutches without becoming dizzy and falling over.

His next shock came the first time he was able to make it as far as the bathroom. The man whose reflection he saw in the mirror had a head of badly cropped grey hair and an ugly half-inch-wide scar running from his forehead down across the hollow where his right eye should have been. He put his hand up to the mirror as if to feel the reflection. Could this really be Teddy Brien, God's gift to the women of Ireland? This wreck? This grey old man?

As his strength increased he began to think about the future. Had the treasure been found or was it still waiting where he had hidden it? If he had that treasure, while he might be a freak, he would be a bloody rich freak. The doctor had said they were going to give him a false eye.

Wonder how that will look. I'll probably take to wearin' shades all the time anyway, an' get the hair done proper. Heard one time that women like the idea of bein' shagged by a fella wearin' cool shades. Adds to the mystery an' all that. Either way, there'll be women for Teddy. Yeah. Where there's money, there's mots.

CHAPTER THIRTY THREE

'It's been a month now since he regained consciousness and he hasn't uttered one word yet,' Teddy heard the doctor say as he entered the ward accompanied by two policemen and another man, a long skinny fellow wearing glasses.

Cops. What now?

One of the policemen was in plain clothes. He came and looked Teddy straight in his remaining eye.

'You're sure he's not faking it?' he asked Doctor Moore.

'Well, if he is he's extraordinarily good at it. People have been talking to, at and about him constantly since he woke up and there hasn't been one syllable out of him.'

'That may very well be,' the plain-clothes man replied, 'but Mister Murphy here tells me that this treasure he's supposed to have hidden somewhere would be worth a lot of money to some people.'

'That's an understatement,' George Murphy put in, 'it would be literally beyond price. Absolutely irreplaceable. Even the few small pieces he overlooked would fetch close to a million if offered to unscrupulous collectors, although why they bother paying huge sums for objects they have to keep hidden is beyond me.'

'What I'm saying,' the plain-clothes man went on, still holding his gaze on Teddy's eye, 'is that if our man Teddy here woke up perfectly aware of what had happened, then he would consider it well worth putting a lot of effort into playing dumb until he could get at the treasure. What would you say to that, Teddy?'

Bastard! Teddy managed to hold his blank stare into the piercing eyes.

So it hasn't been found. Oh, bloody great! Well, I'm fuckin' sure no gobdaw of a cop is goin' to do me out of that stuff, so you can go an' shite.

'Is there no way, no test that could be run on him that would tell us if he's getting the message or not?'

'No. We know he's getting it in the sense that he hears us, but as to the extent of his understanding of what's being said, it's impossible to say.'

'Well, we'd be obliged, Doctor Moore, if you would advise us of any change in the situation, and as far as the museum is concerned, Mister Murphy, it would be wise if you kept this out of the papers. If word got out we'd have to cope with the possibility of criminals or terrorists attempting to kidnap him. We can do without that sort of complication.'

Teddy's false eye, when he got it, made him wonder if he wouldn't have been better off without it. They said the eyelid had been too severely damaged to restore it to working order, so he was left with a staring eyeball that could only be covered by manually pulling the lid over it. Still, not to worry, money would talk later, get some expensive surgeon on the job.

He was transferred to Lourdes Hospital near Dunlaoghaire to have his artificial shin and foot fitted. His prosthesis they called it, and his first attempts at standing on it were blinding agony, so bad that he was close to giving up, and indeed would have, had it not been for the expert insistence of the hospital staff, long experienced in coaxing amputees past this crucial stage in their rehabilitation. In three months he was walking with a limp that varied in it's markedness depending on the soreness of the stump which was unpredictable from day to day. He heard doctors and nurses discuss the possibility of sending him home, and listened in frustrating silence as they came to the conclusion that it would be unwise to let him try living outside the hospital yet, for while he had 'learned' to carry out all the necessary chores his continued lack of vocal communication worried them.

Three more infuriating weeks passed.

The temptation to scream at them to just let him out of there for fuck sake was almost irresistible but he knew that if he once opened his mouth the Garda car would be at the door by the time he had it shut again. Then somebody suggested letting him home with a live-in social worker until they were satisfied he could survive by himself. He hoped she'd be a good-lookin' mot.

He wasn't.

Michael Johnson was a perfectly ordinary fortyish Dublinman, friendly, helpful, not at all condescending, and Teddy couldn't wait to get rid of the stupid bastard.

Teddy's mate, Nick Rogan from four doors down, called in and sat with them for an awkward half hour, Michael explaining to him as best he could the unknown nature of Teddy's speechlessness.

'Well, sure,' Nick said, putting a sympathetic hand on Teddy's shoulder, 'I'm only down the road if you need anything, pal, anytime.'

He needed Nick; he was the one who knew the contact for the yank. Michael went with him to the bank when his social welfare cheque arrived, and then to the supermarket. The social worker was pleased at how quickly he got the hang of it all. Teddy bought himself a couple of pairs of sun-glasses.

To his delight Michael announced after two weeks that he wouldn't need to live in anymore, but would call in every day to make sure things were going smoothly.

Oh, yes, you do that, fucky face. Now just get lost.

He watched from the window until Michael had turned into the next street, then turned the radio up and sang along, whooping at the top of his much-neglected voice which quickly became hoarse from this unaccustomed usage.

Light-headed with the sense of freedom he ran to the door at the clatter of the letter-box. A bank statement. Holy Christ! Over twenty seven grand in the account. I'm well off even without the bloody treasure. He bounded upstairs to the bedroom and masturbated before the dressing-table mirror. Go mad if I don't get a good ride soon. Jaysus, what I wouldn't do to a woman this minute! Must take a ramble out to Foxrock, give the cow a good goin' over. Beat the fuck outa her. Yeah, oh, yeah. Ugly her up a bit for precious Peter. Yes!

When his voice returned he dialled Nick's number.

'Hello.'

'Howya, Nick, it's me, Teddy.'

There was a short silence.

'Teddy... ?'

'Brien, you dope, Teddy Brien.'

'Look, pal, I don't know what you're playin' at but you picked the wrong bloke to impersonate. Teddy Brien's a dummy, hasn't said fuck all for four years.'

'I know. I know, but it's me, Nick, I swear!'

'Aw, yeah, of course it is. Go an' jump in the fuckin' Liffey.'

'Nick! No, wait, don't hang up. Remember the night we got Mary Jackson up the back lane and had a go at her? Only you an' me know about that. She didn't even know she was bein' shafted she was so drunk. Probably wondered where her knickers went when she woke up.'

Another silence, then:

'Fuck me pink! What's goin' on, Teddy, how come you're talkin'?'

'I could talk from the time I woke up. I was spoofin'. Codded the whole lot of them,' he chuckled.

'Why, for the love an' honour of Jaysus?'

'Because I'm goin' to be rich, that's why, an' I mean rich. There'll be a nice few quid in it for yourself, too. Tell us, do you still know the fella who knows the yank that buys oul' chalices an' stuff?'

'Yeah, but that was years ago, maybe the yank is dead or not around these parts anymore. Haven't heard tell of him for a long time.'

'Find out for me, will you?'

'Right, I'll give yer man a buzz an' get back to you. What the hell have you got that's so valuable?'

'A load of oul' holy stuff from hundreds of years ago, mostly gold. D'you know the big treasure chests you'd see in films about pirates? Well, you'd need about ten of them to hold this lot. That's why I had to sing dumb. The cops know I hid it somewhere an' I wouldn't be surprised if they're watchin' me. Another thing, Nick, can you get me a second-hand car fairly quickish, not too recent or flashy. About two an' a half or three grand.'

'You're throwin' it around a bit, aren't you? Have you sold some of the stuff already?'

'No, this is all nice an' legal. They paid me dole all the time I was under.'

'No kiddin'? Right, I'll start lookin'. Are you sure you'll be able to drive, I mean with that foot an' all?'

'I'll drive. You just get the car. An' listen, not a word to anyone about me talkin'.'

Teddy went and withdrew four thousand pounds in cash from the bank.

'Just a little pocket money, heh-heh.'

He treated himself to a pub dinner before downing eight pints of Guinness which the regulars at his local insisted on paying for. Wouldn't shaggin'-well happen if I was broke an' gaspin', he thought. The plain-clothes man in the corner kept count as the pints disappeared.

'Won't be going anywhere important tonight, not with that lot in him,' he said to himself as Teddy staggered to the exit.

CHAPTER THIRTY FOUR

Patsy screamed. The horrible face with the great staring eyeball had suddenly appeared as she went to close the kitchen window for the night. A hand grasped her wrist.

'Hey, Patsy, get 'em off ya, you're husband's back!'

He hauled himself up and in the window.

Patsy ran from the kitchen into the hallway and picked up the phone. As her finger pressed the third nine the receiver was dashed from her hand and the wire ripped from the wall.

'My husband will be home any minute,' she lied in desperation, Peter's job as a concert promoter could keep him out till dawn.

'Your husband!' he grabbed the back of her neck. 'Your fuckin' husband! That's a bloody good one. I'm your husband. Me. I own you, an' I've come for what's mine, right?' He squeezed her neck until it hurt, and his nails dug into her as she tried to pull away.

Tears streamed down her face.

'You're sick. Insane.'

He squeezed harder, making her cry out.

'Please, what good can this do you? Just go and I'll say nothing to anyone, please.'

'Now, you just shut up an' listen to me. You never bothered to get yourself lookin' this good for me, so I'm goin' to do a bit of a job on you so that you'll never look good for another bastard again. An' what's more I'm goin' to get away with it.'

Patsy whimpered in terror. She knew his love of violence of old.

'You see, bitch, it's a terrible provocation for a wife to walk out on her seriously ill husband, any judge would understand that,' he roared with laughter into her face.

'The children, you'll wake them. They'll be upset,' she pleaded.

'Oh, shit, not that one again. Why in the name of Jaysus do women always whinge about their kids before they get screwed? You know what? I don't give a tuppenny fuck about your little bastards. OK?'

He dug his nails in cruelly.

'OK?'

'Yes, yes,' she screamed in pain, 'please don't...'

He let go her neck and gripped instead her dress at the throat.

'Before I fuck you, I want to teach you that no woman of mine opens her legs for another man and gets away with it. First, you're going to confess to the crime. Let's have it.'

Patsy was now crying hysterically.

'Come on, whore, out with it,' he shook her violently.

'Y-yes, all right, please stop.'

'No. Oh, no, no, that won't do. Say it, I opened...'

'Oh, Jesus, please...' '

Say it!' he rasped, his disfigured face so close he sprayed hers with beer-reeking spittle.

Between great convulsive sobs she said it.

'And now dear naughty Patsy must be punished. It's only right.'

He drew back his right hand and brought the flat of his palm against her cheek with a force that would have knocked her off her feet had he not had a grip on her dress. Pausing for a second or two to savour her reaction to this first blow, he then brought the back of his hand with equal force against her right cheek. He grinned with a mad delight as he saw the red weals rising almost immediately.

Grinding his teeth, he repeated the blows, endeavouring to strike her even harder, her agonized yelps exciting his warped mind.

'Hey, Patsy,' he panted, 'd'you know what I'd like to do now, eh? I'd love to drive me fist into that whore's mouth of yours an' smash it to a pulp. But I won't, an' d'you know why? Because I don't want me cock ripped to shreds by broken teeth, that's why.'

Patsy began to slump but he held her up.

'Hey, what d'you think of me new foot? You haven't had a go of it yet. Stand up there a minute.'

He stepped back and aimed a vicious kick at her stomach with his artificial limb. In a weak effort to avoid the kick she turned sideways and slid downwards at the same time, so that the foot caught her on the temple with a hollow thud.

'Never felt a thing!' he marvelled. 'Get up there now an' I'll give you a proper boot in the belly.'

He pulled at her slumped form and felt her unconscious weight.

'Aw, shit, come on now, bitch, wake up.'

He shook her, but her head just lolled. 'Stupid fuckin' cow! Well, if you think you're goin' to get off light by flakin' out on me, think again.'

He undressed her, ripping the clothes from her inert body and violating it in a crazed frenzy.

When he had finished with her he arranged her body in a lewd position facing the hall door.

'There you are now, all ready for precious Peter when he walks in the door. "Hi, Honey, I'm home!" Heh-heh'.

He wiped around the kitchen window with a cloth and closed it, then cleaned the phone and any surface he thought he might have touched. Leaving by the hall door, he paused to look back at his handiwork.

'Oo-ee! What a crack! Wouldn't I just love to be a fly on the wall when the quare lad gets home.'

CHAPTER THIRTY FIVE

'We're looking for a right bloody maniac here, Detective O'Rourke,' the fact that he was not in the best of humours was sharply evident in the tone of Garda Superintendent Maguire as the squad car driven by O'Rourke pulled up outside Teddy Brien's house, 'if you had stayed on Brien's tail last night at least we could have eliminated him and saved time.'

'But I'm telling you, sir, I followed him home. He was barely capable of standing up, let alone get out to Foxrock and attack his wife.'

'Nevertheless, you should have stayed at the house or called in somebody to do it. Look, O'Rourke, whoever attacked that poor unfortunate woman was a psychopath. If there's one thing I've learned in my years in this force it's never to underestimate the cunning of a psychopath. If Brien is our man he will have seen you and put on a show, then watched till you were out of sight and away with him to Foxrock, free as a bird.'

'From what I've heard, sir, Brien could hardly be considered the intelligent type.'

'You're not listening, O'Rourke,' Maguire sounded wearily exasperated, 'I said cunning, not intelligence. Some people equate the two, I don't. The media often credit clever criminals with intelligence if they appear to outwit the police repeatedly. I could point people out to you on the streets of Dublin who should have been locked up years ago, mindless bastards who would put a knife in your back or a bottle in your face without blinking, and it's sickening to see them portrayed as intelligent. I tell you, O'Rourke, no intelligent human being sets out to hurt his fellow man or woman, that's the bottom line. What some people fail to realize is that the very fact that these people are criminals rules out their having any real intelligence. Cunning, yes. Intelligence, no. Any intelligent person can see clearly the stupidity of violence. I mean, just think about it, can there be anything on this planet more stupid than a flying fist?'

O'Rourke was somewhat taken aback at the passion of this unexpected sermon from his superior.

'Well,' he shrugged, 'that's me told off. But surely you must have thrown a few punches in your time, sir?'

'I have, but I've never once used more than the minimum force necessary to restrain somebody or prevent them from harming another person, and I have always bitterly resented being forced to raise my hand against anybody,' he threw open the car door. 'Anyway, let's see what Brien has to say for himself.'

Teddy was asleep when the knock came to the door. He cursed, rolled over and ignored it.

A second, much heavier rat-tat-tat nearly lifted him out of the bed.

'Wha... who the fuck...?'

He stumbled downstairs. He hadn't bothered to undress last night. No point. As he reached the door another thundering barrage of knocks shook it and he barely managed to pull himself up as he opened his mouth to yell at whoever it was to hang on, for Jaysus sake.

He opened the door. Two cops.

'Good morning, Teddy. I'm Superintendent Maguire and this is Detective O'Rourke. May we come in? We'd like to ask you a few questions.'

Fuckin' sure you would! He waved them in past him and closed the door. Maguire handed him a notebook and pen.

'You look like you've had a rough night, Teddy,' he said.

Teddy gave him his blank stare.

'Maybe you could manage to write down a few answers for us. You seem to be able to sign your cheques and the like all right. Where were you last night?'

Teddy took the pen and making it seem like a superhuman effort wrote the word PUB.

'Yes, we know that, but where did you go afterward,' O'Rourke asked. HOME, he wrote.

'We know that, too. The thing is, we think you may have gone out again, maybe taken a little trip south to Foxrock. Nice area for a ramble on a summer night.'

Teddy shook his head.

'Well, we have to inform you,' Maguire said, 'that your former wife was attacked at her home last night. She's still unconscious. Know anything about it?'

No sign of emotion showed on Teddy's face as he again shook his head.

Maguire gazed steadily at him.

'You know, of course, that we'll find out anyway, either when the victim comes to or, failing that, from DNA tests on the semen from the maniac.'

What's he on about now? Semen's the fancy word for spunk, but what the fuck's DNA?

As if reading Teddy's mind, Maguire answered his question.

'Maybe you haven't kept up with the latest advances in detective work, Teddy, it's as good as a full set of fingerprints. If it was you, there's no way you're going to walk away from this, so you might as well come clean now and save time.'

Teddy gave a sneering grin.

'Incidentally,' Maguire said, 'while we're here you could just jot down the location of that treasure you hid in the mountains.' The sudden change of tack caught Teddy by surprise and he hoped he hadn't given anything away before resuming his vacant stare. 'No? Ah, well, maybe next time.'

Maguire took the pen and notebook and put them in his pocket.

'We'll leave you for now, Teddy. Maybe you should keep your doors and windows properly locked in case this psychopath comes looking for you. Can't be too careful.'

Bastard!

'What do you think, sir?' O'Rourke asked when they got outside.

'I certainly wouldn't cross him off the list. I didn't tell him the hospital people don't expect Patsy to pull through. Brain damage,' Maguire replied.

'Didn't look like he gave a damn one way or the other. A cold fish. I hope she lives. It's always better to hear the likes of him condemned straight from the victim's mouth.'

'Unfortunately, O'Rourke,' Maguire's face grimaced in disgust, 'whether the poor girl lives or dies, that's exactly how he'll be condemned.'

Shortly after the police car had left, Nick Rogan drove up in a little Metro.

'It'll cost you three grand but it's in perfect nick. Get in an' I'll take you for a test drive, you can try out that leg.'

Nick drove to the foothills of the Dublin Mountains and joined the northern end of the Military Road that had been built at the beginning of the nineteenth century to give troops access to the rebel strongholds in the Wicklow Hills.

'You can't do much damage up here,' he said, pulling in to the side.

'Stop worryin', will you.'

Teddy got behind the wheel and at his first attempt at moving off the car leapt forward only to be jerked violently to a halt, throwing them against the dash. Teddy cursed and tried again with the same result.

'I'll get it, I'll get it, just say fuck-all and leave me at it,' he said as he started the engine for the fifth time. 'It's hard to judge how hard I'm pushin' the accelerator with no feelin' in this bloody foot.'

Eventually he mastered it and they drove reasonably smoothly to the mountain village of Glencree in Wicklow.

'Jaysus, I'm parched,' Teddy licked his lips. 'Where's the pub in this gaff?'

'There isn't one.'

'You're kiddin'!'

'No, I'm not. You may drive back to Tallaght for the nearest pint, unless you want to drive on down to Enniskerry.'

'I do an' me hole. Let's get back to civilization.'

They drove back across the Featherbed Mountain and pulled in at Bridget Burke's pub at Old Bawn.

'Yer man, the yank, is still in business,' Nick said as they sat with their pints. 'He'll arrange to meet you if you can bring a sample of what you've got for him to see.'

'Yeah, well, we'd better make it quick, the cops'll be onto me soon. I want to get the money an' get out of here, maybe to England or even the States.'

'Why should the cops come at you now? Did they find out you can talk?'

'No, It's somethin' else. I went a bit hard on Patsy last night.'

'Patsy ! I thought she was gone for good.'

'She is. I paid her a visit.'

'Aw, Jaysus, you mean you went to her new place an' broke in on her. Well, you know I'm your mate, Teddy, but I have to say, it, you're a fuckin' eejit.'

'Easy for you to talk, Nick. I hadn't had a proper ride for years. I mean, unless your a fuckin' queer you soon get pissed off stickin' it up arseholes in the Joy.'

'Ah, don't give me that, you've got the shillin's in the bank. I know half a dozen mots that'd do anything you want if the price was right, an' that's on our road alone. I had Danny Jacob's missus meself a few times when I got me redundancy.'

'No, Nick, it had to be her, Patsy.'

'Why, for Christ sake, I mean, no offence, pal, but she's not exactly Madonna, now is she?'

'She fuckin' is!'

'What?'

'You mustn't have seen her lately, mate, but I'm tellin' you, whatever she's been doin' to herself you wouldn't know the bitch, an' anyway, I wanted to teach her a lesson she wouldn't forget in a hurry. Between you an' me, I went out there with every intention of stranglin' the whore. It just didn't work out that way. She got knocked out an' there wouldn't have been any kick in it.'

'Jesus Christ, you're an evil fucker, Teddy,' Nick seemed genuinely shocked, 'an' is that why the cops were at your house this mornin', 'cause she told them?'

'No, she's still unconscious, an' even if she never comes to they reckon they have this new test they can do on a lad's spunk to prove that it was him that done the job. Can you believe that? So I want to get rid of the stuff quick an' get lost before they get the results back. They say it takes a while but I don't know how long.'

'I still think you're stark ravin' mad, Teddy, a bloody fortune waitin' buried somewhere for you an' you go an' risk fuckin' the whole thing up for the sake of a lousy ride. '

'Just shut up Nick, will you. I'll tell you what, you drive back the rest of the way an' drop me at the Horseshoe. Park the car at your place. I don't want the cops to know I have wheels. I'll take a run down the country tomorrow an' get somethin' for the yank. Be the way, d'you think Danny's wife would still be on for it? I could do with someone for tonight.'

'Yvonne? Yeah, I'd say so. Danny's still in the Joy for that shop job he pulled, an' I'd imagine she finds cash hard to come by. She's bloody brilliant, too, but don't try to come the heavy with her, she's no dope. Don't know how she ever got lumbered with a loser like Danny. If she comes across to you it'll be for the three kids. She's crazy about them.'

'Tell her it'll pay well, an' not to come before twelve tonight. I'll stay in the Horseshoe till about eleven meself, have a few scoops. It'll throw the cops off the scent if they see her arrivin' at my place. They'll figure I'm in for the night an' bugger off with themselves till mornin'. I'll slip away in the car around dawn before they have someone back for the day. Try an' get the yank to meet me in Bray around lunch time tomorrow. Ring me after eleven tonight an' let me know. Oh, an' drop the car keys in me letter-box.'

Yvonne Jacob knocked gently at Teddy's door shortly after midnight and as he let her in he saw what Nick had meant. She looked him straight in the eye, showing no reaction to the false one, no doubt forewarned by Nick, and asked him what sort of money he wanted to spend.

'Fifty quid,' he replied.

'Well, you can double that for a start. I have bills to pay, and I'm not a common hooker. I'm only here because one of your sort has left me in financial trouble and I have kids to feed. I give value for money. If you're not willing to pay what I ask you can go and get yourself a cheap tart.'

He knew she wasn't kidding. She was dressed to stun in a miniskirt displaying thighs designed to seduce saints, yet she spoke like somebody who had come to perform an unsavoury but necessary task and just wanted to get it over with.

'Well, do I stay or go?'

'Oh, stay... stay, Yvonne. Yeah, I'll pay you well, don't worry.' He didn't know if Nick had told her he was supposed to be a dummy but to hell with it, she wasn't likely to go running to the cops.

'You can pay me now, then,' she demanded.

'Yeah, right. Jaysus, you look great.'

He counted out a hundred pounds in twenties.

'That all right?' he asked.

'You won't be disappointed,' she smiled.

By the time he let her out at five in the morning she had managed to extract a further hundred pounds from him, offering him extras one by one, favours she rendered him powerless to refuse.

'I'll give you a call again soon,' he said as she left.

'You do that,' she replied, 'as soon as you have five hundred for me.'

Here and there along the road an early morning farm worker turned to see who was about as the Metro sped over the gorse-clad Calary plateau and on through the sleeping villages of Roundwood and Annamoe. At Annamoe he was surprised to see that the old humpback bridge had been replaced by a wider level one. He wasn't to know he had slept through a devastating visit by hurricane Charlie in nineteen eighty six which had caused the destruction of many of Wicklow's quaint old bridges.

He easily located the unusual gatepost and having torn away some brambles that had overgrown the spot, retrieved the small chalice still safely wrapped in its nest of plastic bags which had become home to dozens of snails and worms. He transferred it to a clean bag and drove back as far as Bray. Three hours to kill; the yank would be in the Ardmore Bar at eleven thirty. He drove down to the seafront and had breakfast at the Coastguard Restaurant near the foot of Bray Head, then strolled up and down the mile-long promenade, not looking out of place among the holiday-makers who were already out making the most of the good weather. Soon, if things went all right, he would have his pick of all the beaches in the world, and what the weather was like in any particular place wouldn't matter a shit, he would just move on, follow the sun.

The yank turned out to be quite the opposite to the big, brash wheeler-dealer he had been expecting; a small, quietly-spoken bespectacled man who could have doubled for Donald Pleasance. He made little noises of appreciation as he examined the chalice behind a copy of the previous day's Evening Herald in a secluded corner of the pub.

'And this is a fair example of the kind of things you have? I mean is it all in this condition?'

'I'm no expert, but yeah, I'd say so.'

'And there's quite a hoard of it?'

'Yeah, I just took that little cup thing out to prove I had the stuff, like.'

'Roughly how many of these would you say there are?'

'Of them small ones? Eh, I suppose there must be a coupla dozen.'

'And what size would the larger ones be?' the yank was barely concealing his excitement.

'About the size of them big bowls they use at Christmas for mixin' the cake an' puddin'. There must be about half a dozen of that size. There's loads of other stuff as well, I don't know what most of it is. Things like tops of walkin' sticks, an' others, like little houses, an' crosses of all sizes.'

The yank gazed long and hard at Teddy. He indicated the shades.

'You got something to hide, Mister... eh...?'

'Brien.'

'Mister Brien, I like to see a man's eyes when I do business with him.'

Teddy raised the sunglasses.

'Oh, I beg your pardon.'

'That's OK,' Teddy said, lowering them again.

'Well, my friend, if you've got what you describe then I can tell you we would be willing to take it off your hands, but you should know that there is no way we can possibly give you what a hoard of that size might be worth. You know about the Derrynaflan Chalice?'

'Never heard of it.'

'Well, it was dug up by some guys searching with metal detectors about ten years ago. The British Museum estimated its value at between five and eight million pounds. It's one of your Christmas pudding types of chalice and you tell me there are six of those alone, so you can imagine the fantastic amount of money the complete hoard must be worth, and I'll be frank with you, we are simply not that big. On the other hand, we are probably your only hope of getting rid of the stuff and making enough to see you comfortable for life. And it wouldn't be any good giving us part of the hoard and trying to sell off the rest elsewhere. Unless you know the right people it can be extremely risky selling objects like these. You could find yourself behind bars for a long time, so I'm going to make you an offer you would be wise to consider carefully. Subject to seeing the rest of the treasures, we will buy the lot from you for five hundred thousand pounds, half a million. OK, I know that's only a tiny fraction of the kind of money we've been talking about, but it's as high as we can go. To be honest, I'm almost frightened at the prospect of trying to get such an amount of stuff out of the country, it's way out of our league, but that's our problem. I reckon once it's in the States and spread around a bit we should be able to shift it all right. Think about it, Mister Brien, do you need more than half a million?'

Teddy thought about it. He couldn't even visualize half a million, and he didn't give a shit what these guys made on it afterwards. This was it!

'Right,' he said, 'it's a deal. What do you want me to do?'

The yank took a notebook from his pocket.

'I'll give you an address in County Kildare. You'll deliver the hoard there and when we're satisfied everything's OK you'll get your money. Where would you like it deposited?'

'In me hand. Cash.'

The yank shook his head.

'Nobody runs around with half a million in his hand. Believe me, it's much more secure to deposit the bulk of it in some bank. You could have a certain percentage of it in cash if you wished.'

'I suppose you know about these things. What do you recommend?'

'Switzerland. A sudden deposit of that size in an Irish or even an English bank could lead to awkward questions being asked. It's peanuts to a swiss bank. You'll be given all the details when we close the deal.'

'I want fifty grand in cash.'

'Fine, now when can you deliver the goods?'

'Tomorrow. I want to get out of here as soon as possible. How do I know I can trust you?'

'You don't,' the yank said, handing him an envelope. 'There's a thousand pounds in there as a deposit on this little item. You'll leave it with me to show some people?'

'Yeah. Right. What time do you want me in Kildare.'

'Anytime. We'll be at that address all day and tomorrow night in case you get delayed.'

'Don't worry, I won't keep you waiting. I'll go now to where it's hidden, make sure there are no unexpected snags, then go back tonight and get it out of there.'

'I look forward to completing the deal, Mister Brien. I'll see you tomorrow.'

The yank shook his hand and left the pub.

Teddy ordered another pint and contemplated the moves he would make once he had the money. He had never been further than England but money would smooth the way wherever he decided to go. He would get to England first, anyway, feel his way from there. Jaysus, that Yvonne was good last night. Where the fuck did she learn all that stuff? Maybe I should ask her to come away with me. No. Fuck it, there'll be plenty of foreign cunt.

As he sat planning his future over his pint of Guinness in the Ardmore Bar, Detective O'Rourke was knocking on Teddy's door in Dublin for the third time in as many minutes.

'A woman joined him here at around midnight, sir, and she hadn't left up to four o'clock when our man went off. All the lights were out in the house from two thirty, so they were obviously in for the night. I was back here myself before six and nobody has, left the house this morning.'

'Well, then, Detective O'Rourke, why is it, do you think, that there is no reply to our polite knocking?'

O'Rourke shrugged.

'I believe,' Superintendent Maguire said quietly, 'that we are about to witness a perfect example of the consequences of ignoring what I tried to convey to you yesterday about underestimating psychopaths. Break the glass and open the door.'

Patsy had died during the night and Maguire was cursing himself for not having arrested Brien on suspicion of involvement in the attack on her.

'Get a call out with a description of him,' he said when they had checked the empty house. 'Tell them he may be mute, and stress may. Tell them not to depend on it. The artificial eye and foot should be obvious if there's any such thing as a policeman out there at all. And get a watch on the ports.'

As Teddy drove into the mountains for the second time that day he looked forward impatiently to the coming night. He would get Nick to come along with him in his own car; the Metro would be a bit small for all that loot, and it would be handy to have someone to help remove the stones that blocked access to it. Slip Nick a few grand for now, send for him later when he got settled somewhere himself. Christ, he felt good! After all the pissin' about, life was about to take off for him.

His heart was thumping as he rolled down the hill into Glendalough. Holy shit! The place was crammed with people. He was in a line of cars and as he approached the hotel he noticed that most of the cars ahead of him were turning in left at a point that looked to be uncomfortably close to where the old gateway to the overgrown area was situated.

Getting closer his heart staggered.

Something was wrong. Terribly wrong.

The cars were indeed turning into the old gateway, except the old gateway wasn't there anymore. He looked frantically in the direction he knew the hiding place to be.

Holy mother of Jaysus Christ, there's a fuckin' buildin' there. They've built somethin' on top of the treasure. Oh, fuck, no! A large wooden sign read 'GLENDALOUGH VISITOR CENTRE'.

He stopped the car, blocking the traffic behind him, jumped out and ran into the building, jostling tourists of various nationalities until he stood before the reception counter and bellowed 'No!' into the faces of the two receptionists, one male, one female. He brought the palms of his hands down repeatedly on the counter.

'No! No! No! What the fuck have you done?'

Although equipped with half a dozen languages between them the receptionists found themselves at a loss for a reply to this query and jumped back startled from the counter.

Recovering his composure somewhat, the male receptionist said:

'If you could just calm down a bit, sir, maybe we can...'

'Calm me fuckin' arse, you stupid' bollix,' Teddy roared, leaping into the air so that his head smashed into the man's face sending him reeling backwards with a crash.

Teddy then turned and lunged at the nearest gaping tourists, pushing

223

them so that many of them fell domino fashion with a clashing of cameras and camcorders and a babble of strange dialects. 'It's here! It's here!' he stamped madly at the floor. 'Buried it, they did, the fuckers,' then, seeming to contradict himself he screamed: 'It's gone, the whole shaggin' lot's gone. Oh, Jaysus fuckin' Christ!'

A large man with an American accent approached him.

'Now, see here, fella, you can't just...'

His sentence ended in a groan of agony as Teddy's unforgiving prosthesis connected with his groin. The man's wife screamed:

'Someone get the goddam police! Get this maniac outa here.'

'They're on their way,' the female receptionist shouted above the din. Teddy's sunglasses had fallen off when he had head-butted the man behind the counter and the staring artificial eye heightened the deranged expression on his face while the other one rolled in his head as several men attempted to close in around him.

'Hold him for the police!' somebody yelled, and Teddy went totally berserk, howling like a dog, legs kicking in all directions and arms flailing like a windmill in a tornado. He burst his way through the crowd to the door, leaving more unlucky tourists on the floor in the wake of his raging flight.

People outside jumped out of the way as he threw the steering wheel of the Metro around and jerked the car through flowerbeds in the car-park. Metal screeched against metal as the Metro bounced off cars in its mad bolt for the entrance.

He howled and cursed, tears of rage mingling with the spittle and foam that flew from his mouth. The engine of the little car screamed and whined in protest as he shot into the village of Laragh at close to ninety miles an hour.

This time he didn't even see the truck.

The lush green glens of Wicklow basked once again in the June sunshine, and deep in Glendalough the garden of Camaderry Cottage was alive with the hum of a myriad busy insects. The summer scent of roses wafted in through the open window where Cam was filling his kettle. Pink roses covered the south and west facing walls of the cottage and hung in perfumed garlands around the window frames. He had pulled some of the trailing branches so that they hung right inside the house.

He stood for a long moment, eyes closed, savouring the scented breeze on his face. It was a good world, a beautiful world, if people would only open their eyes and hearts to it.

Old acquaintances who many years before had ridiculed what they termed his eccentricities now came to visit him, some with their lives in turmoil, and wondered at his contentment. Most were better off than himself. He was happy with sufficient to leave his mind easy, and pointed the way to peace of mind for many.

'I was lucky,' he would tell them, 'in that I saw at an earlier age than most the futility of striving after more material things than are necessary for a reasonable degree of comfort, or, to be blunt, I realized greed was a scandalous waste of time. Oh, yes, you may succeed in amassing an impressive store of possessions, but they'll let you down in the end, whereas riches of the mind will be a comfort to you as long as you live, and to your children after you. When my father left me the contents of these shelves he left me the world. But listen to me, now, it's a happy fact of life that as long as you're still above ground it's not too late, and once you accept a few simple facts you'll be amazed how immune you will become to the vagaries of the world. You'll find yourself laughing at pettiness which once would have had you lashing out, and it won't bother you at all if somebody thinks he's better than you, or smarter, or stronger. You'll just put his thinking down to a little deficiency on his part.'

Cam put the kettle over the flame. His neighbours, the Keans, were coming over for a chat. Billy and Jenny had moved to the glen three years ago. The reward from the museum for the items found was quite substantial, and the pieces were now on display with a plaque giving Billy credit for the find. Jenny had immediately suggested they look for a place in the country, and Billy needed no pushing. They bought Primrose Cottage, Jim Price's old place, which had lain derelict since Jim had passed on two years before. It had come at a reasonable price because it was in need of quite a bit of renovation which they delighted in carrying out, and it stood less than a quarter of a mile along the road from Camaderry Cottage.

They found that between the sale of their house in Bray and the reward money they had a few thousand pounds left over in the bank for a rainy day. Jenny got a small car of her own so that neither of them ever felt cut off from the outside world. Billy had said he might as well be out of work in a nice place like Glendalough as in a town, but it hadn't worked out that way. Farmer friends of Cam's in the surrounding hills began to offer him a day's work here and there and before long he found himself having to turn down offers. He and Jenny had never been as free from worry. The children loved it. There were four of them now, the two younger ones born in the glen. The first was a boy and, following the example of Cam's parents, they called him Kevin. When the little girl arrived Cam suggested that as she had followed Kevin they should christen her Kathleen, and so Kathy, now a delightful two-year-old toddler, joined the family.

Cam had relaxed his rule about loaning books in the Keans' case and both Jenny and Billy regularly raided his shelves. The older girls would often run up to Cam's to check on an awkward homework problem and, regardless of subject, he would invariably come up with the volume that would set them straight.

Small running footsteps pattered on the garden path.

'Cammy!' Little Kathy came scampering in the door and leapt into his arms.

'Woosha!' he laughed, lifting her up, 'and how's the terror of the glens today?'

'Kevin's got a ladybird!' she squealed breathlessly.

'Has he now, bedad?'

Kevin came to the door, eyes fixed on a plump forearm where the little insect was making its way towards his elbow.

'See!' He held the arm up for Cam's inspection, 'Ooh, he tickles, but I'm not afraid of him.'

'And why would you be, little man? When you've finished with him you can leave him outside on the roses, himself and his pals are great men — or should I say ladies — for the greenfly. Hello, girls! Come in. Come in the lot of you, the kettle's singing.'

Over tea they discussed the strange tragic events of the previous day in the glen.

'What in the name of God could have caused the poor man to go berserk like that in the Visitor Centre?' Cam wondered.

'Some people I spoke to this morning over there say he kept shouting that they'd buried it,' Billy said. 'D'you think he could have hidden the treasure somewhere under the centre?'

'Surely if that were the case it would have been uncovered during the construction work,' Jenny reasoned.

'That's true,' Billy nodded, 'and besides, who in his right mind would bring the treasure right into the village to hide it when there's a whole wilderness of forest and mountain out there?'

'Indeed, Billy avick, indeed. But on the other hand, who in his right mind would have stolen the treasure in the first place? The poor divil's gone now and we'll never know,' Cam slowly shook his great head. ' "What do you not drive human hearts into, cursed craving for gold!" ... Virgil... now there was a man! Ay, there was a man.'

Other titles available from
Kestrel Books Ltd.

Little Old Man Cut Short
Donal O'Donovan

West Cork, 'a sort of a history, like . . .'
Tony Brehony

Irish Film - 100 Years
Arthur Flynn

Birr The Monastic City
St. Brendan of the Water Cress
Geraldine Carville

Ballads and Poems of the Wicklow Rebellion 1798
Eds: Ruan O'Donnell & Henry Cairns

Insurgent Wicklow 1798
The Story as written by Luke Cullen O.D.C.
Ed: Ruan O'Donnell

Seventeen Ninety-Eight Myth and Truth
Derry Kelleher

Wicklow Gold
Ray Cranley

St. Gerard's, Bray 1918-1998
An Educational Initiative
Brian Murphy

Buried Alive in Ireland
Derry Kelleher

Home Rule as Rome Rule
The Unspoken Unionist and Loyalist Case
Derry Kelleher

The Book of Wicklow
Arthur Flynn